Kringle Falls

Lynn Oliver Hudson

About the Author

After moving around the world as an Army brat, Lynn Oliver Hudson settled in Ohio with her wife, son, and two dogs. She credits her middle school teaching career for her sarcastic wit and humorous worldview. She proudly wears the self-proclaimed titles of science and history nerd. She spends hours on Lego creations and dreaming up epic adventures with her wife and son. Her love of everything supernatural and anything Christmas come together in her debut novel, *Kringle Falls*.

Kringle Falls

Lynn Oliver Hudson

BELLA
BOOKS
2023

Bella Books, Inc.
P.O. Box 10543
Tallahassee, FL 32302

First Edition - 2023

Editor: Ann Roberts
Cover Designer: Heather Honeywell

ISBN: 978-1-64247-501-2

Acknowledgments

Thank you to Bella Books for taking a chance on me and thank you to Ann Roberts for her coaching and continued excellent advice.

Writing this book has been one of the hardest things I have ever done. Thank you to everyone who encouraged me along the way but specifically my wife, Lisa, and my son, Cooper, who listened to and loved me endlessly.

To Emily who started this entire process. She is always willing to jump on any crazy idea I have and see where it goes. This one, however, started with her. Thank you!

To the Coven, long-time friends who read every draft and offered endless support along this journey, thank you so much for your time and your friendship.

To my cousin Kim, thank you for reading the drafts to Aunt Bea, and thank you both for your support and love.

To my parents for providing me with the experiences that allowed me to write this.

PROLOGUE

December 23, 1959

I never knew you could feel magic. It pops and cracks like an engine sputtering to life, a combustible atmosphere heavy with the possibility of ignition. I stood in front of the hardware store, pushing the snow off the sidewalk, very aware of the ethereal presence that was within my reach, and then it was gone. My newfound skills were in their infancy and their power was staggering. Everything in this universe has energy, some more than others. I could feel that energy, any disruptions were like seismic shifts. I felt the figure reappear at the end of Main Street, a hooded figure, consumed in robes, placing two large objects wrapped in brown paper beneath the town Christmas tree. The snow began to pick up. I watched the wind blow it across the sidewalk, covering my work. The figure turned to look in my direction, throwing what felt like a percussion wave in my direction. Anyone else would not have felt a thing. It would take years to control how I reacted to the energy changes around me. As I sat in the old rocking chair, the air knocked from my lungs, I realized I had a lot to learn.

CHAPTER ONE

The heavy, wet dollops of snow were changing to frozen, intricate flakes as I made my way up the only road that led to Kringle Falls. The winding, two-lane pass was a time machine. The years peeled back with each mile marker as I traveled toward my hometown. "Sleigh Ride" crackled on the radio. I was beginning to lose the signal from New Hope. Once I rounded the bend, I knew that the three-decades-old wooden Santa would be waving his newly painted bright mitten. The elves would be loading the sleigh, and the reindeer would be standing proudly, waiting to take Santa on his most important trip of the year. Here, I would hear the first sounds of Kringle Falls's only radio station, *KRIS*, where there was one program: Christmas music, twenty-four hours a day, seven days a week, three hundred and sixty-five days a year.

Reaching down to change the channel, I felt the tires slide across the pavement. My 1986 vintage Land Cruiser handled the roads well, but the spinning started immediately. Snow-covered trees became a blur as I came to a stop with a loud thud. The Kringle Falls Santa, which had welcomed visitors for over thirty years, was lying on the front of my truck. His bright green mitten was still waving, thunking my windshield with each jolly nod. His voice box let out a dystopian distress signal rather than the ordinary holly jolly, "Ho, ho, ho." It was now more of a whale's mating call. I slowly looked above the steering wheel to a post-apocalyptic scene of Santa, his elves, and the reindeer, all scurrying from a crime scene as the smoke from my engine wafted across the merry gang, adding to the illusion of an Armageddon.

Looking over the damage, there was no way I would be able to fix this one on my own. Handiness ran in our family. We could fix just about anything, anything except this Santa, who had been decapitated, his head launched into a nearby tree where it was lodged in a squirrel's nest. The loud chattering from the treetops rained down on the already chaotic scene. Those squirrels were mad and they were letting me know.

"I hear you," I yelled out the window to the squirrels running amuck in the top of the trees. Santa's head rolled from their nest, bounced on a few branches, and landed on my windshield, where a small crack popped into the glass and quickly spread.

A large battery ran the waving hand, incessantly knocking on my windshield, slowly but steadily spreading the crack. I pushed my door open with both legs, shoving piled-up snow out of the way. My only option was to climb over the hood and try to disarm it. That's when I heard a car slowly stop on the road behind me, a finely engineered German engine from the sound of it. I know my machines.

Unfortunately, I had thrown my legs in the air to reach the battery and could not see anything above Rudolph's ass, which proportionately was larger than it should have been. I struggled to get the wires, my legs flailing about as if my life were in danger. Balance and grace were never in my wheelhouse. From the stranger's point of view, I looked as if I were a toy that had just been stuffed headfirst into Santa's bag, now desperately trying to escape. As I strained to reach the battery's wires, I heard a voice.

"Is everything okay?" The firm and serious voice was not the slightest bit amused by what she saw. On the other hand, I chuckled as I pictured the scene. Years of being awkward allowed me to develop a keen sense of humor in these situations.

"Yes, I'm fine. It's just this one wire." My voice strained as I pushed out a grunt stretching for the mechanism. Santa's bag collapsed, sending me backward toward the reindeer. I managed to mount Prancer, the only member of Santa's team still standing. Laughing at the absurdity of the entire situation, I slid down the side of the tall wooden reindeer, using an elf's head as a step, to be standing face-to-face with a very serious woman. A very stunningly beautiful, serious woman. Her eyes were silver-gray, and her blond hair was pulled back. Her presence was unwelcoming. Everything about her had a hard edge, including the expensive suit she wore. Why then, was I so drawn to her? We stood looking at one another as time slowed to a stop. I caught the slightest movement of her eyebrow. She felt something too and quickly looked down to break eye contact, and the world began to move again.

My T-shirt had caught on the reindeer's rough wooden fur, pushing it up in the back. She looked at me once again, a slight smile turned the corner of her lip, as she glanced away. The cold on my stomach was due to exposure.

"Your shirt…" she said slowly, as if I might not understand her. Her opinion of me could only go up.

"Oh jeez, I thought it was cold out here." I quickly pulled it down, stepping away from the reindeer.

"I assume you're okay then?" she said, pulling a twig from my hair.

"I am but I'm not so sure about Santa." I laughed, tossing a glance toward the leaning heap on top of my truck. Presents were strewn all over the roadway, thrown from the back of Santa's sleigh. The reindeer and elves were scattered as if they were all searching for something—perhaps my dignity.

"It seems as though you've made quite a mess here." Her gray eyes were as cold as her condescension. Absurdly beautiful, I mean who looks like this?

"I must have hit an icy patch. My truck started spinning, and the next thing I knew…" I shrugged my shoulders and pointed toward my resting truck.

"This type of weather does require one to pay a bit more attention when driving. There must have been a good song on the radio or perhaps an important text?"

She threw a fake smile at me as she finished her sentence. I'm not sure that I deserved her attitude or was this normal for the tall, exquisitely dressed, thirty-something woman, that stood before me, wafting a wonderful scent? This aforementioned scent would have surely knocked the closest reindeer over had they not already been lying on their backs, legs in the air. I would have been much quicker with my wit had I not been so taken aback by everything about her. How could such a disgruntled human being smell so good and look so perfect? I stumbled over my words multiple times, trying to form a sentence. I wanted her, and I was incredibly annoyed by her. How was that possible?

"I…uh…there was no radio involved here," I lied as my right eye twitched, and I shoved my hand deep into my pocket.

"Shall I call a tow truck?"

"No, my brother owns the garage in town. I can call him. He can help me put the North Pole back together again," I said, gesturing toward the festive heap. "Headed to Kringle Falls?"

"Business."

"I wasn't thinking vacation."

"Excuse me?" she said with a raised eyebrow.

"You have the look of someone who is either going to the reading of a will or foreclosing on a house."

"So, you're okay then?" she quipped.

"I'm good. You don't need to stay but thanks for stopping."

"I'll just wait in my car until someone shows up."

She walked away, carefully skirting the large clumps of snow in her exceptionally shiny, black Jimmy Choos. I was gathering the presents scattered about when I heard a distant horn playing "Jingle Bells" as my brother's truck rambled toward us. He had just purchased the garage, and money was tight. His tow truck resembled Mater from *Cars*, complete with rust and dangling parts. He did, however, take the time to install a horn that played numerous Christmas songs. He adorned the truck with garland and a large wreath on the grill. The wreath was filled with lights that blinked quickly enough to induce a seizure. I watched the woman cringe as she heard the horn for the first time. She seemed embarrassed as she closed her eyes and lowered her head. My brother slid into place behind my truck as the stranger pulled away, offering a quick hand in acknowledgment.

He got out of his truck and saluted her. "Andi, you're home!"

"How did you know I was here?"

He pointed to a small black box on Santa's sleigh. A red light blinked in the corner. "You're live. Some local kids were making off with the reindeer and the elves. We would find them arranged in compromising positions around town. It came to a stop as soon as I installed the camera."

My brother is very serious about Christmas. Every year my family is filled with the spirit of the season. I am surprised he didn't install tracking devices. Christmas in Kringle Falls was serious business.

"That was quite a slide you took, sis."

"Saw the whole thing, huh?"

"I heard the commotion and checked the camera. You forgot the garage is not that far from here, just through those trees. I'm not sure how we'll get this fixed, though." He sighed, looking around at the mess.

"Let's pack up Santa and take him home. We can fix him and bring him back." I quickly gathered the elves and righted the reindeer. Sean collected the presents and retrieved Santa's head. The squirrels quieted down, but I assumed I would be receiving a bill for repairs to the nest, payable in walnuts or acorns.

"Way to make an entrance, Andi."

"Let's just get this fixed before too many people notice." We headed toward town with my Land Cruiser in tow and Santa tied to the front of Sean's truck, like we were bringing him home from a hunting trip, mitten still waving in the breeze, thunking the hood of the old truck.

CHAPTER TWO

Kringle Falls will never change. Big box stores have not found their way into our nestled town, nor would they, as the city council actively worked to keep them outside our borders. Dinners were still under the dark red awnings of St. Nick's Kitchen. Birthday cakes were bought at The Elves' Oven, along with doughnuts and anything else where the primary ingredient was a bag of sugar. The Kringle Falls Book Nook housed all the latest books on the bestseller lists as well as the classics. The owner, Martha, recently opened a little coffee counter that encouraged everyone to stay just a little bit longer. Stores and shops peppered Main Street, completing the picture of a perfect Christmas town. At the end of the street, past the post office, was the Kringle Falls Public Library, my new home. My brother and I drove past it and headed out of town to our parents' house. My dad's workshop would be the perfect place to restore Santa and get him back in working condition before anyone noticed he was gone.

The library was dark, with a closed sign on the door. A large portico sat atop an old wooden door that was more glass than wood. The building, with its Colonial Revival architecture, was stately but lonely. It had none of the decorations of the other buildings in town and sat isolated at the end of the street.

"How long has the library been closed?"

"Maybe a month," my brother said, turning up the radio as "I Want a Hippopotamus for Christmas" began playing. "The librarian that the city hired from up north didn't stay very long. I think you need to be from Kringle Falls to appreciate it here."

"You mean you have to love Christmas year-round?" I laughed, thinking of the Santas that decorated Main Street in July with patriotic swimming trunks and sunglasses.

"It certainly doesn't hurt."

We pulled into our parents' driveway to see our dad working in his workshop. His tools were lined up precisely, and his workbench was neatly organized with projects. My brother came to an abrupt stop, causing Santa to slide down the hood onto the driveway, the green mitten standing straight up in the grill of the truck. The shock on my father's face was something I had not seen since Sean stole the mascot from New Hope High School. For two days we had a hairy, screaming, armadillo in our house. Screaming was an understatement. That was about the time that our dog, Griswold, started carrying around his own back leg and my mom developed a nervous tick related to loud noises.

"Is that the mitten from…"

"Yes," my brother began.

"What have you done?" he asked as his legs swiftly carried him to the mitten sticking out of the front of the grill. My father planted a kiss on my cheek as he passed me. "Hi, Andi-bug, your mom and I are glad to have you home. Sean, what have you done?"

"Believe it or not, this was all Andi. She came into town on two wheels. Luckily, I had the cameras installed and watched the whole thing. We fixed what we could, but we might need a little help with Santa." My dad was already unloading the seven-foot Santa when he noticed that Father Christmas had no head.

"Oh lord, Andi, you've killed Santa." My dad wasn't really known for his dramatics. He was a quiet, organized guy who said what he meant. He reconnected the wires, and Santa's mournful mating call escaped the speaker once again. Our dog, Bark Griswold, shot through the dog door, cocked his head and began to howl. "Gris! You're going to tell the whole town about this. Go get a cookie." Gris let out one last howl and returned to the dog door for the prospect of a cookie.

"What's going on out here? What on Earth is Gris barking about?" My mother turned from the heap of Santa to see me standing in the driveway. "Andi. You're home!" My mom was dressed in her Christmas apron, covered in flour, sugar, and whatever other ingredients she may have been working with. If my father was the picture of planning and organization, my mother was the poster child for flying by the seat of your pants. She accomplished most things by the sheer panic of procrastination. I am sure the kitchen looked like it had just received the first Christmas snow. Behind her wafted the smell of gingerbread and cinnamon. She hugged me, leaving flour on the front of my shirt.

"It's good to be home," I said, holding on to her waist and smelling the vanilla and cinnamon that enveloped her like a cloud.

"What is going on out here?" my mother repeated. She made an audible gasp when she saw the dangling voice box and heard the twisted sounds coming from it. She held on to me tighter, steadying herself. "Sean? What did you do?" My brother shook his head as he walked into the garage with Santa pieces trailing behind him.

"I know, Helen, I'm already on it," mumbled my father, who was able to fix anything but daylight and a broken heart. He rambled into the garage, picking up the pieces Sean had dropped.

"Are you already working on your gingerbread house for the competition this year?" I asked my mom, knowing that the

Kringle Falls Gingerbread Competition was a yearly event not to be missed.

"We have something *big* planned this year." Her arms dramatically unfurled to show me just how big it would be.

"What do you mean *we?*"

"Oh, your father has agreed to help this year. With my baking skills and his handiwork, our gingerbread village will be the talk of the town."

"Village? As in more than one gingerbread house?"

"No need to be concerned, dear, we're just taking the competition to the next level." She winked and made her way inside with a sly grin on her face.

Within the hour, Old Saint Nick was looking good as new. His cheerful voice had returned, and his green mitten was waving furiously at my mother standing in the kitchen with a look of relief I had not seen on her face since she found Aunt Rita's lost fruitcake recipe, the one with the homemade rum in it. The world was right again.

I unpacked my bags in the room where I grew up. My parents generously offered it to me until I found a place. My brother lived in the small cottage out back, so everyone was home for Christmas.

I was anxious to get to the library and start my new job. I had left Kringle Falls to go to school and thought I might find a job curating one of the collections in New York City. I knew, however, that my place was here when my mom called in hysterics one morning, explaining to me that the librarian had left and that this was a sign. I had to come home. I was a bit hesitant at first. Would I be settling for a job that wasn't challenging? Our town had a small library. There are a few rooms, lovely old fireplaces, and a classic mahogany circulation desk. My grandfather built it for the library when he was a young man and my grandmother was the town librarian. He would check out all kinds of books, from woodworking to balloon animals. According to him, she was the reason he was able to raise his IQ a solid five points and earn a few bucks at birthday parties. He offered to build the desk to spend more time with her. It worked. They had been married sixty-seven years when she passed last November. He hadn't been the same since.

I felt like I was carrying on a family tradition, a calling. Books were essential, and it would be my job to take care of them for Kringle Falls, introducing new generations to the countless stories that could take a reader anywhere. I became excited just thinking about it. I grabbed my jacket, slid on my boots, and raced out the door to my truck dangling from my brother's heap of rust.

"Forget your little accident?" my brother said with a snicker.

"I did." I pulled out my phone and hit the Uber app. My brother, still snickering, looked over my shoulder and laughed.

"First of all, I'm surprised you even have service here. Second, no one in this town has even heard of Uber. This isn't the city. You know Archie is the closest thing we have to ridesharing. You should call him quickly. Today is Friday, and the Mahjong Club is meeting at Nick's. All those ladies like to have a little afternoon cranberry cocktail. Archie shuttles them around for free. He says it's a public service. We don't want all those little tipsy ladies on the road in their Buicks."

My mom stuck her head out of the back door. "I already called Archie for you, honey. He said he has another pickup, but he will be here in a jiffy."

Archie ran the only cab company in Kringle Falls. He had a 1969 Checker Marathon Wagon painted the same shade of red as the awnings on St. Nick's Kitchen. It was called Christmas Red in Kringle Falls. He permanently attached a green pine wreath to the grill with a bright red ribbon. The car was roomy and comfortable. He fit every little lady in the Mahjong Club into that wagon, and they never complained. He kept warm plaid blankets in the back seat, if you got a little chill. He would share his hot cocoa with you if you asked, since he always kept a thermos and extra cups in the front seat. In fact, for as long as I could remember, the inside of his cab smelled like hot chocolate with a dash of peppermint, even in the middle of summer.

Archie rounded the curb and barreled down the driveway. Brenda Lee poured out of the cracked windows as he slid to a stop.

"Hi, Andi. Glad you're home. Guessing you want to go to the library? We certainly do need you there. I haven't been able to get a good mystery since it closed. Do you mind if I stop at the inn and pick someone up? I didn't think you would since it is on the way." Archie wasn't much for letting anyone else get a word into a conversation. He was back in the car and putting it into reverse before I had even reached the door. "I'm sorry, Andi, I have a bunch of cookies to drop off too. You'll have to sit in the back if you don't mind." The front seat was covered in boxes from The Elves' Oven. I walked toward the rear, noticing that the entire back of the wagon was also filled with cookies.

"Archie, what's with the cookies?" We all knew that he was both a delivery man and a cab driver, so it wasn't surprising to see the treats, just incredible to see the sheer volume that was currently taking up space in his cab.

"The van broke down over at The Oven, so I volunteered to drop their first few loads off this morning. Those elves can't make enough of their famous Christmas cookies. They only bake them in December, you know."

I did know. Kringle Falls wasn't home to any real elves. The Thorishoffers had been running the bakery since it opened. They were Norwegian but oddly short in stature. They made an incredible Christmas cookie that could only be explained as a chocolate peanut butter swirl that exploded in your mouth, leaving behind the sweet aftertaste of peppermint. When I was a kid, I tried to convince my mom that it was just like using mouthwash, both minty and refreshing.

I jumped in the back of the wagon and pulled the warm wool blanket over my legs. "Where's Charlie?" Archie's shepherd mix usually made the rounds with him. His jingling collar could easily be mistaken for sleigh bells. The boops and snuggles he passed out were not to be missed.

"He's resting up for the mahjong ladies. They all bring treats for him so he wouldn't miss that for the world. Besides, I had to have room for the cookies." I smiled at Archie as he turned around and headed toward town.

A fresh blanket of snow made everything sparkle, especially when the sun slid through the clouds. It was good to be home.

CHAPTER THREE

I wrapped myself in the warmth of the tartan blanket and snuggled back into the seat, resting my head and closing my eyes. My arrival back in town had been exhausting, but it was great to be home. I took a long deep breath, a sigh of contentment, and heard the door open.

It was a newly familiar, wonderful, smell of warmth, coziness, and home. I smiled, groggily lifted my head, and opened my eyes. I was face-to-face with the beautiful stranger from the holly jolly massacre I had just caused.

"Hello again," she said, looking surprised to see me. She slid into the back seat, her finely tailored dress coat opening as she unbuttoned it and sat down. She slid her leather gloves off and neatly stacked them on her crossed knee. Her scarf was tucked, with precision, in her coat, perfectly folded. I watched her for a moment. Her presence was overwhelming. Straightening the blanket on my lap, I tried not to slouch, sitting slightly taller in the seat, attempting to gather myself but unsure why I cared.

"Cold?" she asked, looking at the blanket.

"No, just cozy."

She laughed, a short, unassuming laugh that she had let escape.

"What?" I asked, looking at her curiously.

She adjusted herself to face me. "Is being cozy a qualifier for living in this town?"

"Have you been subjected to an overt amount of coziness?" I raised one eyebrow, ending the question with a bit of sarcasm.

"As a matter-of-fact, yes, aside from meeting you at the holiday armageddon, it's been one long, idyllic, perhaps even quaint Christmas card."

"The way you say that leads me to believe those qualities are not ones you are looking for."

"No, not really," she said, adjusting her gloves from what appeared to be uneasiness.

"Then you came to the wrong place. This town is dripping with Christmas cheer and holly jolly, Yuletide spirit."

"That's exactly right, Andi," Archie interjected. "Kringle Falls is filled with the spirit of Christmas all year long," Archie said as he jumped back into the wagon after delivering half the cookies to the inn. "Everybody ready? You mind if I drop off the rest of the cookies at The Kitchen?"

"Of course not. Nothing like a good warm cookie!" I said, still enjoying the wonderful peppermint and chocolate smells that escaped the boxes.

"Are we making deliveries too?" the stranger asked Archie, leaning forward slightly to hear his answer.

"You'll find that we all help each other here in Kringle Falls."

Archie looked at us through the rearview mirror, winking at me as he put the car in gear. We rolled out of the driveway and onto the street that would lead us to town. The wind whistled through the windows even though they were rolled up. The Christmas music was light and happy, helping to offset the anxious mood of the new passenger that had now filled the car. She seemed rushed as if she were in a hurry.

"I suppose I should have introduced myself when I crawled off the reindeer. Yes, my mother did teach me better than that.

I'm Andi," I said, reaching my hand from beneath the blanket and extending it toward the stranger.

"Theodora. I could tell you my mother taught me better, but she did not."

Her hand met mine. We both held on just a little bit longer than we should have. She turned to look at me. Was she as caught off guard as I was, or had my wool blanket and dry hands just shocked her? We paused for a moment, looking at one another and then slowly let go.

"Nice to meet you, Andi," she said, softly.

"And this is Archie," I said, changing the subject to ease what I perceived as tension between us.

"Yes, the desk clerk at the inn told me about Archie's cab when I found my car with a flat tire. I think it may have been a casualty of your accident."

I had really managed to come into town with a bang. Santa, reindeer, elves, and now Theodora's car. I felt terrible. "I am so sorry. Please, call my brother. I am sure he will be able to help you. And please let me pay for it."

"Thank you. I've already called the dealer in New Hope. Hopefully, it will be good as new this time tomorrow."

"Shall we, ladies?" Archie turned the radio up and began singing "It's Beginning to Look a Lot Like Christmas," slightly louder than the radio. The impromptu concert was a little too loud for conversation. I joined in as we drove toward town. Theodora's face was both equal parts annoyed and nervous as we pulled onto Main Street and stopped in front of St. Nick's Kitchen.

"I'll be right back. Just let me drop these cookies off."

Being the queen of awkwardness, I did not want to be alone with Theodora again, so I jumped out of the car. "Let me help you, Archie. We can get this done quickly."

"Thanks, Andi. Remember, you used to help me make these deliveries when you were still in school."

"Oh, I remember. It was one of my favorite things to do during the holidays. You always paid me in cookies."

We gathered the last boxes of sweet treats and took them into The Kitchen and were quickly on our way again. I was so looking forward to getting to the library and making it my own. I had spent so much of my childhood there that I felt like it was a second home. I pulled the key out of my bag and held it. The red velvet ribbon wrapped through the head of the key, slightly worn from rubbing against the ornate design for so many years. The metal swirls came together to form Kris Kringle's face and beard. He winked as if he was keeping a secret. The key's shaft was engraved to look like a swirling candy cane. It came to me in a green velvet box with a handwritten note: "Please take care of our library and all it contains." My grandmother had written the beautiful script. I couldn't wait to unlock the door and open a new chapter in my life.

Archie pulled in front of the library. It felt like seeing an old friend. I folded the blanket on my lap and opened the door.

"Thanks, Archie. Let me know if you need any more help delivering cookies."

"Sure thing, Andi. Glad to have you home," Archie said before he pulled away. The wind wrapped around me, causing a shiver. And then I heard her voice.

"Am I to assume that you are the new librarian?"

I exhaled slowly and turned to see Theodora standing in the road, carefully putting her gloves on. I sighed heavily and turned back to look at the large stone structure.

"Yes, but I won't be open for a few days. Why don't you check back next week?" I suggested loudly over my shoulder as I ascended the old marble stairs.

"I'm here to purchase the collection," she projected as I moved away from her.

"I'm sorry, we don't have any collections for sale."

"You may change your mind when you hear my offer," she said, walking to meet me on the stairs.

I stopped and turned to face her. "Teddy?"

"Theodora."

"*Theodora*, this is my first day at the library. I have a lot of work to do. Why don't you call me next week?"

"This will only take a moment."

"I really don't want to be rude. Do you have a card or can you give me your number? I'll text you when I can take an appointment."

She looked at me for a moment, finally realizing how resolute I was, and reached into her purse for a card. She handed it to me. "Call me as soon as you can."

I took the card and watched her walk away. I respected that she was willing to walk toward town in those shoes. *Theodora Declan, Whitby's, Senior Specialist, Head of Private Sales.* Why would anyone, let alone a Whitby's representative, be interested in one of Kringle Falls's collections? We had a few historical books from the town's early history, but I knew of nothing else.

I unlocked the door and entered the vestibule. The rich smell of aged wood tempered with just a touch of musty paper greeted me. To the left was a coat room. I clicked open the door to find it filled with boxes. I would certainly add that to my list of things to do. The grand entrance door stood before me. It wasn't locked. It opened slowly under its own weight, letting the sweet aroma of aged books, old wood, and fireplace remnants overtake me. I inhaled deeply, hoping it would take me back to when I was a child. My grandfather's large circulation desk stood before me. Ornately decorated with swirls, carvings, and inlays, it looked as new as the day my pops finished it, except for the tarnished brass return slot that needed a bit of a shine. The computer on the desk looked out of place. It took away from the charm of yesteryear. A door to the right opened into a small librarian's office. I could have sworn I caught just the slightest whiff of my grandmother's perfume as if she sat at the desk gently fanning herself with an old borrower's card.

I sat my bag down on the green blotter, walking past the desk and into the next room. My grandmother called this room "the study." It had a beautiful stone fireplace darkened with age. They were built to keep the entire library warm when it was first constructed. Now they just added ambiance. An old leather sofa faced the fireplace with adjoining high-back chairs. The furniture surrounded a plain coffee table bedecked with silk autumn leaves and a plastic pumpkin, a reminder of how long the library had been closed.

Behind the couch sat two tables, each with adjoining chairs. Tall, wooden bookcases held up the walls of the old room. Two large-paned windows sat on the exterior wall, the aged wood framing the image of the snowy trees outside. My grandfather had made two benches, one for each window. The decorative flourishes swirled on each of the benches' legs, reminding me of the love he poured into everything he made.

Just a few steps outside the door of the study were stairs that led to a landing. The stairs creaked as I ascended them. A small Tiffany-style lamp sat on a table, spilling warm light down into the hall. My grandmother was big on night lights. She placed them strategically throughout her house, helping us find the bathroom while simultaneously keeping away any unruly spirits that may haunt us at night. She was the one who put the lamp there. It had probably been on for years. The lamp also did a wonderful job of lighting the two stained glass windows sitting just above the table. From outside, they glowed warmly. They had been found in the basement of city hall, packed in wooden crates, now they rested here. The windows were filled with geometric shapes connected with one another, forming a less-than-perfect grid. Upon closer inspection, it was easy to see that the windows were a map of Kringle Falls that dated back to 1804. A curious thing about the map, however, was that it seemed to miss a piece. In other words, the map pieces did not connect. There was obviously a portion of the map missing and strangely enough, the piece missing was where the library is located.

I reached the second floor, pausing to take it all in. It was home to two identically sized rooms. The south room welcomed the little ones of Kringle Falls with pint-size bookcases and a large stitched rug of the solar system. A small alcove held long, deep-red velvet curtains with gold trim. My grandmother had salvaged them from the high school when they built a new theater. A large puppet stage took up the entire space. After my grandfather spent so much time on it, my grandmother

felt obligated to have one full-fledged production every year.
My professional-level puppetry skills were proof of this. Small
tables dotted the rest of the room. Opposite the alcove sat half
a sailboat, its tall mast pointed toward the ceiling, the white
cloth of its sail draped from the tip of the mast to the corner
of the room. It was filled with pillows and cushions. The wall
was painted with a lighthouse, sitting on jagged rocks, a white
seagull perched atop a log, grinning a big goofy smile. Trees
were painted on the walls, their canopies stretching out across
the tall ceiling. It was a magical place where I always found
adventure tucked between the pages of a good book.

The reference and periodical section were across the hall.
All of the normal reference books and periodicals could be
found there along with several tables decorated with traditional,
green-shaded brass lamps. The highlight of the room was
a rather large, enclosed bookcase. The oldest volumes in the
library were housed there, large books bound in rich leather.
I had only seen the case open once or twice. Many of the
volumes were handwritten with detailed illustrations of life in
Scandinavia. Some were religious but many were historical.
Nordic myths and legends lived in the books and made up most
of the volumes. They were important not only to the library but
to the town. They were the first books brought to Kringle Falls,
directly from Scandinavia by one of our earliest settlers.

All that remained was a small storage space in the attic
where we kept seasonal items, a few closets here and there, and
a basement that held all the maintenance equipment. It wasn't
an extensive library, but it was essential to the people of Kringle
Falls, and I intended to do it justice. I walked back down the
stairs, feeling the cold overtake me.

The only warmth came from the light on the landing, gently
cascading down the stairs. I could see my breath as I checked the
heat. The old furnace came to life with a few knocks and bangs
as I turned up the thermostat. The materials to build a fire were
easy to find. It wasn't long before the orange and yellow lights
began dancing on the walls of the study. The beautiful light
and the smell of wood smoke reminded me of being a child.

CHAPTER FOUR

Theodora

I rarely, if ever, have found myself walking down the street of a small town in America. Nonetheless, here I am. I had hoped this job would be simple, in and out. It was getting rather close to Christmas, too close for my liking. This business excursion was not going as planned. Had I known I would be walking what seemed like miles to the only restaurant in town, I certainly would not have worn these shoes.

This entire trip had been one mishap after another. I had been packing for a very quiet holiday far from anything resembling Christmas when Becks called, asking for a "big" favor. Since she is my boss, the asking part was only due to the respect she had for our friendship. I ultimately had no choice but to say yes. So here I am, walking down a sidewalk covered in snow, hoping my feet will not freeze before I get back into town. For someone who could take or leave Christmas, mostly leave, this was not the best assignment. This place was dripping with holiday cheer.

There was a charming bookstore much closer than the diner. I decided it best to warm up there rather than risk frostbite. The two-story colonial had been recently updated, painted white with copper shed dormers over the windows. The hanging sign, attached to the building with a wrought iron bar, moved in the breeze. Had I not seen it I might have passed the quaint building thinking it was a residence.

The bell jingled as I opened the door. I expected nothing less. The warm scent of cinnamon assaulted me as a smartly dressed woman popped up from the counter and offered a greeting.

"Good afternoon. Welcome to the Book Nook. Is there something I can help you with?" Her glasses rested on her nose, her brown hair sitting neatly on the shoulders of her Christmas sweater. A large sleigh bell affixed around her neck, jingled with her movement.

"I think I will just have a look around, thank you."

"Of course. When you find something you like come to the back. We have a new café. I'll make you a cup of coffee."

"Thank you, that's very nice of you."

She went on about her business and I looked around the shop, wondering how long it took to create so many Christmas-related displays. I doubted there was anything here that would hold my attention but I looked anyway. The various genres of fiction were readily available. There was a cooking section, science, religion, current events, and finally history. My interest piqued even though I was sure it would only have a few books on local history and maybe a compendium of the American experience. To my surprise, there were several books on European history, even a few on Russian history. I had, of course, read them all but I was still pleasantly surprised to find them. I pulled a familiar volume from the shelf and made my way to the back of the store.

The intimate room had a few small tables that circled a fireplace. The gas logs glowed with warmth. I settled in a chair by the hearth, letting the heat thaw my chilled body. The woman from the front quickly followed.

"Martha." She extended her hand to me. "Would you like a cup of coffee or maybe hot chocolate?"

"Theodora. Coffee would be nice, black. Thank you."

The shiny new machine spurred and hissed as it came to life. She pulled a porcelain cup and saucer from above the coffee machine, poured the coffee, and placed a small candy cane on the saucer. She took a muffin from the small pastry case and placed it on a plate as well.

"On the house. You look a bit peckish." She sat everything down on the table beside me. "*Natasha Dancing*, good book. I read it for the second time a few years ago."

"It is interesting, isn't it?" I felt foolish, having judged this woman before I even had the opportunity to talk to her.

"Very interesting. A fan of Russian history?" she asked, walking back to the coffee counter.

"You could say that. I studied Russian history and culture at Oxford."

"Impressive. What brings you to Kringle Falls?"

"Business actually," I said, sipping the coffee and letting it warm my throat.

"Well, I hope you are able to wrap things up before Christmas and get home."

I smiled politely as she walked back toward the front of the store, leaving me to my thoughts.

No one considers that Christmas is not for everyone. Some of us just like to retreat from the world and wait for "the most wonderful time of the year" to pass. With any luck, I would be able to acquire the collection and be out of town by tomorrow afternoon. I had a feeling the new librarian was going to be difficult. She was very insistent about not meeting with me today, not even for a moment, not to mention the ridiculous way in which we met in the first place. That alone should have served as a warning to steer clear but for some reason, she intrigued me. To be honest, I expected someone twice her age and certainly not as beautiful.

Turning the pages in the book, my fingers softly ran down each page as I thought of her skin, exposed as she stood before me, hair tousled from the rendezvous with the reindeer. A short breath escaped my mouth, unconsciously, as my mind wandered to our first encounter. The heat rose quickly onto my face, and I realized my mind had drifted somewhere it had not been in quite some time. I reminded myself I was here on business, and nothing was more important than finishing this, or any, venture I was assigned, certainly not romancing a small-town librarian.

The woman returned with a book. "This is one of my favorite Christmas books." She held a copy of *The Snowmaiden*, a Russian fairy tale.

"Mine as well." I took the book, a little surprised. The worn cover once displayed shiny silver snowflakes but were now worn to dull shapes.

"I thought you might like it."

"Where did you get this?" I asked, very interested in the book.

"An estate sale. We often purchase old books and resell them here. I couldn't pass this one up." The bell on the door gently rang, signaling a new customer. Martha excused herself and was gone once again. My hand slid across the cover as images from my childhood ran through my head like a silent film, black and white, stark and unforgiving.

This town was very peculiar. I needed to conclude my business and leave before any more surprises presented themselves.

CHAPTER FIVE

I heard something jingle; the old sleigh bells moving on the leather harness welcomed someone through the front door of the library.

"Andi, you're home." Jessica charged at me, wrapping her arms around my waist before I could say anything. We had been friends since we both formed an alliance against Sparky Mildewski in the second grade. He had taken it upon himself to tell everyone in our class that Santa didn't exist. Together we shut him down by lunch that day. And that was the beginning of our friendship.

"I saw the smoke coming from the chimney, and I thought I would take a chance. I hoped you were home. You should have called," she said, chastising me.

"I haven't been here long. You were next on my list, I promise. I just wanted to get in here and see this old place again. I didn't realize how much I missed it."

I walked into the study and fell onto the soft leather sofa, propping my feet onto the coffee table, and letting the fire warm my legs. Jessica joined me. We sat shoulder to shoulder, soaking in the popping and crackling fire, content to sit in silence, enjoying the moment.

She always broke first. "It'll be nice to have you home again," she said, poking her arm through mine. "Just like old times. Jules is happy you're home."

I glanced over to see her eyebrows raised. "Really? I'm sure she has way more to do than be concerned with me." Julia was Jess's older sister. To say we had a history was an understatement. We dated through high school and tried to keep it together through college but found it difficult with both of us being so far apart. And let's face it, the world opened once we left Kringle Falls, at least it did for me. It wasn't ever the right time or the right place for us. I still considered her my friend, and in some respect, we would always have a connection. Jess, however, wanted us together. She thought having her best friend as a sister-in-law was the best of both worlds.

"She's back in town for Christmas. Maybe you should call her," she said with a grin.

"Jess, I have so much to do here. Besides, we gave it a good try. It just wasn't meant to be."

"We'll see about that. I always knew you would be back," she said, standing and looking at her watch. "I have to go. I promised my mom I would help with her gingerbread house."

"I understand. Helen is in full competition mode. What are you guys building?" Calling my mom by her full name always made Jess chuckle.

"Whoa, that's top secret. I'm surprised you even asked," she said over her shoulder as she headed for the door. "I'll give you a call later. Maybe you can come over for dinner? I know my family would love to see you."

She was out the door before I could answer. I loved her family dearly and had missed them since Jules and I broke up. It would be nice to spend time with them again.

I locked the door as I didn't want any more surprises as I worked. The circulation desk was neatly organized, with no books needing to be reshelved. Everything seemed to be in its proper place.

A small display had been created about regional writers. An October calendar hung behind the desk. Another display sat on a round table in the entryway. An easel held a placard: *Haunted Hudson Valley*. I began to gather the books and clear the table for a more seasonally appropriate display. Working through the afternoon, I was delighted with my progress. I took a moment to sit in the librarian's office and take a break. I could still feel my grandmother in this room, smell her perfume, and hear her laugh. She was still with me.

Her oversize desk took up most of the space. A large window sat opposite the desk and looked out at the snowy pines behind the library where the red birds danced about in the trees. My grandmother told me once that red birds were a sign of angels, so I knew she was here.

A book fell from the desk to the floor, landing on the spine to reveal its pages. "I know, Nona, I need to get back to work." A breeze blew through the room, rapidly turning the pages until they stopped on what appeared to be some kind of blueprint. It was a detailed pattern for a desk. I had always felt my grandmother around me but looking at the book, this was the first time she really tried to communicate with me and I felt a little uneasy.

The book was filled with patterns and images of antique furniture. Inspecting the desk pattern, I realized that there were numerous secret compartments, sixteen in total. I sat the book on my lap and reclined in the chair, carefully looking at my grandmother's desk. It was a beautiful escritoire. A hinged door dropped down to reveal a writing space and numerous drawers and pigeonholes. Two large doors sat in the center, between the compartments, with no obvious way to open them. The small strip of wood that framed the cabinet was carved into holly, and there just below the doors, a holly berry had a slightly larger gap around it. I wouldn't have noticed it had I not been looking for something. Pushing it in, the doors clicked and opened to reveal three drawers. By this time my interest was piqued. This was Da Vinci Code-level stuff, and I was more than excited to see what was hidden in the desk. I opened all three drawers and found the usual writing and library supplies, nothing out of the ordinary.

The top drawer was hard to see into. I pushed my hand inside, feeling for the back when my wrist slid across a loose bolt. Pulling it toward me caused the entire box that held the three drawers to dislodge. The compartment that was revealed was about six inches wide and four inches tall. In the middle of that small space was a hand-carved figure of St. Nicholas.

He stood in the center of an intricately carved wood wreath. He held his staff in one hand while the other held the hand of a small child, her long hair tied up by a ribbon that formed a large bow. She looked to be cradling a book, the writing too small to read. A doll with long flowing robes was tucked under her arm. Gently, I reached out to touch it. It eluded my grasp and slid back into the cabinet, startling me. *Did I touch it?* That's when I heard a click from the other room. The figures spun slowly and "Let It Snow" faintly played.

My heart beat quickly and my head began to spin. Something was happening. The St. Nicholas figure moved forward again. The loud click echoed from the other room. *What the hell is happening? Am I imagining this? Is that figure moving on its own?* My fight or flight response was kicking in and now I was thinking flight.

My phone rang and vibrated in my pocket, it might as well have been a taser, the way I shot from my seat, putting my back against the wall so I could see both the desk and the door. Realizing it was my phone, I pulled it out to see my mother's goofy grinning face. She was holding a bright red gingerbread-man-shaped spatula. I knew she was in no mood for shenanigans, compelling mystery or not, so my only option was to answer the phone.

"Mom, can I call you right back?"

"Andrea, do you have any idea how much molasses it takes to provide my walls with the stability they need? It's an obscene amount." I sat quietly for a moment, stunned that this was her emergency. "Are you there?"

"Yes, Mom, I do remember you telling me about the extra molasses."

"Andrea Lynn Thatcher, keep your voice down."

"Mom, calm down. I'm at the library and no one heard me."
I was exasperated at the crisis my mother had created while
looking at the open desk that stood before me.

"Andrea, I need a case of molasses. Can you pick it up on
your way home? And I need it sooner than later. Can you leave
now?"

"Yes, I can leave now."

The phone clicked and I imagined my mother absent-
mindedly placing her phone in her apron as she went back to
the gingerbread emergency at hand.

St. Nicholas moved back into place as if it sensed my hand
moving toward it. I replaced the shelves and closed the desk.
I turned off the lights and quickly made my way down the
hallway to the door. The light cascading down the stairs was
briefly interrupted by what I thought was someone's shadow. I
stepped back into the entryway and looked up the stairs to see
an empty landing. I must have been seeing things.

Quickly I ran outside, listening to my favorite sound of the
bells on the leather harness jingling as I shut and locked the
door, thinking in the back of my mind that I heard footsteps
behind me.

CHAPTER SIX

The gingerbread emergency was averted as I came home with a case of molasses. I was told, however, never to purchase that much molasses at one time again. It would only raise suspicion about what was happening at our house. My mom was a top competitor every year, and she swore Dottie, from Dottie's Grocery, was her arch nemesis. Unfortunately, all ingredients had to be purchased from Dottie, which put us at a slight disadvantage. In the past, my poor dad had driven to New Hope in the middle of the night, and I wasn't going to ask Archie to do that.

Dinner was filled with conversations about the sturdiness of this wall or ingredients for stained glass windows for that wall. I took part in the discussion, but my mind wandered back to the library and the mysterious compartments I found. I hoped to get up early the following day and get to the bottom of what was happening.

I woke up to the smell of gingerbread. It reminded me of being home on Christmas break. My mom's oven worked continuously through Christmas Eve when the competition took place. The stove warmed our house but so did the strands upon strands of Christmas lights, garland, the fireplace my dad refused to let go out, and most of all the spirit of the season. I jumped into my reindeer slippers, tripping over the antlers and gaining my balance before scampering down the back stairs, hoping I would be fortunate enough to land some of my mom's famous pancakes. I looked and felt like I was ten.

"Pancakes? Oh dear, I don't have time for that. I'm at a very precarious time for my walls right now. I'm adding weight to the second floor, and everything must be just right."

"I'm sorry, Mom…did you say the second floor? Don't tell me you have an elevator planned too."

She was quiet for a moment too long. I looked over and caught her wink and smile at me. "Honey, go on up and get your shower and stop at The Kitchen on your way to the library."

If I didn't know any better, I would have thought that she was trying to get rid of me. I quickly got ready, anxious to get to the library, and headed out. My car was still in my brother's shop, so Archie was nice enough to pick me up if I helped with a few deliveries again. Our final delivery was The Kitchen. We dropped off the cookies and I stayed for breakfast.

St. Nick's Kitchen was part diner, part nice restaurant. It was the only eating establishment in Kringle Falls, so it had to function on a few different levels. The old building held two floors and Nick and Cecilia Nettlepot moved into the second floor when the kids all went to college. They wanted to be closer to the thing they love almost as much as their family. The back of the old brick building held a surprisingly modern kitchen. They had just spent the last few months renovating everything. I got timely updates from my mom, who called Cecelia her best friend. How their friendship survived the competition of December, I will never know, but it did, and it had for years.

I waved to the happy couple making breakfast for a half-dozen customers and headed to my favorite table. It was tucked into a small corner by the large fireplace. There were two dark-green wingback chairs at the table. They sat against a bookcase, shelves filled with leatherbound books about Christmas and the town's history. I would have to talk to the Nettlepots about sharing some of their lovely volumes with the library.

The warmth from the fire filled the space under the table and toasted my cold legs. The youngest Nettlepot, Erik, was home from college and was helping. He brought a carafe of water and a small glass.

"Coffee or cocoa?" he asked very sleepily.

"Not used to the early hours yet?"

"Not yet. They run a tight ship around here."

"Cocoa, please. With plenty of whipped topping."

It was the holidays, so I was going to splurge a little. Besides, the Nettlepots' creamy, decadent cocoa was not to be missed. I settled back into the soft chair, enjoying the warmth of the fire and going over the events of the last day in my head. I recounted the movement of St. Nicholas in the secret compartment and hearing a click somewhere in the outer rooms. Why a click? What was moving? There was still a missing piece to the puzzle. Why hadn't my grandmother told me about it? Surely, she knew.

My hand traced the outline of the plaid bow that wrapped itself around the glass lantern sitting on the table. I stared at the dancing flames as my mind wandered through the events of yesterday.

"May I?"

A strange but familiar voice brought me back to the restaurant. I looked up to see the beautiful stranger gesturing to my seat.

"Of course," I said quickly, not realizing the words had left my mouth. I was again struck by how comfortable I felt around her.

Theodora, I wouldn't make the mistake of calling her Teddy again, quickly sat down. A bit of her cold exterior seemed to have melted.

"I apologize for the way we met. I'm on a deadline, which tends to put me a little on edge."

"I was thinking pretentious." It came out before I realized what I had said but let's face it, she and I had not met on the best of terms.

"That's fair. I was a bit of a Scrooge yesterday, and I regret taking it out on you," she said rather politely.

"Everyone has their days. Kringle Falls is a nice place where everyone goes out of their way to help each other. We can be a lot for some people." I smiled, hoping to make her feel more at ease.

"Your first impression of me must have been terrible. I could have at least been cordial. In my defense, you were wrestling a reindeer. It wasn't the welcome I expected when I came around the bend." She smiled from just the corner of her mouth. "I have no excuse other than this trip was scheduled for me at the last minute, and my boss heavily emphasized the importance of it. I, however, should not have taken that out on you or anyone else for that matter."

"I accept your apology."

"Was I apologizing?"

"There it is!" I said quickly with a sly smile on my face. "I knew it wasn't that easy. Some of that snarkiness had to be your personality."

She grinned and laughed under her breath.

Erik delivered my hot cocoa. He waited for Theodora to decide what she wanted.

"Just coffee, black, please." He nodded and walked away. "I think perhaps, we should start again. Hello, my name is Theodora Declan." Her long, elegant arm reached toward me. I smiled and returned the gesture.

"Andi Thatcher. Nice to meet you." I would have thought the silence that followed was awkward, but I sat back in the chair, taking in the situation. Theodora sat across from me, her gray eyes framed with no-nonsense glasses. Her blond hair rested on her shoulders with wisps of bangs across her eyebrows that moved when she blinked.

"You're the new librarian then?" she asked, tucking her hair behind her ear and easing back into the chair. She picked up her newly delivered coffee, taking a quick sip without even cooling it.

"I am, although I'm not sure that *new* is the correct word. My grandmother was the librarian. I spent countless hours there with her."

"I have to say that's a bit of a relief to hear. Then you know why I'm here. This is an important acquisition." Her phone began to ring. She looked down at it, lifting it as if she was surprised. "I'm sorry, I must take this."

She quickly stood and walked toward the hallway that led to the restrooms. Opposite the men's room was a small sitting area with a single chair and a table holding a small Christmas tree. She walked quickly toward the chair and sat down, crossing one leg over the other, intertwining them. Even though she sat relaxed, she exuded power and confidence. Listening carefully to the caller, she raised an eyebrow and slightly bit her lip. She quickly responded to what was being said with either impatience or a touch of anger. Finishing her sentence, she ended the call and promptly returned.

"I apologize, but can we continue this conversation another time? Something has come up that requires my immediate attention." She removed money from her purse and placed it on the table.

"Yes, another time…"

She was already through the door, reading her phone intensely.

I enjoyed this new interaction. Theodora was intriguing. Each of our interactions offered something new and I couldn't wait for the next one. But what did she mean when she said that I knew why she was here? Questions were piling up and I had no answers. I needed to get to the library.

I quickly ate my favorite breakfast, hazelnut waffles with a dab of chocolate spread and bananas. It wasn't long before I found myself walking down Main Street toward the library. Snow was gently beginning to fall. I wrapped my scarf around my neck and picked up the pace.

The library's mailbox was filled. I stopped to pull out as much as possible before I bounded up the stairs to the front door. Jules was sitting on the handrail, two cups of cocoa in her hands.

CHAPTER SEVEN

Theodora

The opportunity to talk with the new librarian had presented itself and yet here I was squandering that chance. My phone rang and I assumed it was Becks asking about my progress. I was shocked to see Maksim's name appear on my screen. I quickly excused myself to answer the phone.

"Is he dead?" I asked immediately. Silence on the other end. "Maksim, is he dead? That should be the only reason you would call me."

"Theodora, you should really have more respect for the man who raised you."

"He can't even be bothered to call me. He gets you, his crony, to do all his dirty work. And you and I both know he did not raise me. What do you need, Maksim?"

"Your father has some paperwork he needs you to look over and sign. He's selling the house in Switzerland."

"I own that house. It's in my name. He can't sell it." The anger was stewing inside of me, growing to an eruption. Maksim was representing a man who was my father in name only. This house had been in my mother's family for decades. She passed it on to me. It was all I had left of her. My father made a game out of taking things that I loved.

"I'm sorry, Theodora, but according to Swiss statutory succession rights, even with her will, he can claim ownership over the house. Please sign the paperwork and make this process easier for all of us."

"Are you sure he's not dead?"

"I'll expect the paperwork no later than tomorrow morning." And the line was silent.

Once again, I felt as if I had been left alone, to fend for myself. This feeling was familiar. It didn't hurt as much as it used to. The first time it happened I was five and standing alone in a train station in Bremerhaven, on our way to Vienna. The platform had been busy. One train was loading, another unloading, people were moving quickly. He boarded the train without me and didn't notice I was gone. I sat on a bench, my feet not able to touch the ground, holding my doll, carefully tucking her robes around her so they wouldn't touch the dirty station floor. When the platform finally cleared, I sat alone but I wasn't scared. That bench offered more safety than he ever had.

CHAPTER EIGHT

"Why didn't you call?" Jules asked, hopping down and attempting to hand me the steaming cup. She was never great at reading a situation and was oblivious to the stack of mail that she knocked out of my hands, forcing her hot chocolate on me.

"I just got in. How did you know I would be here?" I said, fumbling on the ground to pick all the pieces up.

"Are you serious? We were together for years. I know you like the back of my hand."

I resented the comment. We had been together for a while, and we were still friends, but my life had changed. I had changed. I wasn't necessarily who I used to be.

I reluctantly took the hot chocolate and opened the door. I wanted to get back to the mystery at hand. There was no time to socialize, and I wasn't going to bother to hide it.

"I just dropped by to say hi. We can talk another time if you'd like," Jules said, taking a step back.

The wind caught her brown hair, blowing it behind her shoulder while the intermittent sun pulled out the red highlights.

It was good to see her face. And yes, she did know me quite well. That level of comfort takes a good deal of time to cultivate. Should I tell her about what I had found? Maybe I needed to find out more information and just keep this to myself.

"No, I'm sorry I was rude. Please, come in." We both stepped into the vestibule. The entryway rug was slightly turned up. Catching the corner with my toe, I fell forward, once again scattering the mail and landing in Jules's arms as she turned to see what was causing the ruckus.

I recovered to find myself facing her, my arms gently resting in her hands. It had been a while since I stood here, but the feeling was the same. I missed this. I missed her. Maybe I just missed the familiarity of it, the touch of someone else. Slowly we moved toward one another, breathing together. I was close enough to smell the chocolate and cinnamon on her breath when a loud, junkyard rendition of "Jingle Bells" began to blast the library. Sean was sitting in his truck with a grin that told me he was very proud of himself.

"Andi, your truck is fixed. Want me to drive you to the garage so you can pick it up?" My brother was yelling very loudly and enunciating the words quite clearly as if I couldn't understand him or speak English. I smiled at Jules and she smiled back.

"Wrong time, wrong place, as usual," she said, stepping away from me and opening the door to the outside. I sighed, picked up the mail, and waved to my brother.

"I'll be right there."

"It was good to see you, Andi. I hope we can get together again soon."

There was disappointment in her voice. It wasn't uncommon to hear. I let her go and walked to my brother's truck.

"That seemed a little intense," he said, putting the truck in gear.

"You have terrible timing."

"Or perfect timing. It's all how you look at it. Do you want to go down that road again? You and Jules were great for each other for a while. Don't let her hold you back."

"Is that what you think she did?" I asked, surprised.

"A lot of your story was about her. There are two people in a relationship. I think she forgot about that. Look, there are a lot of fish in the sea. I think you need to find someone else." I was surprised by his candidness but thankful at the same time.

His old truck continued down the road that was becoming snow-covered. Christmas music played on the radio as usual.

"Sean, do you know about anything related to the library?" I asked, hunting for information but not sure of the questions to ask.

"I know lots about the library. What are you asking?" Sean had spent just as much time after school and working at the library as I had during the summer. It was our second home.

"I know. I mean anything specific? Anything unusual?"

"Like the stained-glass windows?"

"I know about those. How they found them in the basement of city hall and had them installed at the library."

"That's what everyone thinks." Sean looked like a teenager holding on to a juicy secret.

"What do you mean?"

"According to Pops, those windows appeared one Christmas Eve under the town Christmas tree. It was late, the gingerbread competition was over, and he was cleaning up in front of the hardware store. The street was empty. Christmas lights and streetlamps were the only things lighting the town. He saw someone walking around the big Christmas tree in the middle of the square. The snow had picked up, making it difficult for him to see who it was. He called out to them. The stranger turned, looked at Pops, and began to finish whatever he was doing quickly. Pops was pretty young, so he took off running after the stranger. He ran through the woods, leaving no trail for Pops to follow, so he walked back to the Christmas tree. The storm had gotten bad. There were two large packages wrapped in brown paper and string. They were addressed to the town."

"What? When were you planning on telling me this?"

"Pops told me a long time ago. He said it was a family secret."

"Sean, I *am* family."

"You were young when he told me this. I didn't think anything else of it. Nothing was ever said about it again. Is that what you're talking about?"

"No. I don't know. Maybe?" I told Sean everything I had found at the library so far. He didn't seem surprised.

"Andi, you and I both know this place is special. Kringle Falls is a magical town from another time. Everyone who lives here knows it. Our family has a special job in protecting some of its secrets. You coming back here to be the librarian is not an accident. It's all fate, Andi. It's supposed to be like this."

"Who are you?" I looked at my brother like he was a stranger. "We've never talked like this."

"We're adults, Andi. We can have adult conversations," he said as if he were chastising me. Something I had never experienced.

"I know we're adults, Sean. I'm learning a lot of new information right now. I'm just trying to process everything." We pulled into the garage. My truck sat in one of the parking spots, clean and ready to go.

"Oh, wow, Sean. It looks great. Thank you so much. What do I owe you?"

"Just drive carefully and keep me filled in with what you find at the library. And promise you'll make any late-night runs to New Hope for Mom's secret ingredients. Oh, and take Gris out in the morning so I don't have to come up to the house. That should cover it."

"Consider it all done. Thanks, Sean."

I practically ran to my truck. It felt good to sit in my worn seat again, listen to the radio and just go where I needed to go without having to deliver cookies along the way.

I pulled out of the garage parking lot and drove toward town. I would finally be able to go back to the library and get to the bottom of what was happening. Turning onto Main Street, I spotted the red awnings of St. Nick's Kitchen. Two long, wood benches sat in front of the restaurant. They were draped with pine garland and tartan plaid bows. A lantern sat between the two benches, glowing despite the blustery day. The door opened. A tall, well-dressed woman stepped out onto the sidewalk carrying a bag. She turned her face from the wind. It was Theodora. She was still quite elegant even trying to avoid the blustery conditions. I had two choices, ignore her and head to the library or stop and see if she needed a ride. Even though I entertained the notion of a decision, I would never have left her in that weather. Elegantly rolling down a window is not an option if you're cranking it like your life depended on it. "Get in. This weather is getting worse."

She turned slightly. Removing her glasses, she squinted through the wind to see me. Once again, time slowed to a stop. Everything—the snow, the wind—it all slowed like we were part of a *Matrix* movie and yet again she left me holding my breath. Time continued, she smiled, nodded, and walked in front of the truck. She opened the door, letting the snow whip and whirl into the front seat. Setting the bag on the floor, she slid into the truck. Her scent spun in on the wind and wrapped around me. I took a slow breath and could feel my heartbeat. She looked at me and paused, our eyes adjusting to one another. Her hand rested on the console, less than an inch from my own. I could feel her. A half smile curled the side of her lip. The silence between us should have been awkward. I returned my gaze to the road, immediately upset with myself for being the first to do so.

"Back to the inn?" I asked, hoping to lower the temperature in the car. She seemed to pause as well. Perhaps she was as taken aback as I had been and was also processing. I could only hope.

"Um, yes, yes, the inn. I mean no. I was hoping to talk to you. I'm sorry I ran out like I did this morning. Something rather urgent came up and I had to deal with it."

"No problem. Maybe another time? I need to get a little bit of work done at the library, and you look like you have a late breakfast. How about this evening?"

"This evening is perfect."

"Great, I'll come to the inn. Seven?"

"Shall we make it dinner?" she asked without hesitation.

"Yes, dinner…yeah, that would be nice. So, dinner at seven. It's a date." Long awkward pause. "Or not a date. Just a dinner

CHAPTER NINE

The library seemed warmer than before. I had left a few lights on, but that wasn't why. It felt different. It felt alive. The key seemed to leap from my hand into the lock and turn on its own. The building wanted me here, and I was happy to oblige.

I quickly opened the secret compartments in the desk, watching St. Nicholas and the little girl spin. I listened for the click from the other room, but instead, the two figures lifted, revealing a long wooden box. The box had a green inlaid design that looked like holly. It skirted the edge of the lid and was dotted with small red bejeweled circles. The box's interior was red velvet. Tucked into the soft cloth was a slightly tarnished gold key. The key had a long shaft but nothing at the end.

I was startled by the grandfather clock in the entryway, coming to life. It struck the hour and began to play "O Come All Ye Faithful." The notes of the song danced gracefully through the rooms. Whatever was happening was magical. I could feel it.

Where did the key belong? The St. Nicholas figure moved, turning around, locking and unlocking something in the other room. Something was opening and releasing. I needed Sean's help. I called him quickly, and he was swift in his arrival, not wanting to miss the intrigue of the new mystery.

"What do we need to do?" he asked, looking around.

"One of us should move the key in the desk while the other listens for what is unlocking out here." I had hoped he would walk toward the office.

"I got the desk. You stay here and listen." He ran to the office, and before I realized it, he was causing the figure to turn. The click came from the vestibule. It was muffled and faint. I opened the large glass door and yelled for Sean to move the figure once more. The click was much lower now and seemed to be coming from the floor.

"One more time!" I yelled and waited for the recognizable sound. Standing in the middle of the vestibule, I could feel the click through my feet. It was on the floor. I removed the old rug to uncover the original foundation. The wood slats ran perpendicular to the front door. Kneeling closer, there was a thin line forming a rectangle, hidden between the edges of the slats. I easily could have missed it had I not been looking for something. It was well camouflaged and very smooth. There was nothing to lift or slide that could be seen. I ran my hand across the thin metal strip, tracing around the length of the rectangle. There was a small notch at the far end, hidden by the baseboard. A small, circular incision could only be seen if the baseboard was lifted slightly. And then it hit me; the key from the desk. I threw the old, heavy door open and ran back to the office. The small box sat on the side of the desk. I quickly grabbed it, withdrew the key, and showed it to Sean with a smile.

"What is it?" he asked, puzzled.

"A key. I had no idea what it was or where it went. Now I know. Wait for me to yell, and activate the figures again." Feeling for the keyhole, I heard Sean in the distance.

"Wait, I'll tell you when." My finger found the small round hole. I slid the key into it and yelled to Sean. The same click echoed in the entryway, followed by something new. The metal line in the floor began to lower, pulling down a segment of the floor with it. Dust and dirt rose in the air. I pressed down on the trapdoor, but it wouldn't budge. I pushed on it to stand up, and it moved forward. Pushing my fingers into the gap, I held the door in the palms of my hands and thrust it forward. Metal wheels of ancient, rusted pulleys that had held it in place for who knows how long, screamed as they woke up. The smell of old, damp rock slowly moved into the room. There was a spiral staircase that wound down into the darkness. Dust coated the stairs like a blanket and it was obvious no one had stepped on them for years.

"Sean! Get in here."

He was through the door before I could finish my sentence. "Whoa."

"Have you seen this before? Did you know it was here?" I asked, wondering if Sean had kept another secret from me. He quickly bounced across the open hole and grabbed the shades attached to the front door, pulling them down as far as they could go.

"Not at all. This is the first time I've ever seen this."

We both stared into the darkness, wondering what was at the other end. The spiral staircase was beautifully built. Someone had put a lot of attention to detail in the embellished iron steps. The ornate pieces that formed the stairs were covered in swirls and flourishes. Timepieces were tucked inside each decorative element. St. Nicholas, dressed in many different robes, also adorned the heavy steps. This metal staircase had been sculpted by a true craftsman, and whatever lay at the end of it must have been worthy of its adorned beauty.

Sean pulled a small flashlight from the inside of his jacket and took the first step onto the staircase.

"What are you doing?" I asked, very surprised that he believed he was going first.

"I'm going down to check this out. Do you think I'm going to let you go down there first? Mom and Dad would kill me if anything happened to you."

"And they would kill *me* if anything happened to you. Your chivalry is wasted on me." I grabbed the flashlight from Sean's hand and stepped down onto the first step. It was surprisingly sturdy. I felt as if I could jump on it and the stairs wouldn't even budge. "So far, so good. Maybe just one of us should go down, you know if anything happens."

"I don't like this, Andi. Please let me go down and look. I promise I will check it out and be right back up."

"I can do the same," I said, sliding my hand along the cold metal handrail. The dust accumulated under my fingers as I took a few more steps. I was descending into what looked like an old stone well. With each step, the darkness crept up, covering me until I found myself at the bottom of the stairs.

Turning on the small flashlight revealed a narrow wooden door cut into the wall. It wouldn't budge. The light from the flashlight traced the door and landed on a small keyhole. It was not the shape of the key that opened the passageway. I looked around, slowly taking the flashlight along the wall and floor. Could there be a key here? A clue to a key? After looking for quite a while, I decided to come up and brainstorm with Sean. Ascending the staircase, I heard the grandfather clock chime. This time "Let It Snow" merrily escaped the old clock. The steps were eye level, allowing me to see the intricate engravings. Kris Kringle was enveloped in gears and timepieces. Of course! That was it—the grandfather clock.

The old wood floor moaned and groaned as I stepped toward the clock. Opening the glass door, I searched for anything that would hold a key. Nothing appeared to be there. And then I saw it. There was a small round hole where the hands came together. A smile formed on the corners of Sean's mouth. He ran to the newly exposed cellar. I slipped the key in the hole and waited.

"That's it," yelled Sean. "You did it! How did you know?"

I left the clock, walking quickly back to the passageway. "Look at each step. It's the clock pieces. Pops had to know something about this. He practically built this library. Whoever did this didn't want it to be found."

"Are you going, or am I?"

I grabbed the flashlight out of his hand and scampered down the steps before he knew what was happening. The wood door was cold to the touch. It creaked as I pushed it open slowly. Cold, damp air poured out of the entrance. Darkness enveloped the room. It was difficult to tell how large it may have been. The flashlight illuminated the uneven cobblestones on the floor. I momentarily paused, not knowing if I wanted to lift the flashlight and reveal the room's contents. My hand shook with excitement and a slight bit of fear. I drew my breath in, held it, and illuminated the room.

It was filled with different boxes. Small and square, large and rectangular, circular, some constructed out of metal, others out of intricately carved wood. They were all gorgeous, and each took an experienced craftsman to make it. There must have been over a hundred, if not more. All of them sealed with wax.

Slowly I approached the closest containers. I heard Sean enter the room and stand behind me.

"What is this?"

"I don't know. There are so many," I said, shining the flashlight around the room. "Look at this one. It looks like a Black Forest carving. Look at the bears and wolves, the leaves and branches."

"Is that St. Nicholas?" Sean asked, looking closely at the container.

"I think so. It must be. Look at his staff."

"Are we going to open it?"

"We can't. It's sealed with wax. That means someone didn't want it opened. We need to do some more research and figure out what's going on. Why are these even here? Who put them here?"

Sean nodded. We both took a few minutes, walking around and perusing everything in the room. These were delicate, beautiful, old artifacts. They were a collection. And then I realized what Theodora had been looking for. This had to be what she wanted. It was obviously important, or she wouldn't be so aggressive. I wonder what she knows and I don't?

Unsure of what we found, Sean and I returned everything to its place. We were working quietly, knowing that the two of us were pondering the artifacts' purpose and meaning. We soon found ourselves resting on the couch, staring into an empty fireplace, sitting in silence, yet I knew both of our brains were spinning.

"What's next? Research? You're excellent at that."

"It's kind of in-the-job requirement," I said, laughing. "I'm afraid to start researching. I will never get this place open. Let me get some work done, and then I can do a little research this afternoon." I honestly just wanted some time alone to think about everything that had happened to this point. It felt as if things were changing quickly.

"Sounds like a plan. Why don't I drop by later, and we can work on this together? I can bring some dinner back. Mom won't even realize we're gone since we're a week away from the contest."

"That sounds awesome." And then it hit me. "Wait, I can't do that. I have a date tonight."

"A date? With Jules? I knew you couldn't hold out. I'm telling you, Andi, you've been down that path, and there's nothing new there."

"No, it's not with Jules, and it's not a date, per se."

Sean turned around, his eyes lighting up. "Who then?"

"Do you remember the woman from the Santa incident?"

"The grinch one?" Sean said with a smirk.

"Yes, actually, her name is Theodora."

"Yep, that's a grinch name." Sean couldn't help himself. "What kind of parent names their child 'Theodora'? That's a lot to saddle a kid with, don't you think?"

"I don't know, but I will find out soon enough. We are having dinner at the inn tonight."

Sean looked at me with an assuming smile, make that a smirk. "I'll check in later, I want to hear everything about Teddy."

"I wouldn't call her that. It doesn't go well."

Sean snickered as he walked out of the library. Pressing down on the floor where the trapdoor was located, he made sure we had put it back into place.

Sean and I were close in age. Even though he was my older brother, we never had the traditional older/younger sibling relationship. We had always been more like friends. We talked a lot. When I went to school in New York, we never missed a day texting or FaceTiming. He was smart. When he left for school, I wondered if he would ever return to Kringle Falls. He did, with a degree in philosophy, but very unsure what to do with it. He was a substitute teacher for a while and then realized that he could make a living from his tinkering. When Wilbur Harris, the town mechanic, retired, Sean borrowed the money from our parents and bought the garage. He not only could fix anything and everything, but he'd also developed quite a few inventions and gadgets. It was the reason there was only one bay open in the garage. People in town dropped off everything from cars to toaster ovens, and just like my dad, he could fix it all.

The afternoon passed quickly. I occupied myself cleaning up around the library and setting up a new display for Christmas. A town named Kringle Falls needed a permanent Christmas display in its library. It was nice to work and keep myself busy, but my mind kept wandering back to the desk in the office and the collection of antique boxes in the cellar. Why were they there? Who put them there? Should we open one of them? Tomorrow was Sunday. My mom would be furiously baking, and my dad would be her pit crew. Maybe Sean and I could spend the day here researching and getting to the bottom of this. Meanwhile, I needed to get to the inn. I think I had a date, maybe.

CHAPTER TEN

Theodora

Finally, the librarian and I could have a moment alone. I've never taken this long to close a deal. Becks wasn't really into micromanaging me, but I'm surprised I hadn't heard from her. This client was important, otherwise I wouldn't be doing this job.

The banter had been flirty, to say the least. Each interaction with her led me further down a path I didn't care to go. It was a means to an end. If I needed to gracefully walk that path, while she watched, I had no problem with that.

I had spent the afternoon in this over-the-top Christmas-themed suite. There were more nutcrackers in this room than in all of Bavaria. I wondered if they added more for the holiday or if this was standard year-round fare.

I had worked diligently to find a way to keep my mother's house and had a few leads. I hadn't heard from my father, or his associate, in well over a year. I was happy with him out of my life and almost felt disappointed at the prospect of him being alive. He must have been experiencing some type of personal or professional failure. His typical modus operandi was to direct his pain and anger toward me. That would have explained the call from Maksim.

I closed my laptop and reclined on the couch, resting my head on the soft leather. The fireplace had a solitary flame dancing its last song. The clock on the mantel chimed. It was late afternoon, but I still had time to rest before dinner. Trying to outwit a narcissistic bastard was exhausting. I pulled the soft throw over me and closed my eyes.

My father was driving. I sat in the back of the car trying to stay warm. The snow slid past the windows as he drove too quickly on the treacherous roads. He was angry and careless. Sliding back and forth across the leather seats, I tucked my doll beneath my arm and desperately held on to the door. He turned to see me holding on with everything I had, and he started to laugh, a cruel, maniacal sound that told me he was enjoying my fear.

The sound that escaped my mouth brought me back to the Nutcracker Suite. Instinctively, my hand went to my chest, and I began to breathe slowly and deeply, lowering my anxiety and casting that man from my head like an exorcised demon. The clock on the mantel chimed once again and I realized I had been asleep much longer than I thought. I had to get ready for my date.

Dressing for dinner was a little more difficult than I expected. Three outfits later I settled on a red dress and found myself looking in the mirror, wondering what the librarian would think of it. My heart raced with anticipation. I spent the next several minutes assuring myself I was still in control and that this was business. Was I dressing for the task at hand or was I dressing for a sporty librarian who had worked her way into my thoughts?

I went downstairs with time to spare. I needed the advantage. This was her hometown and that gave her the edge. This was a little out of my comfort zone. I had carefully orchestrated my life by not caring what other people thought and treating everything as a business transaction. If my father had taught me anything at all, it was to treat everything like an exchange where the only goal was to come out on top.

I chose a seat by the fireplace and positioned myself facing the door. The butterflies in my stomach told me that I wasn't as concerned with business as I was with making an impression. This was dangerous territory, but I was determined to venture into it.

CHAPTER ELEVEN

I drove home quickly, as I had let time slip away from me. The inn is casual when serving dinner, but I had a feeling that Theodora was rarely casual. Much to my mother's dismay, I chose not to change my jeans. She assumed the hole above my knee had been made at the library, and I could at least take the time to change them but thank goodness, she'd said, I was wearing a sensible brown belt that matched my boots. I threw a hooded cardigan over my white T-shirt and applied a bit of makeup which told me yes, this was in fact, a date. Usually, my hair sat on top of my head so that I could keep it out of whatever project I happened to be working on. I was a huge fan of the stereotypical beanie or baseball cap and had quite a collection to prove it. I had been blessed, or cursed, with thick, brown hair and what I liked to call lazy curls. A hat of any kind came in handy to keep them under control. My grandmother often referred to my hair as thick as molasses. I took it as a compliment because she always smiled when she said it. I hoped I wouldn't be dressed too casually for Theodora, but then again, I wasn't even sure if this was a date.

There was something between us. I had felt it in the truck. Call it chemistry, an attraction. It felt like the magic that's in the air on a late summer evening when you look into the trees and see all the fireflies light the canopy like twinkling Christmas lights. I was positive she felt it too. I guess I would find out for sure at dinner.

It had snowed on and off all day. As I drove toward the inn, the snowflakes that danced in front of my headlights began to pick up. I knew these roads like the back of my hand, but the mounting snow and ice didn't care about that. I carefully drove the rest of the way, knowing I would be late.

The Kringle Falls Inn was beautiful any time of year but seemed to come alive at Christmas. Pine and ribbon, dotted with white lights, decorated the front porch while wreaths hung in the windows. Large lanterns flanked the stairs, lights warmly glowing from within. An old sled sat by the door, presents stacked on it with ice skates waiting for someone to take them on a spin. Adirondack chairs made from old skis circled a slowly burning small, round fireplace. Wool blankets were slung over the chairs from the last guest who warmed themselves by the fire. I laughed to myself, wondering if Theodora had noticed them. The inn was nothing if not cozy.

The Driscolls had owned the inn for as long as I could remember. They liked to keep it in the family. The Driscoll brothers had taken on the inn when their parents were too old to care for it. They still ran it together with the help of their wives and older children. We all hoped it would be in the family for many generations to come.

As nervous as I felt, this was a date. With trepidation, I slid my hand around the large brass door handles and stood still for a moment, as if I knew opening that door would change my life forever.

Theodora sat in the parlor, one leg crossed over the other, wearing a radiant red wrap dress with frills trimming the edges. Her long legs ended in black velvet heels.

We looked at one another. She was dressed for dinner and I was dressed for a college bowl game. Unconsciously, I exhaled a long deep breath. She looked…like she didn't belong in Kringle Falls. The corner of her mouth lifted in a slight curve as she waited for me to make my way into the parlor. This was becoming her signature smile.

"You're late," she said playfully.

"I am."

"Apology accepted," she whispered, walking by, close enough for me to catch her wonderful scent. I already felt as if I was losing ground. This was most certainly a date, and she was bringing her best game. There wasn't a bowl game within a hundred miles that I could blame my clothes on. Did I have time to go home and change? Thank goodness my belt matched my boots.

I needed to get back my home-field advantage. I hurried past her to talk to the host, the young Nathan Driscoll. He had just returned from his first year at college. I coached his soccer team until I left for school myself.

"Nate, it's so great to see you. How is Columbia?" I said this much louder than was necessary, as I made both Nate and Theodora jump.

"Andi, it's awesome. It's a little harder than I thought, but I think I'll make it. Where would you and…" He looked around me to glance at Theodora. "…Ms. Declan like to sit?"

"How about the table by the fireplace?"

"Perfect. Right this way." He weaved his way through the tables and pulled out a chair. I stepped to the side, allowing Theodora to take the seat. He set a small menu in front of us. "We apologize for the shortened menu this evening. The weather is worse than expected. We're a little understaffed in the kitchen."

"No problem, I completely understand. It was tough getting here. Thanks, Nate."

"Of course, Andi. Can I get the two of you started with a bottle of our house wine? I know you like the Merlot." I looked across the table at Theodora, who bowed slightly and nodded in approval.

"That would be nice, Nate." He walked away and I still didn't have the home-field advantage. She was steadfastly calm and relaxed. "The weather is terrible. I'm sure you noticed."

"I did. I'm surprised you're here at all. I appreciate your tenacity." She smiled, leaning forward to take the glass Nate had just filled and set on the table. "I hope you find that it's worth it."

"I guess we'll know soon enough."

My heart was beating quickly, and my hands were clammy. I felt like I was in junior high trying to tell a girl I liked her for the first time. According to my mother, my outfit was appropriately juvenile. She would have been so ashamed had she known I was on a date.

I picked up the glass and took a much larger gulp than I had intended. Not wanting to draw attention, I quickly swallowed and felt the searing pain of too much liquid going down my throat. I coughed, took a deep breath, and attempted to gain my composure. Leaning back in the chair, I crossed my legs and carefully set the wineglass down on the table. The lone tear that ran down my cheek helped me to look anything but casual.

"Nervous?" she asked with apparent nerves of steel.

"No, not at all. You?" I managed to get out right before a veiled burp.

"Nothing to be nervous about. Finally, I have the chance to talk with you." She smiled, tracing the bottom of the wineglass with her finger.

"So, you're here on business? Something about a collection?" For this to be a week before Christmas, whatever this "collection" was must have been important. "I'm sure your family wishes you were home right now."

"My family is my father, biologically speaking, but I haven't seen him in years."

"Oh, I'm sorry."

"No need for apologies. I do quite well on my own." She seemed to sit taller as she wrapped her self-made armor around herself tightly.

"I have no doubt that you do."

"I suppose you're from Kringle Falls," she asked, already knowing the answer to that question.

"Guilty. I did leave for a few years to go to school, and I worked in New York for a while, but when the librarian job came open, I knew I had to come back. There is no place like Kringle Falls."

"Indeed. It's certainly an everyone-knows-everyone kind of town. I barely know the people who live in my building."

"I got that feeling in Archie's cab earlier. You were out of your element."

"No, pressed for time. The client is urgently pressuring my boss, who in turn is pressuring me."

"Sounds intriguing. How exactly do I fit into this?"

Nate arrived just in time to subvert the conversation. "Ladies, have you decided on dinner?"

"I'll have the lobster mac and cheese," I said, placing the small menu back on the table. Nate nodded as he filled my glass again.

"Make that two." He set down a small breadbasket and left. Theodora looked around, sat up in her chair, and leaned toward me. "To be honest, I know very little, but I have been told that this is a very private matter. I suppose it was one of the reasons I was sent here. I am very good at what I do."

"You certainly don't mince words, do you? And you have an exceptional perception of yourself." I smiled as I felt the playing field shift in my direction.

"I never understood hiding one's talents or not showing the world what one is capable of," she said, reclining back in her chair.

"Humility. It's certainly okay to be good at what you do and show others those strengths, but there is something to say about the strong and silent type," I said, watching the fire flicker and warm her gray eyes. The corner of her mouth raised in her now familiar half-smile as she took a drink.

"I can certainly see your point when access to what you want is easy. When you must fight for everything that is yours, the world looks a bit different. We all don't have the opportunity to live in a Christmas movie," she said, raising her glass and acknowledging not just the beautifully decorated dining room, but the town. I felt naive and foolish.

"You're right. Life here in Kringle Falls is idyllic. We are a small town, and we often don't let the outside world in. I've been very fortunate. I apologize."

Her face warmed as she blinked twice, trying to erase the last bit of the conversation. "Well, that certainly turned serious, didn't it? Perhaps we should enjoy our wine and get to know each other a little."

We talked through dinner. She told me about boarding schools and going to college early to gain her freedom. I felt she was gifting me with information she didn't often share with others, and I gladly accepted it. I told her of my grandmother and her influence on my life, how I left with a love of books but returned with a love of preservation and history and understanding our place in that history. She listened intently, asked questions, and was genuinely interested in my story. I hung on to every word she said, listening to stories that outlined a fascinating life. She was beautiful with a dash of sadness. I wanted to know all her stories, and I wanted to share all of mine.

Dinner was over when I looked outside for the first time in over two hours. The snow had piled up significantly. I sighed heavily, knowing that I needed to leave soon. Hours felt like seconds. I could easily spend the rest of the evening in this very chair, watching the words escape her lips while the air around us seemed to pop and crack like something was coming to life. I was not ready to go.

"I hate to say this, but you should probably go. The roads are already snow-covered." She paused for a moment and thoughtfully looked toward the lobby. "Or maybe you should stay here? Certainly there are empty rooms."

I loved that she was worried about me. "I should go home. I've driven in this my whole life."

"Is that a bit of humility speaking?" She laughed with that sly smile escaping her lips as she looked down, tucking her hair behind her ear. My heart took an extra beat. She was not the woman I met a few days ago on the road to Kringle Falls. There was still ice to chip away, but I felt it would be well worth the effort.

Our conversation continued for another hour. We both felt as though no one else existed. Other guests had come and gone. Nate had stuck his head out of the kitchen a few times before we realized we were the only ones left in the room.

After hours of talking, we never discussed why Theodora was in town. I quickly offered to pick her up the following morning, and we could speak at the library.

Reluctantly, we left our table and slowly walked to the foyer. The inn was quiet except for the popping of the fire and the soft notes of Doris Day singing "Let It Snow." Theodora's eyes had a distinct sparkle. I wanted desperately to reach my hand out and gently entangle my fingers in hers. We were close enough. My hand felt warm. We were closer than I thought. There was an electrical charge between our skins. I took a deep breath, closing my eyes as the air rushed in my lungs. Her scent coursed through my system. I felt her fingers in mine. I opened my eyes to see her standing there, breathless, wanting to speak, looking at me intently. No one had the advantage here. We were both in new territory.

"Is this, okay?" she asked, hesitantly.

"Yes." The word escaped my mouth as I exhaled.

"Good." She leaned forward, so close to me. I smelled her magnificent scent and felt the warmth of her face. Every inch of my body was tingling as she leaned into me, her hips against mine. The world was starting to go white. Her hand slid further into mine, our fingers tightened together. She was holding me up. I waited, her warm breath against my ear and the heat between our faces.

"I'll see you in the morning. Don't be late," she whispered, lessening the strength of her fingers and slowly stepping away from me. I can't imagine what I looked like, standing there, barely able to move as my vision came back to me.

"Yes, tomorrow morning. I will be here around ten." As I tried to form words, I wasn't even sure if I was making sense. She walked toward the stairs, turned, and smiled as she slowly began to ascend the steps one by one. She knew I would watch until she went out of view.

CHAPTER TWELVE

I don't remember driving home, and it wasn't from drinking too much wine. The snow blew past my windows, and the images of dinner whirled in my head. I couldn't get rid of the giddiness inside of me, the kind that makes you whistle when you don't want to, greet perfect strangers, and maybe even skip a little.

I arrived home to a warm kitchen. Gris was stretched out on the hearth having his back warmed by the low fire that sizzled in the grate behind him. His back paw was solidly in his mouth, and he was sound asleep. My dad had the same look on his face as our dog, lying across the "good" Christmas pillows, tool belt still wrapped around his waist, gentle snores escaping his nose in unison with Gris. My mom was organizing gingerbread walls. Sean was working on the base, eating the mistakes of the evening. All was right in the Thatcher house.

"Hi, honey. Jules stopped by to see you. We weren't sure when you would be home, so we asked her to stay for dinner. You just missed her."

My mom absolutely loved Jules. If there were a way she could get us back together, she would in a heartbeat, and she was constantly working at it. I'm sure Jules would always be part of my life, but we had moved on. Now I needed my mom to do the same.

I asked if they needed help but didn't wait for a response before I bounded up the back stairs and settled into bed. I wanted to process the night and think about what had happened. I lay in bed and watched the snow gently fall, piling up on the branch outside my window. Despite my excitement, sleep came easy and for the first time in a long time, I slept peacefully.

I wasn't expecting the clock to read 9:15 when my eyes opened for the first time. I threw my blankets off and quickly stumbled through a shower. She was going to think the harried look was typical of me. Jeans, boots, and my favorite sweater were going to have to work for today. The curse of thick hair is that it takes far too long to dry. I slid down the back stairs to my family sitting at the kitchen table—plus one.

Jules sat in her usual seat, eating my mom's pancakes. Sean had a half-smile on his face as he looked down at his plate.

"Oh, honey, so glad you're up. I was just getting ready to call you."

"Mom, I have plans this morning."

"Nonsense, honey, sit down and have some breakfast with us. You must eat." I sat down across from Jules and smiled at her. She looked very at home.

"You're here more than I am," I said as I grabbed one pancake and threw it on my plate.

"I've been trying to catch up with you. I called and texted, but you didn't answer."

I took my phone out of my back pocket and looked at the screen. Sure enough, there were four missed calls and thirty-four messages, most of which were from Jules.

"We were getting worried about you last night when Jules said she couldn't get in touch with you. And then Sean came over and told us you were having dinner at the inn. Who were you meeting?"

Everyone stopped and waited for an answer. Even Gris dropped his paw and listened. "Someone I just met, actually. She's in town on business."

Jules's attention was piqued. "Must have been a good dinner if you didn't even hear your phone ring."

"Yes, it was a delicious dinner. And I'm sorry, but I have to go. We are meeting to discuss some library business this morning."

"So, she's in town on library business? That seems a little odd," Jules said with just a hint of jealousy in her voice.

"Honey, why don't you see if you can reschedule? We thought that we could get the tree and decorate it this afternoon. I asked Jules to hang around and help." My mother was relentless. I hated to break her heart, but that wasn't happening today. I told Theodora I was picking her up at ten and that's where I planned to be.

"Mom, I wish you would have checked with me. I can't reschedule this meeting. Besides, I have to work at the library when we're done. There is so much to be finished before I open next week. I can do the tree tonight if you'd like." I knew that Jules couldn't be here this evening because her family had regularly scheduled family dinners on Sunday nights that she would never miss.

"Honey, Jules won't be able to help."

"That's fine, Mrs. Thatcher. I think that was the idea anyway." Jules got up, took her plate to the sink, said goodbye to my family, and walked in my direction. She reached out to hug me as part of her goodbye, moving to kiss me on the cheek, at least that's what I thought. I felt her warm breath near my ear.

"We're good together. You know I'm right. Call me after your meeting." She ran her hand along my back in an old familiar way. A way I used to love but now just made me uncomfortable.

"Well, that was rude, Andrea." My mom brought out the big guns.

"Mom, Jules, and I are over. We're friends, that's it, but if you keep this up, that might not even be the case."

"Oh, honey, you guys are good together. She comes from a great family right here in Kringle Falls. She's perfect."

"You're right, Mom. She is perfect, for you. If the two of you would like to be alone…"

I heard Sean snicker.

"That's enough, Andi," my mom said.

"I'm sorry, Mom, I didn't mean to be sarcastic or hurtful. I know you mean well, but seriously, it's over between us."

My mom's face softened a bit. "I just want you to be happy, Andi."

"And I will be, Mom, just not with Jules. Thank you for loving me so much, but I got this." I squeezed her, kissed her on top of her head, and said goodbye.

Sitting on the old leather chair by the fireplace was a soft tartan blanket. It smelled of fireplace remnants and gingerbread. I tucked it under my arm on the way out the door. I heard my mom behind me as I opened the back door and headed toward the truck.

"Did Andi just grab a blanket?" my mom asked with a hint of confusion in her voice.

"I think so." I heard the smile in Sean's voice. "Must be chilly at the library." He snickered before he could get the full sentence out.

I jumped in my truck and positioned the blanket just right in the passenger seat, smiling the whole time. I didn't even let my truck warm up before I headed toward the inn. It seemed like forever since I had seen Theodora, even though it was only a few hours. I admit the attraction I felt for her was unlike any I had ever experienced. Of course, she was a fascinating, dynamic woman, but it was more than that. Being with her felt right. I felt whole. But there were still so many questions. Why was this collection so important to her? Was she feeling the same way? I felt like an entire world of possibilities lay before me and my truck could not get to her fast enough.

CHAPTER THIRTEEN

Theodora

Usually, sleep comes easy for me. I learned when I was very young to compartmentalize, putting everything in neat little packages to stuff down as far as I could. Successfully navigating life with that skill set allows one to sleep easily. But last night was different. I left the librarian, Andi, and returned to my room. My mind was in overdrive. Her words, my words, formed a narrative, a new chapter and it didn't have a place in my book, even so, I read it repeatedly until I needed to escape my own head. The parlor, I decided, would be a welcome distraction. The nutcrackers were closing in on me.

The lobby was quiet, and the lights were low. Snow was streaming past the side windows, pushed by the wind that howled down the chimney. It was well past one o'clock. The inn was asleep.

The chair by the fireplace was warm against my legs as I settled into it, pulling the blanket from the side across my lap. A chuckle escaped my mouth when I realized I couldn't remember the last time I casually used a blanket. This place was getting to me.

Just an hour ago, Andi and I had stood at the bottom of the stairs, oblivious to anyone around us. The acquisition of this collection was of the utmost importance. That piece of information rested in the forefront of my brain. I wrestled with any other thought that tried to replace it. The thought of Andi standing in front of me, the heat of her body as we brushed against one another. I had tried desperately to maintain some sense of dominance and be the one in control, but I felt it slip away when my face touched hers.

Keep your eye on the ball Theodora. This job was no different from the countless others I had successfully completed in my career. This was just a means to an end, and I intended to use it.

Besides, Andi was not my type. She wore jeans to dinner. She probably had a T-shirt on under her sweater with some grinning cartoon animal plastered on it. And that truck of hers was a heap. How many other things had she hit before Santa on that fateful afternoon?

Footsteps softly approached from behind. Nate placed a cup of black coffee on the table beside me. It sat perfectly in a saucer surrounded by tiny, iced Christmas cookies.

"Decaf," he said with a warm smile. "You don't look as if you need any help staying awake."

"I don't. I just can't seem to fall asleep tonight. I don't usually have this problem. Thank you," I said as I picked the cup up to smell the wonderful scent of a Christmas blend.

"No problem. Is there anything else I can get you?"

"No, thank you." He tucked the tray under his arm and headed back to the dining room which was lit only by the light streaming from the kitchen. "Do you know Andi very well?"

"It's been a while. She was my soccer coach in middle school. She went away to college, but she'd come home in the summer and run a camp for all of us. She even helped me write a couple of my essays when I was applying to college."

"She sounds like an all-around Eagle Scout," I said rather smugly.

"I don't know about that, but she certainly did help me. Her whole family is like that. They would help anyone who needs it.

It's just the way they are. If you don't mind me saying, it looked like the two of you had a good time tonight."

"Not at all, I did have a good time. It was a business dinner." I heard the words leaving my mouth but wasn't sure where they had originated.

"Really? Looked like a little more than a business dinner."

Nate smiled at me and once again headed back to the kitchen. I sat in the cozy room listening to the Christmas music as my body began to relax. I knew it was time to return to my room as the last embers of the fire collapsed through the grate.

Sleep began to settle over me as I pulled the heavy blankets up and over my shoulders. I watched the snow rushing past the windowpanes as my eyes became heavy. No time passed before I found myself sitting in our house in Switzerland. I could hear my parents talking in the other room. Their voices were raised. I slid from my bed and tiptoed past the small Christmas tree my mother had put in my room. The wooden ornaments were different figures, all representing St. Nicholas. Each year she and I would decorate the tree with the tiny figures as she told me the story of each of them. We would finish by placing a beautiful snow maiden on the very top, her robes flowing down the tree. I stopped for a moment to watch the white lights slowly twinkle. The voices became louder. I moved to the door, wanting to hear their every word.

The door creaked slightly as I opened it. The conversation stopped. I stood breathless, waiting for it to resume, watching them through the slit between the door and the frame. My father started for my room. My mother grabbed his arm and spun him around. He looked at her hand as it touched his arm. He hated that she touched him. She slowly let go.

"Darling, let's go for a ride. We can finish our conversation," she said softly as if she loved him with all her heart.

Even then I knew what she was doing. She called for the nanny and told her they were leaving and asked her to stay with me. It was the last time I saw her.

CHAPTER FOURTEEN

The roads were covered in snow as I made my way to the inn. A morning like this was meant to be spent in bed with a warm blanket and a hot mug of cocoa. I rounded the bend to see Nate clearing the driveway.

"Hey, thanks for clearing this off for me," I yelled to a very cold Nate, who had been outside for some time. His cheeks were rosy, and he was bundled like a toddler getting ready to go out and play in the snow.

"No problem. It's heavy snow." He walked toward my truck dragging the snow shovel behind him. "She's been down in the parlor since a little after nine," he said, nodding toward the front door. "I thought she was coming down for breakfast, but she's been sitting in the chair by the window, and I'm pretty sure she's been watching for you."

I felt my core warm and spread up my neck as my cheeks flushed. "Thanks, Nate."

"No problem, Andi," he said, raising his eyebrows and smiling an assuming smile. Pulling past him, I parked and quickly got out of the truck to find her standing at the top of the stairs that led to the inn.

"Good morning!" I said with an uncontrollable smile on my face. She held two cups in her hand, holding one out for me. "Thanks, coffee?"

"No, hot chocolate. I didn't think you were a coffee kind of girl," she said with a great deal of certainty. She was right. I have always hated coffee.

"What about yours?" I asked, pointing to hers.

"Coffee, black. I like it simple."

"Good to know," I said reaching for the cup. We moved toward each other, both taking a step and pausing for a moment as I took the warm drink, my fingers touching hers and lingering. "Should we go?" I said hesitantly, not wanting to let go.

"I'm looking forward to seeing your library."

She looked incredible and surprisingly casual. Her jeans were barely visible as her brown boots came to her knees. Her oversize sweater wrapped around her. A tartan plaid scarf circled her neck, draping casually across her sweater. Her hair was slightly more relaxed, tucked behind her ears.

"You might need a coat. It's a little chilly in the library. At least until I get the fire going."

I heard her laugh. "Is this library in 1890, on the prairie, maybe? Trust me, I'll be fine." She continued to snicker as she opened the door and saw the blanket stretched across the seat. Her chuckle became a laugh. "Why am I not surprised?" she asked, folding the blanket on her lap. She looked surprisingly comfortable in my truck. I could get used to this. We waved to Nate and headed toward the town.

"Do you mind if we take a detour?" Theodora asked, adjusting the blanket around her legs.

"Not at all," I said too quickly, knowing I would say yes to any extra time with her.

"I need to head to New Hope. Is that too far away?"

"No, what do you need, if you don't mind me asking?" I would have said a cross-country journey wasn't very far if it meant being with her.

"My boss sent some documents she needs me to see right away."

"She couldn't email them?" I asked, puzzled.

"No, they're of a…delicate nature. A colleague of mine left them in a safety deposit box on the way to his cabin."

"Safety deposit box? That sounds official."

"We take care of our clients and their privacy. So, New Hope, how far is it?"

"It's about an hour away but I can shave some time off if we cut through Hogmadog Pass. Most people take the highway, but the pass is beautiful this time of year."

"Is it safe? There's been quite a bit of snow lately."

"She can handle anything," I said, patting the dashboard.

"Famous last words," Theodora laughed. She pulled the blanket up to cover her hands and settled into the seat.

"Christmas music?" I asked, turning the radio up to let the sounds of a Motown Christmas filter through the car. Her knee began to move up and down with the music. "It's catchy, isn't it?"

"I've never really been a fan of Christmas music, but Motown, the Supremes, Ronnie Spector, I have listened to them since I was a kid."

"Okay, I'm going to need to unpack this. You don't like Christmas music? How? Christmas music can change my whole day. It makes me feel at home, warm and cozy, and so happy."

"And all of that is associated with memories, correct? Warm, happy times you probably spent with your family? The music you love is the music that was played year after year and those memories come flooding back when you hear those songs."

"Exactly," I said very naively.

"I didn't have that. Christmas music reminds me that even when I was with my father, the staff put up the tree and wrapped a present or two. Christmas was just another day. I usually tried to find a good book and spent the day reading, hoping it would go by quickly." The car was silent for a moment or two except for the knocking of the truck and empty notes of the Christmas music that now fell flat around us.

"I'm so sorry. I don't know what else to say. That must have been hard." She didn't look at me but stared at the pine trees that rushed by the window. "Hey," I said, reaching over and placing my hand on her arm. "Are you okay?"

She shook her head, as if trying to break a trance, and squeezed my hand, quickly letting go while she returned a half-smile.

"Yes, I'm fine. Just a little tired. I didn't sleep very much last night," she said as her demeanor quickly changed. She sat up a little taller in the seat, adjusting her armor.

"Why is that?"

"I had a few things on my mind."

"Really? Anything I can help with?"

"No, I got it but thanks," she said, surprising me with a wink.

We took the road that led to the shortcut. The sky became cloudy, and snow began to fall as we drove closer to the mountain pass. The road was clear but would not stay that way for long. I held my arm firmly on the console, letting her know I was there, hoping to convince her that I understood what she was feeling but there was no way I could. My family, my life, was filled with nothing but love and support. She leaned toward me, our arms touching, and a flood of butterflies unleashed in my stomach. The heat between us was enough to warm the truck.

As we approached the pass, the sky began to darken. Large flakes covered the windshield quickly, unable to be cleared by fiercely beating wipers. Begrudgingly, I withdrew my arm from the console, trying to steady the wheel. The road had become slick. I tested it by hitting the brakes and fishtailing to the side. Theodora reached for the armrest.

"You do know how to drive in this right?" she asked, keeping her eyes on the road.

"What? Of course, I know how to drive in this. I've been doing this my entire life. I was just testing the road and hoping you would grab me instead of that armrest." Realizing how cheesy that must have sounded, I felt my cheeks turn red.

"If I recall correctly, it was your expert driving that allowed us to meet in the first place," she said, raising her eyebrow. She was wonderfully gracious for ignoring my stupid attempt at flirting.

"That's fair," I said, almost forgetting the incident where we first met.

The gray fog of snow encircled us as we traveled over the pass. The headlights illuminated only a few feet in front of the truck and that distance was quickly decreasing as the minutes passed.

"Maybe we should pull over and wait a few minutes. It looks like it's getting worse."

"That might be a good idea. There's a turnout just ahead. We can pull over and wait to see if the weather clears up a little." The break in the road came upon us quickly. I pulled as far to the right as I could, not wanting to leave us vulnerable on the side of the road.

"Do you have a thermos of hot chocolate handy?" Theodora asked, snickering as she drank the remaining coffee in her cup.

"Come to think of it, I might just have something," I said, reaching behind the seat.

"C'mon!" Theodora quipped as I leaned toward her, fumbling around on the floor. Her scent was warm and comforting, flowers rain-kissed on a spring day, their bouquet resting softly on her skin. I took longer than I should have hunting around behind her seat just to be close to her. Finally, I pulled out a box of The Oven's famous Christmas cookies.

"Not exactly hot chocolate but I think it will do the trick."

"Aren't you full of surprises?" She unlatched her seat belt and turned toward me.

"I try." I set the cookies on the console and turned to face her as well. "I have some hot chocolate left if you would like to share it with me." I lifted the holiday cup in her direction. She split a cookie in half and handed me a piece as she took the cup from my hand and gently sipped. She could make drinking cocoa look seductive. She was really good at this game. She handed it back to me, her lipstick smudged on the lip of the cup. Adrenaline flooded through my veins, causing my heart to pound in my chest. My temperature was rising because I watched her drink something. I was in trouble. The entire population of North American monarch butterflies was flying right through my stomach.

"Are you okay?" she asked with the corner of her lip curled up in an overconfident smile. Her eyes ran up and down my body. I imagined myself falling from a height and landing like a superhero in a panther-like pose. Visualizing was all I had right now.

"I'm good..." That's all that escaped my lips before the hot chocolate ran from the lopsided cup into my lap, pooling between my legs. My panther quickly turned into a three-legged cat on its ninth life.

"I'm sorry, what were you saying?" she said with a giggle.

"I was saying that I think you're making it hard for me to concentrate right now," I said, grabbing my scarf and mopping up the warm chocolate that was beginning to drip from the seat. She was watching me with eyes that were sparkling. Some of the ice had melted away and what was left was an ocean of deep blue. She took a bite of the cookie and slowly chewed, carefully analyzing me.

"I like that," she said, very self-assured.

"Yeah, I know," I said, trying to mop up the chocolate that would not only stain but become a sticky mess. The snow outside the truck was my only option to clean up the mess, and it would have to be quick. The wind rushed in, filling the cab with frozen confetti. I turned to shield my face and caught a glimpse of a warm light in the distance. Finishing the cleanup, I jumped back in the truck and turned on the windshield wipers, throwing the snow off the window. The path that lay ahead of us was now visible. The golden light glimmered in the distance, like a lighthouse on a distant shore.

I had driven this pass more times than I could count. There was nothing along this road. I was certain of it. Yet here we sat in a whiteout watching the light cast a ghostly glow from a phantom building.

"What is it?" Theodora asked as she wrapped the blanket around my shoulders, warming me by rubbing her hands along my arms. I should have tried this stunt earlier.

"No idea," I said as I attempted to focus beyond the windshield.

"Maybe we can wait there until the storm passes."

It was a good idea. The weather was getting worse, and I would feel better if we could wait this out somewhere safe. These crazy mountain storms had a way of whipping themselves into a frenzy and sticking around for a while.

I slowly let the clutch out and began moving forward in the deepening snow. The tire treads desperately tried to reach the road. We slid from side to side but finally began to move toward the cabin, watching the lights intensify in their brightness.

The provincial cabin sat in the snow, rough timbers holding it together. It looked as if it might blow away with the next gust of wind.

"Let me check it out," I said as I jumped from the truck, leaning into the wind and shielding my face from the sharp sting of the snowflakes that felt like tiny little ninja stars. I walked up the step onto the front porch and felt it give way. I fell backward into the waiting arms of Theodora. She was much stronger than I had imagined.

"You didn't think I'm one of those wait-in-the-car kind of girls, did you?"

She steadied me, leaving her arm around my waist as we both walked toward the door. It clicked and opened on its own. The warm air rushed from the room, surrounding us and pulling us in. The door slammed behind us, locking the wind out. Eventually, our eyes adjusted to the dim room. It was lit by a roaring fireplace that had been sparked by the open door. Strings of Christmas lights hung from the ceiling, looping around rough timbers and hanging from the bar that anchored the room. The lights were the old classic C9 bulbs that generated enough heat to keep the room warm without the fireplace. Framed images hung on the walls with old ski and travel posters. Long tables, lit by candles of various sizes, sat in the middle of the room. Wooden booths hugged the walls. Old lanterns hung from the ceiling, glowing on rusted chains. Doris Day sang "Let It Snow," again, the notes escaping an old jukebox in the corner. I guess this was our song.

"Now this song I know," Theodora said, letting go of my waist.

"I would hope so," I said, thinking of the night before, standing in the parlor of the inn, cheek to cheek, barely able to breathe as the song played gently in the background.

"Ladies, this storm is unforgiving. I'm glad you stumbled upon us." The angelic voice came from behind the bar. It landed softly on our ears, bringing both comfort and familiarity. It belonged to a tall woman, with long silvery hair cascading down her shoulders. Her porcelain skin was ageless, and her grace was apparent as she effortlessly placed two heavy steins on the bar. "We have a house glogg that will warm you right up." She scooped the steaming drink from the large black cauldron sitting on the bar. The spicy scents escaped quickly from the open pot, almost smelling better than Theodora. "On the house," she said as she pushed the large steins toward us.

We looked at each other in agreement and sat down on the heavy barstools. As my eyes adjusted to the dimly lit tavern, more details began to emerge. Bookcases dotted the room, small and large, tucked into the walls like nooks and crannies holding mysterious treasures. A beautiful gray cat with a splash of white on his head sauntered in front of the fireplace, stretched, and took residence on a cushion that rested on a shelf.

"Nysno, his name is Nysno. He runs the place." The tall stranger laughed as Nysno stretched once again and rolled to the side, stomach elongated to face the warm fire.

"It's funny, I've lived here my whole life and I don't remember this place," I said.

"We've always been here. Sometimes we're just a little hard to find," she laughed, and gave us a wink. "What brings the two of you up here?"

"We're heading to New Hope."

Theodora jumped into the conversation. "Andi was under the impression this was a shortcut." She smiled and elbowed me.

"You two are cute. How long have you been together?" the woman asked.

"Us? Oh, we're not together. We just met," Theodora quickly added as she stumbled over her words. "I'm here on business and Andi has been nice enough to help me out."

The tall woman paused and looked at both of us. "Give it time. You two have a connection."

"You may have something there, Randi." A voice came from the dark corner of the bar. "I saw it when they walked in." I looked in the direction of the voice, waiting for a face to appear. "We don't tend to see many new people around here. It's good to see a fresh face."

The stool slid against the stone floor and a well-dressed, middle-aged man stepped into the focused light of a bar lamp. His suit was dark, perhaps blue, maybe black. A white shirt set the background for a tight Merovingian tie, crimson in color. His kind eyes were set in a face that showed his years. He reached toward me. I took his soft hand, gently shaking it.

"Andi," I said, "and this is Theodora."

"Thomas. Nice to meet both of you."

"You look familiar, Thomas. I'm sure I have seen you around town."

"Perhaps," he said mysteriously as he pulled his seat into the light. "I do come to town a few times a year."

"Thomas is a world traveler. He doesn't stay in one place very long," Randi chimed in as she filled our mugs.

"That's enough for me," I said, placing my hand over the top of the mug. "Someone is going to have to drive us out of here."

"It's not going to be me so fill it up!" Theodora said loudly as she pushed her stein toward Randi. I looked at her and laughed at her uncharacteristically loud and brutish behavior. "Was I loud?" she asked as she covered her mouth and let out a small burp.

"Little bit," I whispered to her and laughed.

"Why don't the two of you head over to that table by the fire and get warmed up? I'll bring you out some of my famous winter stew." Randi finished filling up Theodora's stein and vanished through the door behind the bar.

"Sounds like an excellent idea. Nice to have met you," Thomas said as he returned to his place in the corner, picking up a newspaper that was not written in English.

Theodora and I stood at the same time. She immediately grabbed my arm. "How much of that have you had?" I asked, watching her gingerly stand beside me.

"Half, three-fourths…most of it?"

"Thirsty or nervous?" I asked.

"A little of both."

I didn't mind that she was holding my arm. Every touch of hers released a migratory group of butterflies through my stomach. She literally made my knees weak.

We walked to the table by the fire. The snow was still falling heavily outside the window. The table had a padded bench secured to the wall with two pillows resting on either side. Opposite the bench were two chairs. The fire danced and lit the table in hues of yellow, orange, and red. I slid into the bench hoping that she would join me. I wanted to feel her leg against mine and have her lean into me. I saw her hand on the chair as she began to pull it out. My heart sank.

"Oh, honey, don't sit in that chair," Randi said as she walked toward our table with two large bowls in hand. "And the other one is too close to the fire. Why don't you sit on the bench with Andi. It's nice and cozy over there." I couldn't thank Randi enough for her suggestion and quickly slid over to accommodate Theodora. "And, honey, you need to get some food in you," she said as Theodora plopped down into the seat. The steaming stew sat in front of us, the wonderful smells lifting into our noses. As expected, Theodora rested against me.

"You're a lightweight, aren't you?" I asked, laughing as I enjoyed the weight of her against me.

"Hardly. I would never call myself a lightweight. Did you have any of it?"

"A few drinks but I didn't down it like you did. Besides, when my throat started burning, I thought it might be a good idea to stop."

"All I can say is that Randi must be pretty heavy-handed." She burped again as she grabbed the stein.

"All right, Champ, let's go easy on that." I took the mug from her hand and set it back on the table. "It's still early. Let's save the heavy drinking for later." She snickered as she clumsily found her spoon. *Note to self: she's adorable when she's tipsy.*

The stew tasted as good as it smelled and warmed our cold bodies. I felt a little sleepy as I took the last sip and rested back in the seat. Theodora joined me, leaning against me as she sighed with contentment. I hoped the snowstorm continued to rage. She rested her head on my shoulder and I let her scent wrap around me, intoxicating me. Closing my eyes, I leaned my head against the warm wood of the bench. Randi brought me back to Earth when she picked up our bowls. She smiled at us like a proud aunt and winked at me.

Suddenly, the tranquil atmosphere of the tavern was disrupted by a loud bang as the front door blew open and snow poured in. The wind howled as it rushed up the chimney. Two dark figures stepped into the comfort of the warm room. They stood, shaking the snow from their clothes as the door slammed shut behind them.

"Konrad, Viktoria! Got grueze iuch."

"What was that?" I said quietly, as I listened to Randi greet the strangers.

"God greet you," Theodora mumbled as she straightened up in the seat. "It's High German." She burped again. This time covering her mouth.

"Let's get some coffee in you. How do you know that, by the way?"

"I'm fluent in German and lived in Austria. I haven't heard it in a while. It's an older phrase."

The two made their way to the bar, continuing to talk to Randi in what I assumed was German. Thomas joined in from the back of the bar, once again coming into view. The four laughed as they carried on what could only be called a conversation between old friends.

Theodora needed coffee. I approached the bar and was met with the smiling face of Konrad. He said something to Randi who looked at me.

"He is asking if you are new here. He hasn't seen you or Theodora before but says you look familiar."

"I live in Kringle Falls, ten minutes from here." Randi translated for him. He and Viktoria laughed loudly. Randi noticed the puzzled look on my face.

"They're laughing about everyone's misfortune in getting caught in the snowstorm. Mother Nature has her own agenda." I took the coffee and returned to the table. Theodora was resting her head against the back of the bench.

"Interesting couple," I said, placing the steaming cup in front of her. "Black, just the way you like it." From the look on her face, I was pretty sure she saw two mugs. "It's the one on the right." A smile lifted the corner of her mouth as she chuckled and wrapped her hands around the mug.

"I knew it. It was on the left." I watched her sip at the coffee. She was even more beautiful now. Once again, she leaned back against me. I could sit here forever.

Relaxing into the cozy seat we shared, I let Theodora settle into the curve of my body, leaning in as much as I could to support her, but not wanting to be too forward. We were both quiet and it wasn't awkward. There was no silence that needed to be filled. It just felt right.

Looking around the room for the first time I noticed picture after picture hanging on the walls. Some framed, some simply tacked to the wall. Some looked as if they could have been taken today, others a hundred years ago. Just beside our booth, next to a beautiful painting of a large reindeer, was a picture of a couple decorating a Christmas tree right here in this tavern. The young couple stood frozen in time in the black and white image.

I slid away from Theodora to inspect it closer. The young couple had familiar faces. She was decorating a Christmas tree, wrapping garland around its branches. He sat on the very bench I had just left, ornament boxes stacked in front of him. He was watching her with so much love. I stepped closer to see their faces. It was my grandparents, and there in the reflection of the mirror, above the fireplace, was Randi, standing behind the bar as if it were yesterday. I slowly turned to see Randi standing in almost the same spot, watching me. She smiled, as a slight nod moved her head.

I had so many questions. They would have to wait. I needed to think, and we had to get to New Hope. It was getting late and the storm seemed to have passed. Randi made us coffee and cocoa to go. When I reached for the cups, she held my hand for a moment.

"We're here if you need us."

I thought it was an odd thing to say but it still brought me comfort. I thanked her and we made our way back to the truck. I opened the door for Theodora and offered my arm as she pulled herself up into the seat. The truck started easily. We continued our trip to New Hope. The horizon brightened as the road opened. The snow whipped behind the truck causing a whiteout behind us. The tavern vanished.

The trip to New Hope was quick. I dropped Theodora off at the bank and took the opportunity to visit one of my favorite bookstores. It was just a few doors down, The Night Owl. I had wandered in when I was a teenager during a weekend shopping trip with my mom. It was filled with unique books, some new but mostly old, many dusty and showing their years. In the back, behind a heavy tapestry, was a small section of local history books. A familiar chair sat in the corner, bathed in the light from a window that lifted to the ceiling. A gray cat was curled up in the chair. He had a recognizable splash of white on his head.

"Nysno?" I asked, realizing how foolish I sounded. He pushed his head into the cushion and purred. "That's impossible," I said to myself.

"What would that be?"

I turned to see an older gentleman, with tousled white hair and wire-framed glasses, standing behind me. His crisp white button-down shirt peeked out from a red Fair Isle sweater. Upon closer inspection, the sweater's pattern was reindeer, elves, and candy canes.

"The cat, he looks familiar."

"She wanders in from time to time. This seems to be her favorite chair. I call her the Gray Lady."

"As in the Gray Lady Ghost?"

"Seems fitting, doesn't it? She sneaks in and out like a ghost. She used to give me a jump but now I just give her a scratch behind the ears and go about my business." He skirted past me and placed a book on the shelf.

"I saw a similar cat not too long ago, an hour or so in fact, at the tavern on the pass between here and Kringle Falls."

"Tavern? Is it new? I didn't know there was anything up there."

"Me neither. We happened upon it in the snow. It got treacherous as we were driving over."

"Interesting," he said as he looked at the shelf. "There's a book around here on local mountain legends." He pulled an old book out, the corners tattered, and the cover worn. He handed it to me. "You might like this. Let me know if you need anything."

He left me and the Gray Lady to peruse the book. She moved to the side as if to tell me to have a seat. I sat in the soft chair as she circled and settled beside me. Her warmth was very comforting. The book was published in 1952. The cloth cover was dark green with gold trim. The title was simple: *Mountain Legends*. The inside cover held a detailed map of the surrounding mountains, beautifully hand drawn. Kringle Falls rested in the lower left-hand corner of the double-page illustration. Symbols dotted the map identifying the mysteries that were afoot. This would be an incredible display for the library. Part of my love of being a librarian was the research involved. Everything had a bit of mystery that was begging to be solved.

I thumbed through the book and found the usual lake monster and Bigfoot. A story about a crusty old woodsman that wandered the forest and a secret military bunker used for CIA experiments.

"Well, Gray Lady, I think I'm sold. I'll take the book." She purred softly and pushed her head into the palm of my hand.

"Make a new friend?" Theodora was standing in the doorway to the small room. The light from the window softly fell on her face. She was beautiful.

"Does she look familiar to you?" I asked, wondering if she would see the resemblance.

"No, why? Should I know her from somewhere?" She lowered her head, hiding her laugh from me.

"Funny." I nudged her as I walked by.

"Did you find something?" She was still snickering as she pointed to the book under my arm.

"Local history. It will be perfect for a display in the library." We headed toward the checkout where we found the older gentleman waiting for us.

"Did you find what you were looking for?" he asked, wrapping the book in paper.

"I'm not sure that I was looking for anything, but I found something thanks to you."

"I'm glad I could be of service. I think you might find some useful information in the book." He tucked his card in the wrapped book and handed it to me. "Merry Christmas," he said with a smile.

We grabbed a quick sandwich to go and decided it was best to head back to Kringle Falls. Our short trip had taken most of the day. We skipped the pass and took the long way back to town. I didn't mind spending the time in the car with her. I hoped that she would talk about the documents she saw at the bank, but she was pretty tight-lipped, and I didn't want her to think I was prying. So, we talked about little things—the fact that she doesn't like onions on her sandwich and I like tomatoes. She is just as comfortable in heels as she is in tennis shoes and my baseball hat collection is embarrassingly large. I drove just under the speed limit, wanting to hear all her stories. We returned to the scene of the crime, Santa waving in the middle of the holiday menagerie just outside of town.

"His arm is really moving." Theodora noticed the difference right away.

"We had to use a new motor. I didn't think it was too noticeable but maybe Sean was right. He said it looked like Santa was an angry crossing guard at the elementary school, impatiently rushing everyone into town."

"Your brother seems very funny," she snickered as we watched the frantically waving Claus pass by the window.

"Should we go to the library or call it a day?" I asked, hoping she didn't want to end our time together.

"I think we should go to the library if that's okay with you?"

Those butterflies were on the move again, blazing a trail through my stomach. "Absolutely." The back seat held remnants of our day—a tartan blanket, a few cookies from The Oven, a couple of coffee cups, and an old book. From the look of it, we had a pretty great day.

CHAPTER FIFTEEN

Just as expected, the library was cold even with the furnace running. I made my rounds, turned on the lights, and finally started a fire in the study. Theodora sat on the couch, watching me pile up the paper and kindling.

"I turned on the kettle in the office for you. It should be ready soon," I said, crumbling the paper and pushing it into the grate. It was exceptionally quiet. I could feel her behind me.

"You left New York to come here?" she asked, sounding surprised.

"You act as if I gave something up."

"You didn't?"

"Not at all. Look at all I gained." I stood up as the fire began to burn. Throwing a couple of logs on the grate, I sat back down on the couch. "This place may not house collections of international or historical importance, but it is important to the people of this community, and it's a long-standing tradition in our family. That means more to me than any high-profile job I could be doing in New York."

"That's quite admirable." She was looking at me as if she were recalculating what she thought of me.

"I grew up here with my grandmother. She was the town librarian. Any free time I had I spent here. She taught me the importance of books, but not just books, stories and how everyone has a story worth telling and worth hearing." I paused for a moment, realizing how much I missed her. I felt so close to her sitting here in this study, where she told me so many of those stories.

"She meant a great deal to you, didn't she?" Theodora reached out and put her hand over mine, gently folding her fingers into my palm. It caught me off guard. Holding someone's hand is such an intimate gesture. Her soft skin warmed mine, sending heat up my arm, breaking from the collar of my sweater and quickly toasting my cheeks. I could feel my heart beating in my chest and the blood leaving my head. She looked so calm and collected. I wish I knew if I were having the same effect on her.

"She did, and as long as I'm here, I feel like she is too." I folded my leg underneath me and turned to face Theodora. Our hands were entwined now. Hers were warm and strong and held mine. It was the most comfortable I had felt in a long time.

"What are you thinking?" she asked softly.

"There's a lot more to you than what you show people."

"Isn't that true for everyone?" she asked, turning her glance away from me. I reached to touch her cheek and bring her gaze back to mine. She allowed it to happen, slowly closing her eyes as a breath escaped her.

"Maybe, but you...you're different. I'm not sure what it is, but I would like the chance to find out." I gathered my courage and traveled what seemed like a long distance between us hoping she would meet me halfway. She only moved toward me after I had strongly committed. She smiled, knowing exactly what she was doing. Her hand left mine and edged up my waist. I could feel her breath and the tip of her nose on my cheek. I closed my eyes and exhaled.

The library door burst open to reveal my brother, carrying a giant Christmas tree and belting "Jingle Bells," with Gris in tow.

We both jumped. Theodora held her chest and looked shell-shocked. Shaking my head, I remembered how Sean had the absolute worst timing. He bounded into the study, shaking the snow off the tree. Gris let out a few bellowing barks while his backside wiggled out of control.

"Found the perfect tree…" He looked at both Theodora and I and paused for a moment. "Oh, I'm interrupting. I can just leave the tree and let you take it from here. Looks like you already have things under control. No need for my help."

Theodora attempted to hide a muffled laugh. Sean turned and headed out the door, knowing full well that he was interrupting. I was sure my mom had sent him.

"Sean! Come back. I want you to meet someone." He came back in, pulling his hat, adorned with reindeer antlers, and his mittens off, and then stuffed them in his pocket. "Sean, this is Theodora Declan. She is a representative of Whitby's. She's in town on business."

"Wait, you're the grinchy woman from the Santa accident." He stumbled for a moment, trying to retrieve his foot from his mouth. "That is not what I meant."

"No, that's certainly fair. I wasn't in the best mood when we first met. Hopefully, I can have a second chance," she said with her charming smile that had already won Sean over. Reaching her hand out to Sean, he graciously accepted. "And who is this?" she asked, bending down to let Gris sniff her hand, which he did in passing on his way to jump into her lap. He leaned against her, snowy paws all over her jeans, delivering big, wet kisses. She took every bit of it and loved on him like he was her own. In my entire life, I have felt like you can always get a true sense of a person's character by how they treat animals.

"Nice to meet you!" Sean said, smiling at Gris rolling around in her lap. "Hey, Andi, I thought you might want a tree for the library. I hope you don't mind. I just brought one by, guessing you'd be here."

"No, I think it's a great idea, Sean. And yes, you knew I would be here because I *told* you I would be here. Thanks for thinking of me. We can put it over there in the corner." Pausing for a moment, I remembered one of my favorite memories. "I loved to sit here and read *The Snow Maiden* once the tree was up and decorated. My grandmother would put it up right after Thanksgiving."

"*The Snow Maiden?*" Theodora asked, surprised. "That's my favorite story. I've read every version a thousand times. Not many people know about it." The side of her lip curled up as she said this like she was tallying the things we had in common.

"I've been collecting every version of the story I can find. I want to make a special collection here."

"I probably have a few I can add to that collection for you." I noticed Sean shuffling back and forth, keenly aware of his third-wheel status.

"Okay then, I'm going to leave this here, and, Andi, I will call you later. Theodora, nice to meet you…again. Hey, can you take Gris home for me? Thanks." He was out the door before I could say anything. Theodora and I looked at one another and laughed.

"I think I will lock the door." I didn't want to be surprised again and hoped we could get back to where we were. "Where were we?" I asked, realizing how cheesy it sounded as it hung in the air between us.

"I think we need to decorate a tree." She paused for a moment. "It's been years."

"Since you decorated a tree?"

"Yes…" she said slowly, staring distantly at the fire. Gris settled in beside her and laid his head on her leg, his back foot in his mouth. I looked at him like the traitor he was, and his tail started to wag slowly.

"Sounds like the perfect thing to do then. My grandmother has some boxes of decorations upstairs. Why don't we bring them down, see if we can use them, and then go from there."

She agreed, stood from the couch, and placed her scarf under Gris's head, kissing his nose. I really liked the soft side she was showing me.

I walked to the doorway and held my hand out to her. She reached for it. I led us upstairs to find the decorations and hopefully get back to where we were.

CHAPTER SIXTEEN

She let me lead her up the stairs, our hands fitting comfortably together like they had known each other for years. The light from the stained glass windows lit each step. Large snowflakes tumbled out of the clouds, and their shadows cast small falling circles through the colors of the windows. Just below the gray ceiling of the sky, hung the sun. Soon it would fall below the horizon, and the day would turn dark, but right now, it was magical. There are moments in your life that you look back on for being perfect, everything seems to align, and you know... you just know. Holding Theodora's hand and walking up the stairs, I knew. This was one of those moments.

Ascending the staircase, I took in the moment. And then I felt her stop. I turned to see the vibrant light dance across her face. She was looking at the window.

"That's it. That's why I'm here."

"The window?" I asked, surprised.

She walked up the step to the landing, placing her hand lightly on the window. "This is what brought me here."

"What do you mean?"

"The person I represent saw this window on social media. Somehow it tipped them off to some kind of collection. I was sent here to find it."

"Who would post a picture of the windows on social media? Wait a minute. The librarian. The one that just left. She wasn't from here. She came from up north somewhere. It must have been her. I don't think anyone from around here would think the windows were all that special."

"They must be very special, or as I said, *I* would not have been sent here."

"How is Whitby's getting along without you?" I asked, snickering.

"I'm good at what I do."

I liked the little bit of arrogance she possessed. In anyone else, it would have greatly annoyed me, but in her, it was part of her charm. She exuded confidence. "So, you were sent to buy the windows?" I asked, still perplexed as to why she was here. "That's all the information they gave you? So, you're actually more of a super sleuth," I added, becoming more and more impressed with her. Intelligence was definitely a turn-on for me. The more I learned about Theodora, the more I was drawn to her.

"Have you heard of the Voynich Manuscript?" she asked with an eyebrow raised. I felt it was a test.

"MS 408," I said, tossing the ball back in her court. She looked slightly surprised and a little impressed that I could refer to its reference number in Yale's Beinecke Rare Book Library. I mean, what kind of librarian would I be if I didn't know Yale's rare book library?

"Yes, exactly, MS 408. It was the summer after I got my MFA from Yale."

"You've seen it then?" I hoped to hear an eyewitness account.

"Unfortunately, no, even though it's housed there, only a select few have seen it. But it did catch my attention—a fascinating historical mystery. So, I've become somewhat of a history detective for Whitby's. It certainly isn't what I started to do but I love it."

"That's incredible," I said immediately, wanting to know more, realizing we were off topic.

"These windows are the first piece of the puzzle. Do you know anything about them?"

"I do, but I'm not sure you'll believe me." We sat on the stairs that led up to the next level. I told her the story that Sean had recently relayed to me about the stranger leaving the windows under the tree in the center of town.

"And your grandfather never saw the man who left them?"

"Nothing," I said, shaking my head. "He followed him into the woods, but there was no trace of anyone, not even footsteps."

"Well, this is becoming quite an interesting mystery, isn't it?" She turned to look at me. "I'm glad you're along for the ride on this one."

"Me too," I said quickly, unsure of where this would take us.

CHAPTER SEVENTEEN

We decided our best course of action would be to decorate the tree, share any knowledge we knew, and begin to unravel this mystery. I decided to keep the staircase and the sealed containers to myself for the time being. I knew they had to be related, but who was Theodora working for? What did they want? There were too many unanswered questions. I needed to tread very carefully. The mystery that resided in the basement was much bigger than Theodora and whatever was happening between us. I felt a strong sense of guardianship over this library and its contents. I had to keep that in the forefront but everything about her made that very hard to do.

A tree needed decorating, but neither of us was brave enough to cut the ropes that held it together. I knew my brother's ability to pick a tree. Sean had one type of tree: full. When we were kids, he would choose all our trees—by walking into them. If we couldn't see him, it was a good tree. And Theodora, well, she saw him wearing antlers. She knew he meant business. We stood silently, debating the safety of releasing the ropes.

With a healthy amount of bravado and a touch of courage, Theodora grabbed the scissors and cut the ropes. The tree, which had been runner-up for Rockefeller Center, had branches that seemed to span the room. The smell of fresh pine filled the small space like a Christmas bomb. Gris raised his head and let out a few warning howls, clearly telling us to get out of the way.

"So, it runs in the family," she said, laughing at me as I pushed away the branches that were trapping me.

"Christmas spirit? Absolutely. You may have to have a certain amount of it to even live here." She laughed. I hoped that with any luck, I would be making her laugh for a long time to come.

We decorated the tree with a mix of old and new ornaments, the delicate old figurines of St. Nicholas alongside the new garland I had made from tiny little wooden books. Shiny glass ornaments and old tin ornaments all found a place on the tree this year. The old white lights cast a warm glow in the room. A few of them blinked slowly, allowing the tree to twinkle. We stepped back, leaning against the back of the couch, and paused for a moment to look at our work.

"It's quite lovely," she said softly. Our hands touched as they rested on the couch. I slid my fingers over hers. Gris noticed and stood up, resting his chin on our hands, his eyes looking up and darting back and forth between us. We both laughed as his tail began to wag quickly.

The music changed and Diana Krall began to croon "The Christmas Song." Theodora stood and faced me, taking my hand in hers and pulling me toward her. Our bodies met, slowly moving together, the anticipation building. Our hands searched for each other's waists; every touch of her fingers was electric. Together we swayed, slowly our bodies tightly merged, our warm breaths mingled together as we looked deeply into one another's eyes, so close I could almost taste her. We lingered for a moment, the heat between us growing. She took a small step back, inhaling deeply.

"This is highly unusual for me," she whispered. Oh, dear lord, this was her first time on our team. It had to have been written all over my face. "Oh my god, no, not that! I mean that I don't normally…relationships are difficult, and I don't…"

"Things are happening quickly, is what you mean?"

"Yes...they are." She glanced down, interrupting our connection.

Standing there, sharing intimate space with her, I tried to be casual, but alarm bells were going off in my head. She wasn't exactly an open book. There was so much more to her than what she showed. I was treading in dangerous territory, well beyond the bounds of where I felt comfortable. I was looking for a life raft when she caught my gaze again. The adrenaline began to flow like I had just pushed off the top of a steep incline and was racing down a hill, my skis on fire. The only difference was that here I had very little control.

We leaned toward one another, lips barely touching, her warm breath setting fire to my skin. I felt the soft touch of her hand on the back of my neck as our lips met. I was well out of my safety zone when our kiss deepened, flipping an ignition switch that launched a white heat through my entire body. I exhaled deeply and she replied with a soft moan. We no longer swayed with the music but held one another tightly, her fingers in my hair as I held her face.

Our lips parted, her tongue tracing my mouth before diving in to take my breath away.

We were far from the reality of the library when a loud crash quickly pulled us back. Gris barked like he had treed a squirrel, running to the foyer to investigate. Theodora stepped forward, placing herself between me and whatever had created the noise. We stood waiting for another sound as Gris bounded up the stairs. The sound of the outside came pouring down the steps. We looked at each other, thinking the same thing: The Kringle Windows!

Bounding up the staircase, we were relieved to see the windows were still intact. Snow blew down the stairs to the first landing from the broken upstairs window. A large branch from a maple tree protruded from a broken frame, and a few of autumn's leaves were left over still quivering on the branch while snow piled up on the windowsill.

"It must have been the weight of the snow. The branch broke. It's not unusual to lose a branch or two each winter but this has never happened."

Theodora looked out the broken window, down to the ground. "Looks like the base is on the ground. It shouldn't be too much trouble for us to pull it off the roof."

I liked a woman with a plan. We didn't need to call anyone. We were quite capable of handling this ourselves. Jules was never one to take the initiative. This felt good.

"There are some pieces of plywood in the attic. We can use one of those to cover it until I can get someone out to fix it," I said, wanting to be sure to add my two cents.

Theodora and I made quick work of the branch and the broken window. We worked well together as a team. The wind and the snow began to pick up. Storms had a way of sticking around Kringle Falls, and for some reason, I didn't mind this one at all.

We found ourselves back in front of the fire. We were warming up and drying off after our battle with Mother Nature. Gris stretched the length of the cushions, fast asleep, choosing not to help us. The wind howled outside. It was late afternoon but looked as dark as evening. We pushed Gris down, sharing one of the cushions. "Your hands are so cold," I said, holding them between my own. "Let me make you something warm to drink." I started to get up as she pulled me back toward her.

"I'm fine," she said, wrapping the blanket around our shoulders and pulling me toward her.

"I thought you were the one who was cold?" I leaned into her as if I had done it a thousand times.

"Is there any written history on the windows?" she asked, trying desperately to keep us on topic. I would have been happy to sit on that couch, wrapped in a blanket with Theodora for the rest of the day. There were, however, other forces at play.

"Not that I know of. I was under the impression that they were found in city hall years ago. Sean only recently told me the story of the stranger on Christmas Eve."

"It makes one wonder, doesn't it?" I looked at her, puzzled, waiting for her to finish her thought. "What else isn't exactly as it seems?"

CHAPTER EIGHTEEN

The snow piled up quicker than we anticipated, or maybe we didn't take the time to notice. We started with what we knew, sharing information. I played my cards close to my chest, wanting desperately to trust Theodora but feeling that the hidden room beneath the vestibule was undoubtedly bigger than she or I realized at the time. My gut wasn't all in yet, something was holding me back.

We spent the evening looking through the books on the area's history. We learned about the Finnish roots of the town. The influx of immigrants from Finland in the mid-19th century was apparently why our town even had a library. A gentleman named Konrad Jolnir arrived from Finland in 1867. He brought a collection of books with him that served as the first volumes of the Kringle Falls Library. The books were locked in a glass-covered case in the study. We searched for a key but were unable to find one. I made a note to visit my grandfather and ask him about it. He had built many of the bookcases in the study and surely had a spare key. Those books had to hold information, pieces to the puzzle.

I showed Theodora the book I had purchased at The Night Owl. Local legends were always interesting, especially when it came to cryptids, or anything related to the paranormal. I had been fascinated with all things spooky since I was a kid. I remembered begging my grandmother to purchase books about ghosts, legends, and the supernatural. She was a firm believer in otherworldly events and spent a lot of time fostering my interest in them.

"Isn't the road we took to New Hope the Hogmadog Pass?" Theodora asked as she perused the book.

"Yes, did you find something?"

"There is a whole section on the pass."

"That's interesting. What does it say?" I watched her scan the book, her beautiful eyes moving back and forth, quickly ingesting the information on the page.

"It seems like there are a lot of phantom sightings up there."

"Like ghosts? People who have passed on the trails? Or some kind of portal?"

"It's not necessarily people, although it can be, it seems it's more like a place. I'm not sure if it is some kind of thinning of the veil where we can step into another dimension or just the ghostly appearance of a place, like some kind of imprint." I wondered if she believed what she was telling me.

"Is that possible?" I wanted her to say yes. She seemed so logical and analytical. Would she think this absurd?

"I think there's a lot in this universe that we don't understand. Any intelligent human being would be foolish to think the world doesn't hold a few surprises for us."

"Agreed. Are you thinking about that little tavern we happened upon?"

"It crossed my mind." She was looking at me carefully, trying to read my expression.

"Yeah, mine too. I have lived here my entire life and I've never seen that place before. Funny how it showed up just when we needed it." We both sat silently for a few moments. "But that's crazy right?"

"The analytical, no-nonsense side of me says yes, that it's completely out of the realm of possibility." She hesitated, not sure what to say next. "But my gut tells me something else is going on here." I agreed with her completely. Something was happening. It felt like an otherworldly storm was forming, gaining intensity. The air was sparked with electricity and was heavy with the events that existed around us, ready to take their place on the stage.

The lights flickered with the wind a few times, but it was expected. Gris would howl at each flash, strictly from his side, of course, barely lifting his head. It wasn't worth the effort to completely stand and howl. The wiring wasn't the greatest in the library, and the storm was still churning outside. We were caught off guard when a powerful gust of wind knocked out the lights. The fire was small and barely lit the study. We waited for a few minutes to see if the lights would return. The wind roared outside while the cold air cascaded down the stairs from the boarded-up window. Luckily, I had stacked quite a bit of firewood on the hearth.

"I guess we should check the condition of the road. I can probably get you to the inn," I said, walking toward the large wood and glass door that led outside.

"I don't believe we'll be going anywhere tonight. It's not safe," Theodora said, not bothering to leave the couch. I hoped she was right but thought I should at least make it look good in the meantime. She had done a good job of distracting me to the point of not noticing the foot of snow that had piled up against the front door. The roads were impassable, and there were no signs of anyone attempting to drive down Main Street.

I returned to find her staring at her phone. The bright screen was filled with swathes of dark blue and touches of light blue around the edges.

"Is that the radar? Looks like we are going to be here a little while." I tried to hide the excitement in my voice with a veiled attempt at sounding worried.

"I'm afraid so. Looks like there is still quite a bit of snow out there."

I was concerned about the cold. The temperature hovered in the low twenties. We had to keep the fire going. I threw on a few logs and stuffed the crevices with newspaper. The fire roared to life, filling the space between the couch and chairs with heat. I warmed the tea kettle on the fire and found some instant soup in the librarian's office while Theodora put cushions on the floor and made a makeshift tent in front of the fireplace. To my surprise, she pulled out a few pieces of jerky that she gave to Gris, who happily accepted them. I wasn't used to someone pitching in and helping. My golden retriever qualities were some of my best.

"Do I want to know why you keep jerky in your purse?" I asked, watching Gris inhale his dinner.

"Probably not." She looked at me and smiled.

"Well, you've made Gris your new best friend."

She smiled and rubbed under his chin as he gobbled up all her attention. "Thank goodness coziness is a qualifier for living in this town," she said sarcastically as she gathered a few quilts that sat on a table in the corner. I didn't have the heart to tell her that I had just removed a quilting display. She probably thought we just left them laying around in convenient places for people to use. We settled into our tiny tent, faces toasty from the fire, slowly sipping the soup to keep ourselves warm. There was a long silence before she spoke.

She was staring off into the fire, both hands around her mug, the steam rising into her face. Like two kids at a sleepover, we were lying on our stomachs, propped up on our elbows, ready to exchange our secrets. Gris pushed his way into the tent. He was eyeballing the space between us, but to my surprise, Theodora carefully guided him over to her side. He stretched out beside her, flopped on his back, and hoisted his legs in the air. It wasn't long before he was snoring. We both laughed and then let the silence settle again.

"This is a bit strange, isn't it?" she finally said.

"It is...Are you talking about the mystery collection, the Kringle windows?"

She chuckled, swallowed, and dropped her head below her mug. "No, not at all." She took a sip of soup, sat it on the hearth, and turned on her side, resting her head on her palm.

"Us then?" I asked quietly.

"Yes, us. This isn't something I do all the time. In fact, I've never done this."

"Second time this month for me. Why do you think the quilts were on the table?" I enjoyed making her laugh. I don't imagine she showed that side of herself to many people.

"So this is what you do then? Lure unsuspecting women to the town library?" She raised an eyebrow.

"Absolutely. Worked like a charm in New York. A revolving door in the library. I had to move here to get a break."

"Ah, look who is confident now," she said, smirking. "I feel as if there's something you're not telling me." She looked at me with her startling gray eyes. Of course, there was something I wasn't telling her. We were literally lying above a hidden room. I wanted to tell her everything, but could I trust her? I leaned toward her to offer a kiss in hopes of changing the direction of the conversation. She made me travel the distance yet again. I stopped just short of our lips meeting, keeping eye contact to let her know I was issuing a challenge. The corner of her lip lifted in a smile as she stood her ground. We were in a standoff that I knew I would lose. I pretended for a few brief seconds that I was in it to win it before I gave in. And then I melted from the sheer amount of electricity that rippled through my body as I felt her warm breath on my partially open mouth. Her hand gripped my face in a power move that almost caused me to lose consciousness. She backed away, only slightly, and looked intently into my eyes. "You're changing the subject."

"I am doing no such…" The words stumbled out of my mouth as her eyes sparkled. She was enjoying watching me scramble.

"You don't need to finish that." Again, she kissed me, slowly, deeply. Any witty comment that had entered my head was gone. She retreated to her side of the tent, looking very proud of herself as she took her soup in both hands. Her look changed to inquisitive as she said, "Tell me something about you that will surprise me."

"I cheated on an art history test in college." I thought perhaps it was good to start small.

"Hmm." She looked off into the fire and then returned her gaze to me. "That's not surprising."

"It was the only time it ever happened. I was mortified. I couldn't even call home for a week because I was sure my mom would know."

Theodora snorted at this revelation. "Mortifying but not surprising. Everyone has one or two indiscretions in college."

"All right then, *you* tell me something surprising." Since I was not good at this game, I would need an example. She thought carefully for a few moments. She obviously had more than one example she could share. I was intrigued.

"I spent a year abroad, during college. I studied in the Czech Republic, in Prague."

"That's both impressive and surprising. Well done."

She laughed at my response. "Have you been?"

"Prague? No, someday, though."

"It's beautiful. I needed a change. I had been in America for almost eight years. I decided on Prague. The Charles Bridge, the cobblestones of Old Town, it's where I became interested in history, the folklore and legends of a culture. Prague is filled with the mystical, the supernatural." Obviously, this was her passion, you could see a spark ignite when she talked about it. She held a lot of secrets, and I had a feeling this little nugget of information was just scratching the surface.

"Your turn," she said, quickly changing the conversation.

"My turn?" I traced the top of my mug slowly, contemplating what I might tell her. "I certainly don't have anything as exciting as the Czech Republic," I said, wondering what I could reveal about myself that would surprise her. "I don't recycle," I clumsily blurted out.

"Not what I expected and not entirely surprising, but okay." She glanced down for a moment and then continued, "I know something you are incredibly good at, if I may?"

"Of course." I looked forward to hearing what she had to say.

"You're very good at deflecting. Humor is your defense mechanism."

I paused for a moment and raised an eyebrow. "I come from a long line of deflectors. The Thatchers are a hardy group of nontalkers. We're action people. My parents are currently working through their latest argument by constructing the largest gingerbread town ever made. Is it healthy? Who knows, but they've been married for almost forty years. So something must be working."

"You're not a talker?"

"I wouldn't say that. I've watched my parents for a long time. I've worked hard to change a few of the personality flaws passed on to me. What about you?"

"I never spent much time around my parents. My mom died when I was young. I was more of a burden to my father. He sent me away rather than raise me." The words escaped her like any other story told a million times. Theodora wasn't pained by what she said. It was a matter-of-fact.

"I'm sorry. Sounds like a lonely childhood," I said, sliding my fingers into hers, not yet comfortable with our new closeness but wanting her to know I was there.

"No reason to be. My childhood taught me to be analytical, look at situations without emotion, and evaluate accordingly."

"That seems very military-like," I said, trying to understand her lack of emotion as it was the opposite of what I had seen in the last few hours. She looked down at her mug and hesitated. Taking a slow sip, she swallowed and paused for a moment before she looked at me with a great deal of trepidation.

"It's helped me my entire life, until now."

"Now?" I asked hesitantly.

"Yes, now. I feel like I'm in dangerous territory."

"Yep, I've had a few warning bells go off too." Was she saying this was good or bad? I couldn't tell so I matched her energy. My warning bells were telling me I might be getting in over my head, but I was more than willing to take the plunge.

We fell asleep telling our stories to each other, close but not close enough. Fortunately, Gris was not giving an inch and pushed Theodora in my direction. The room was cold and the fire was dwindling. I didn't want to get up and lose what little warmth we shared. She slept peacefully, not showing any signs of the trauma she carried. I tucked her hair behind her ear and let my fingers linger on her cheek. She smiled sleepily and kissed the palm of my hand. I covered the three of us with the wool blanket and three quilts we had compiled. Gris sighed loudly and turned on his back, paws in the air. Lazy dog. I rolled over and looked out the window, watching the snow begin to wane. My eyes were heavy. Her arm slid around my waist as she pulled me toward her. Her face was nestled in my hair and I felt her warm breath on the back of my neck. Her arm relaxed and she began to breathe heavily. I slept, better than I had in weeks, months, maybe years. Gris jerked a few times and whimpered, obviously chasing something through a flowery field in his dreams. The wind began to die down outside. The old sounds of the library quieted, and the building was at peace too. In that state somewhere between sleeping and wakefulness, I heard the tapping of the branches against the windows. I wish I had realized there was no longer any wind.

CHAPTER NINETEEN

Theodora

I woke up when Andi's dog stretched, pushing his oversize paws into my back. My body was stiff from not moving all night and my arm was still wrapped around Andi. She was sleeping peacefully. The blankets trapped our warmth, which I was adding to as I felt her body against mine. My fingers slid under her shirt and glided across her stomach. She sighed with contentment. What had I called this? "Dangerous territory"? I had no business trying to chart this course. This was proving to be an added distraction I didn't need. I had a job to do and I realized this might be a good time to look around.

It was difficult to leave the warmth of our cozy tent, but Gris readily took my place. The dark, powerless library was frigid. The smell of old books permeated the air. I let my finger run along the spines of the volumes that lined the shelves. In a flash, I was back in Bremerhaven, my finger tracing the outline of books as I walked along the shortened shelves in a school library. My father was meeting with the headmistress to discuss my placement while the secretary had been sent to retrieve me from the train station. I was merely an afterthought to him.

Twinkling lights and images of the Christkind reminded me it was Christmas. In the center of the library sat a holiday display complete with a small tree. Books sat on their ends like presents waiting to be opened. That was the first time I saw *The Snowmaiden*. I carefully took the book and crawled under the table to hide from the world.

My doll sat propped on my lap, her dress flowing across my legs, keeping them warm. I liked pretending to read to her. She was my friend. I knew she would keep my secrets. *The Snowmaiden* was beautiful and kind. Underneath that table, feeling lonelier than I had ever felt, I pretended the fair maiden was my mother and the story was about us. And then I heard the door to the library open.

"Are you sure you want her to start this week? After the holidays would be acceptable." The feminine voice must have belonged to the headmistress. "We only have one day left. Our students will be going home to their families. I'm afraid your daughter will have nowhere to stay."

"Miss…I'm sorry what was your name?" my father said dismissively.

"Ulbrict, Dr. Ulbrict."

"Miss Ulbrict, everyone has a price and I am willing to pay yours if you would see a way to take care of my daughter until the new term starts." I knew that my father was opening his jacket to retrieve his wallet.

"You don't wish to spend Christmas with your daughter? Forgive me for being forward but she's only five."

"I have a much-needed vacation planned. You have children, correct? She'll be fine with them. As I said, I will pay you more than enough to make it worth your while."

There was a pause. I knew the headmistress would say yes. People had a hard time saying no to my father.

"I will take care of her."

"Perfect, I will have the full tuition wired to you plus extra for your trouble. This should get you through the holiday." I knew he was handing her money.

"I haven't even met her yet. Is she here?"

"Your secretary returned so I am sure she is here somewhere. She is probably hiding. She likes to do that."

"You don't want to say goodbye?"

"No, I don't have time. I will have her things shipped here." I heard the door shut behind him and he was gone. I sat beneath the table, breathing softly.

"You can come out now," she said, offering her hand as she kneeled.

I stared at her, not knowing whether I should trust her or not.

In an instant, I was standing back in the cold Kringle Falls Library, annoyed that this memory took up space in my brain. I had spent years wrapping these memories up tightly and putting them away. I underestimated how the smallest trigger could bring them rushing back.

Cold air pooled around my feet, streaming in from the small office. I followed it to the window beside the librarian's desk. The chair had been pushed aside and the window was slightly ajar. Snow had drifted on the windowsill, some of it falling to the floor.

Gris surprised me when he nudged my leg and leaned against it. I scratched his chin. That's when I noticed the footsteps leading from the window.

CHAPTER TWENTY

I was awakened by the bright light that warmed the study. The fire had gone out sometime through the night. The remnants of wood smoke lingered in the air. Despite the cold conditions and less-than-perfect bed, I didn't remember sleeping that well in quite a while. It was a solid sleep, a content sleep. And then I realized the source of that feeling was missing, and so was my dog.

I found her sitting in the librarian's office, her hair not even tousled, her face rested and beautiful, but worried. Gris sat on her lap, his head nestled into her neck.

"Traitor," I said, watching his tail tap against her leg at the sound of my voice.

"He was cold," she said, sticking up for him. Her slight smile did not hide the worry that covered her face.

"What is it?" I asked as soon as our eyes met.

"I'm not sure, really. I came in here to look for the key again and found the window ajar."

The window behind the desk was slightly open. Snow had blown in, resting on the sill and on the floor, a testament to how cold it was in the room. In the snow were footprints that disappeared onto the rug.

"That's strange," I said, walking toward the window.

"This is what I'm really concerned with," she said, pointing to the desk. The corners of the desk had been chipped away. Someone knew the desk held secret compartments.

"I think I might know why."

Theodora looked at me, puzzled. I reached over her to the desk, pressing the holly button and watching the doors dislodge. The bolt slid forward to remove the three drawers and before us was the St. Nicholas figurine, standing with the little girl. He moved toward us and we heard the click from the other room. Her face went from puzzled, to surprised, to hurt.

"I should have said something earlier. I'm sorry."

"It's all right. We've only just met. You have no idea who I am or why I'm here."

The line sounded like a preprogrammed response. It was obvious her brain was battling the feelings she felt. We were both apprehensive about where we found ourselves.

I grabbed a stool and sat before her, placing her hands in mine. They were ice cold. The oversized sleeves of my sweater fit perfectly over both of our hands. Suddenly she turned away.

"I don't know what this is or what's happening here," I said, making her look at me. I like you. This is all new to me. The way you make me feel…"

"Is terrifying."

"I wouldn't go that far but yes, it's overwhelming, it's intense."

"It's terrifying." Again, she tried to pull away. Gris reached out and began licking me on the face as he transferred over to my lap, his large paws balancing on the tops of my legs.

"Fine, it's terrifying, but it kind of feels like the ride of a lifetime and I'm here for it."

She let go and walked to the window to look out at the snowy trees. "Ride of a lifetime? You make it sound like an adventure. To be honest, this isn't how I operate." She stood against the window frame, not as tall as before, and leaning forward, in a protective stance. She was uncomfortable and had no idea how to process what was happening. I joined her at the window, pulling her toward me. Her head rested against the glass as she lifted her eyes to meet mine. "You're here for it, huh?"

"Definitely. And I trust you." I did. I couldn't explain why or how but I trusted her.

"Why? I've done nothing to earn that trust," she said, looking out the window.

"Neither have I, but here we are. Do you trust me?" I hoped the answer was yes. She continued to stare off into the distance. I couldn't tell if she was looking for the right thing to say or contemplating her answer.

"Completely," she said, bringing her focus back to me. Her answer was deliberate and filled with certainty. Her cheeks became flushed, from what I assume was anticipation, as she lifted her arms to my shoulders, her hand gently caressing my face. This time she came to me. Her scent washed over me as I pulled her close, my body aching to feel her. Just as our lips were about to touch, Theodora asked, "What is that?"

I opened my eyes to find her staring out the window at something in the snow. "I'm pretty sure it can wait." I pulled her toward me again.

"Look, up there," she said, pointing to the top of the adjacent wall. I followed her gaze to see that the service head had been pulled away from the wall. The three wires dangled precariously, barely attached. The streetlight at the corner was working, and the Christmas lights in the house down the street were blinking. The library was the only dark building on the street. "Stay here," she whispered to me, pushing past me and walking quietly to the door. She stepped swiftly and quietly into the study, returning with a fire iron. She looked down at the footprints and followed them out into the entryway. They did not return.

I pulled a small steel club from my desk. My father knew I didn't like guns, so he gave this to me before I went to college. If you unscrewed the handle, a long, sharp blade revealed itself. Normally, I used it for a letter opener. I was suddenly happy to have it. Gris, the absolute worst guard dog in the world, stumbled back into the study and threw himself into our tent.

I followed Theodora up the stairs, slowly stepping around the small pieces of snow left behind. She held the fire iron like a weapon. It seemed like she had done this before. I wasn't sure if that was comforting or frightening. She waited for me on the landing, listening cautiously. There was a slow knocking upstairs. She motioned with her head for us to move forward. We carefully ascended the steps. The cold air steadily increased, causing me to shake but Theodora was steady and strong. She reached the top of the stairs first. Her hair was moving in the wind. The board had been removed from the window. How had we not heard this?

"This is odd, isn't it?" she said, walking up to the window. I suspected she thought whoever had visited us was no longer in the library.

"I know I slept well, but this is ridiculous. I didn't hear anything last night."

As we covered the window again, a scuffling sound came from the office. We looked at one another and bounded down the stairs. The office window was completely open. Theodora was through it in an instant. It was at least an eight-foot drop, if not more. She chased a figure in a dark, hooded jacket running into the woods behind the building. The birds flew from the trees, rudely disturbed from their winter slumber. I found the key to the front door and quickly followed, meeting Theodora as she came around the building.

"Are you okay?" I asked, reaching for her arms as she met me.

"Fine," she said, not even out of breath. "I would never have caught whoever that was in these boots."

"Did you get a good look?"

"About my height. I couldn't see their face. Black boots, jeans, and black gloves. Nothing discernible."

"I don't get this. What's happening?"

"Looks like someone cut the power to break into the library."

"Surely they knew we were here," I said in disbelief.

"I don't think they cared." Theodora headed toward the door. "We need to talk about the desk and get to the bottom of this."

I showed her the desk, the secret compartments, and finally the hidden room.

"This is incredible," she said as she walked down the spiral staircase, her hand gently gliding along the iron handrail. "How many times have you been down here?"

"Just once. Sean and I found it. We didn't touch anything. We thought we needed more information."

"I can't believe you didn't open one of the cases," she said, looking at the ornate containers.

"Trust me, we wanted to. They are all sealed with wax. Someone went to a lot of trouble to make sure they stay closed. And someone put them *here* for a reason. There must be more to this story."

Theodora walked deeper into the room, slowly taking in the countless cases. "This is astonishing. They all look so different." She turned to look at me. "This has to be what I was sent to purchase. I was told to offer whatever was necessary to obtain this collection. Money was no object."

"These aren't for sale. I'm sure you understand that. They are here, in Kringle Falls, for a reason, and obviously, someone else is interested in them as well. I've always felt like a protector of this library and everything in it. All these cases fall in that category." I didn't want to sound angry, but this library had been in my family for as long as I could remember. We were its protectors, and we took that job very seriously.

"Andi, I understand your sense of duty," she said, walking back toward me, her face coming out of the shadows. She looked so much softer than she had the first day I met her, almost like a different person. "I'm not going to ask you to do anything you're uncomfortable with. If you allow me, I think we should figure this out together. You said you trusted me."

"I know," I said, moving to meet her. I was at a loss for words for how she made me feel. Of course, I trusted her, and yet I had absolutely no reason to. Famous last words or the beginning of something that would change my life forever. Time would tell.

CHAPTER TWENTY-ONE

Theodora made easy work of securing the windows in the office. I quickly checked the other windows and woke Gris, who had buried himself under a blanket and was sound asleep. After the windows had been checked, I carried Gris to the car. Theodora didn't bat an eye. In fact, she held the door for me as I hauled that lazy dog to the back seat of my truck. She tucked the blanket around his shoulders. That alone told me she was my people. We decided to go to my grandfather's house, inquire about the key to the locked bookcase and hopefully get some answers.

Cell service had been spotty the night before, and the phone lines were down. I couldn't believe my mom hadn't sent Sean out to find me. Leaving Theodora at the inn, I promptly went home to face all the questions my mother would have about my whereabouts. Sneaking in the door and up the front staircase was easy. Gris gathered enough energy to follow and returned to his slumber on my bed.

My shirt still smelled like Theodora. I sat on my bed with it cupped in my hands, thinking of the night before. A tinge of embarrassment reared its ugly head. How was I this giddy over someone I just met? Something deep inside me was trying to tell me it was more but I still had questions. To say this was confusing and overwhelming was an understatement. I quickly pulled myself together and made my way down the back staircase, almost running to get to my truck.

"Andi, you're up. Sorry, I didn't have time to make breakfast, honey. We're getting closer to the big day." And by the big day, she didn't mean the birth of Jesus; she meant the gingerbread contest. She hadn't even noticed I had been gone all night. My father had been in his workshop trying to "rig the centerpiece," whatever that meant, and was currently sprawled on the couch, still wearing his toolbelt and drooling on my mom's good Christmas pillows.

"No problem, Mom, I'm just going to head to the library."

"You've really been working hard, honey. I can't wait to see all that you've done. Make sure you get something to eat at Nick's."

"I will, Mom, love you." I dashed out the door, completely relieved that no long explanation was needed and I could get back to the inn and Theodora.

"Andrea. Lynn. Thatcher." My brother's voice was oddly stern. "Where exactly were you last night? And more importantly where exactly was Ms. Declan?" I turned to see his face with a very ornery look on it. "Look. At. You." He giggled while impersonating a pretty good middle school gossip girl.

"Sean, nothing happened. We got snowed in at the library, and the power went out."

"Andi, I have seen you drive through literal feet of snow with no problem. And, no judgment here, I hope you didn't do anything to scar poor Gris. He's such a tender soul."

"He's a useless soul. He slept all night." I paused for a moment, wanting Sean to know I was serious. "Listen, someone tried to break into the library last night. I think they were after whatever is in those cases."

"Are you guys okay? What happened?"

I recounted the events of the night before. Sean suggested we visit our grandfather for his insight. Sean quickly dropped his middle school persona when he decided he needed to "secure" the library. My family was nothing if not prepared for any emergency. They lived for it. I left Sean heading to play security guard at the library while I went to the inn.

Nate was in his usual attire, shoveling the parking lot. He perked up when I pulled into the U-shape driveway. "Hey, Andi! Can you believe this snow?" He picked up a shovelful and heaved it on an already huge mound.

"I think your dad needs to invest in a snowblower for you. It would certainly make your job a lot easier," I said, walking past him.

"Tell me about it. We're all about saving money around here."

I felt terrible for him. He looked tired and overworked.

"That was quick." Theodora was behind me, standing on the stairs. Carefully tucking her hair behind her ear, she looked as if she might be nervous. She wore an oversize fishermen's sweater, black tights, and black ankle boots. Her hands plunged into the deep pockets of a long flannel jacket.

"You look...incredible."

"You clean up pretty well yourself," she said, walking down the steps. I admit that I had dug in my closet a little and would typically not have dressed up this much to see my grandfather. Most people would never consider putting a sweater over a T-shirt as dressing up, but it qualified for me. Usually, one of the biggest perks of being in a relationship with another woman is that your closet instantaneously doubles. Theodora was in for a sad surprise if she thought that would be the case for us. Unless she had an affinity for basketball shorts, I think she was going to be disappointed.

She slid her hand into mine and waited for me to lead her to the car. She was giving me the illusion of control and I took it.

We decided to stop at Nick's for breakfast. Kringle Falls was the picture of an idyllic Christmas. The streets were draped in pine and baubles, glistening in the sun and new snowfall. People were busily moving along the sidewalks, carrying colorful packages. There was a holiday twinkle about town. Magic electrified the air. It was certainly the most wonderful time of the year.

Nick's was busy. Town visitors poured in wanting breakfast at the festive restaurant while residents vied for their regular tables.

"Looks as though we have to wait for a while," Theodora said as she looked at the line and the overflowing restaurant.

The table by the fireplace had just opened. Mr. Nettlepot scanned the line and spotted us immediately. With a wink of his eye and a wave of his hand, we were quickly seated next to the warm fire.

"Impressive," she said as Mr. Nettlepot pushed the chair in behind her.

"We take care of each other in Kringle Falls," he said, placing a menu on the table and patting my shoulder as he went by.

"I've never been in a place like this before," Theodora said. "There's something about it."

"Nick's? There is. It may be the only restaurant…"

"No, Kringle Falls. I've never been anywhere like this before. I imagine that if I had had a home, it would feel like this."

Her face was filled with joy. There was the slightest bit of sadness in her eyes, but my guess was that it would always be there. I wanted to hold her hand, but this was so new. Despite everything we had been through already, I still felt as if I were on a date in high school, edging my hand closer. I took a deep breath and reached for her. She smiled, a warm, trusting smile that let me know she felt the same way. Her fingers slid into my hand and the adrenaline released in my body. Her touch brought down any defenses I had in place. It clouded my thinking and left me wanting so much more—more than what would have been legally allowed in the middle of Nick's for sure. I held on tightly just to stay grounded.

"This is a great place to call home," I managed.

"I would love to have a place like this to call home." She returned the tight hold on my hand.

"It must have been hard, living in different places. I can't imagine not having a place to go back to, a place to call home."

I could tell she was carefully contemplating her words. "I had a place to go back to. I just never would have called it home." She was excellent at placing the feelings she had about her father in a steel box, locking it up, and throwing away the key. It allowed her to be very matter-of-fact when discussing him.

"I'm sorry. It's a terrible way to grow up."

"I wouldn't go that far. It's made me who I am today. My father discounted me a long time ago. I've had many wonderful people come into my life. I was smart enough to let them leave their impression, eating away at his darkness."

"Darkness?" It was an interesting word choice.

"He doesn't possess a good side. There were times that I would swear I could see a dark haze around him. It started when I was little. It was around all his friends too. I'm sure it was just my imagination or my mind playing tricks on me. I just hated him so much. It would have to manifest itself somehow."

"Wow. I don't even know what to say." I held both of her hands, leaning toward her. "I wish…I wish I could give you part of what I had. I wish I could share that love and acceptance with you."

I would've said more but Mr. Nettlepot delivered our breakfast. "I took the liberty of making Andi's favorite, chocolate hazelnut waffles with fresh whipped topping. She has me put the banana on the side with a few strawberries so she can pretend it's healthy." He leaned toward Theodora to deliver this information in a loud whisper while winking at me. "Andi, I haven't had the privilege of formally meeting this young lady."

I knew one thing for sure, if Mr. Nettlepot was privy to new information, then Mrs. Nettlepot would know within minutes, which meant my mother would know it within the hour, if not sooner.

"Mr. Nettlepot, this is Theodora Declan. She is in town on business."

He glanced down at our hands and smiled. "Sure, business." He twisted his mustache while raising his eyebrows above the frame of his glasses, obviously not taking anything we were trying to hand him. "Any friend of Andi's is a friend of ours.

And it looks as if the two of you are pretty good friends." He snickered to himself as he walked quickly to the kitchen. I was sure he was on his way to tell his wife everything. This was quickly confirmed when Mrs. Nettlepot threw open the kitchen doors and began scanning the busy dining room. Upon finding us she looked positively giddy.

"Well, that should do it. My mom will know within the next five minutes."

"Oh, no. Is that going to be a problem? I'm so sorry." Theodora was genuinely concerned. "We shouldn't have been so forward in public."

"No, not that. Not that at all. They're happy. Look at Mrs. Nettlepot. She can hardly control herself." We watched her clumsily fumble to get her phone out of her apron pocket while pulling her glasses off her head. She was frantically texting someone who was certainly my mother.

"My father would have burnt this place to the ground," Theodora said, cutting her waffle and tasting it for the first time. She stopped chewing and looked at me surprised.

"What? Is something wrong?"

"Holy shit," she murmured. Two words I never thought I would hear from Theodora's refined mouth. "This is incredible."

A burst of laughter left me as I watched her chew slowly, enjoying every bite. The look of pleasure on her face was one I could get used to.

CHAPTER TWENTY-TWO

My grandfather lived right outside of town, not far past the library. Not long after he and my grandmother were married, he decided to build the cabin. He wanted her to be close to the library, knowing how much she loved it. They raised their family there, my mom and her sisters, and built a wonderful, ordinary life filled with love. At least that's what I thought.

My grandfather was in front of the cabin when we pulled in. The small pine trees that spotted the front yard had just been adorned with lights. He stood in a pile of extension cords, holding a small piece of crumpled paper.

"Andi-bug!" he yelled, shoving the paper in his pocket and walking quickly toward me. I heard Theodora giggle behind me.

"Pops! It's so good to see you." I hugged him a bit longer than I should have, but I knew that time moved quicker than any of us realized, especially after losing my grandmother.

"Pops, this is Theodora," I said, anxiously awaiting his approval. She stepped up to extend her hand.

"Very nice to meet you, sir."

My grandfather grabbed her hand and pulled her toward him, placing her in a bear hug. She looked very uncomfortable until she realized Pops wasn't a casual hugger. She relaxed and allowed it to happen.

"Nice to meet you, Theodora," he said, letting go. "Can I call you Teddy?"

I froze, allowing the awkward silence to pool around us.

"I can honestly say that until I met you, no one had called me that before."

"First time for everything, right, Teddy?" He slapped her on the back and walked up toward the house, passing me as we went. "I like this one." He smiled at me and nudged my shoulder. I saw the slightest smile creep onto Theodora's face as she looked down, shoved her hands in her coat pockets, and followed us into the cabin.

It was warm and filled with the decorations of my childhood. Small colored lights hung from every crevice of the wooden structure. His Christmas tree sat in the corner, filling the entire cabin with the scent of pine. He hadn't missed a single decoration. It must have been so hard unpacking everything without my grandmother this year.

"Pops, it's beautiful. I'm sorry I wasn't here to help you."

"It's okay, Andi-bug. Sean helped me find it and bring it in. He also helped me decorate it. You know your grandmother picked this tree out last year." He took his jacket off and placed it on the hook by the tree, pausing to look at it. He was thinking of his wife. He sighed heavily, and turned quickly to the kitchen, pushing down the pain of his loss. He pulled three mugs off one of the open shelves and turned to us with a smile.

"I know, Pops. You two planted all those trees along the ridge, hoping they would be Christmas trees for all of us."

If nothing else, he and my grandmother were the keepers of the family Christmas traditions. When Pops first built the house, they came up with the idea to plant as many trees as they could in the hopes that one day it would turn into a family Christmas tree lot. Even as they continued to grow, my grandmother would decorate as many as she could. I'm not sure any of us would have the heart to cut them down now.

"Let's see, Teddy, you look like you drink coffee, black, and Andi-bug, hot cocoa, heavy on the whipped topping. Is that about right?" Theodora laughed and pulled out one of the barstools that sat opposite the counter looking into the kitchen. I joined her, pulling my stool close to hers and leaning into her as I sat down. "Teddy, you work with Andi-bug in the city? We haven't met any of her friends from New York."

"No, I came here on business."

"What kind of business do you have in Kringle Falls? We tend not to get many out-of-towners for work. If you don't mind me asking, of course."

Theodora paused for a moment, not sure how to proceed.

"She works for Whitby's, Pops. She was sent here to retain one of the town's collections."

His face changed from jovial to concerned. "Is that so." He turned and fumbled through the pantry. Even though his cabin was a little cluttered, he knew exactly where everything was located. He was hiding his look of concern and gathering his thoughts. "Andi, can you help me bring in some firewood? I need to keep that fire from going out." He scooped up the canvas firewood bag and headed for the door. "Teddy, we'll be right back. Make yourself at home." My grandfather was out of the house and on the porch before I could get off the stool.

I shut the door behind me and saw my grandfather standing by the woodpile, looking out into the trees that lined the side of the cabin.

"Do you know who she is, Andi?"

"What do you mean, Pops?"

"Can you trust her? Do you know why she's here?"

"I know, Pops. And yes, I trust her."

"I know that look, Andi. I looked at your grandmother that way."

"Pops, I can tell you that I've never felt this way before."

He sat me down on the bench beside the woodpile, placing his hand on my knee. "Andi-bug, if she's the one, you'll know it. And there's nothing like it. The first time I saw your grandmother, my whole world stopped. And I want that for you more than anything but there is a lot to lose here, Andi. Are you sure you can trust her?"

"I don't know why I trust her but I do."

He sat quietly for a moment as if contemplating the destiny of the world. Scooting over on the bench, he wrapped his arm around my shoulders. "That's going to have to be good enough for me." He may have said one thing but the look on his face showed me he was still worried. He kissed me on top of my head. "Let's go inside. I have some things to share with you."

CHAPTER TWENTY-THREE

My grandfather rekindled the embers and made two hot chocolates and one coffee. He set our two cups on the coffee table and settled into his chair. "Come join me, ladies."

Theodora moved to the couch. I sat beside her, folding a pillow onto my lap.

"I hear you're a pretty big deal," my grandfather said, much to my embarrassment. Theodora laughed with a mouth full of coffee. Her cheeks became rosy as she coughed to clear the hot liquid.

"Pops! You don't have to share everything," I said, very embarrassed.

"Andi-bug, it's pretty obvious. I'm not sure how long you have known each other, but I know that look. Your grandmother and I looked at each other that way. It's a feeling and you both know it."

"Okay, Pops, let's slow down. We just met. I should probably introduce her to Mom and Dad first."

"Oh, you haven't met Helen and Henry yet?" Pops asked Theodora.

"Helen and Henry? No, I haven't had the pleasure," Theodora said, looking at me with a smile. She was taking all this in stride, not very bothered by it. I would have been running for the hills by now. Perhaps she had some kind of CIA training that allowed her to remain calm in stressful situations.

"Well, I'm not surprised," my grandfather continued. "It's competition time. Around here, the Kringle Falls Gingerbread Competition is the biggest event of the year. Helen has been planning for it since she came in second place last year. Spent the whole summer making architectural drawings. I've never seen anything like it."

"Wait a minute, Pops, if I'm not mistaken, you shoved something in your pocket when we pulled into the driveway. Could that have been the diagram of all your Christmas lights?" I said with a snicker.

"Maybe. Helen comes by it honestly," he said, laughing as he pulled the diagram out and threw it on the coffee table. He picked up his mug as his expression changed. Sitting back in his chair, he looked at Theodora. "So, you're here for a collection?"

"Yes, an international buyer is very interested in a private collection here in Kringle Falls."

"And who is the buyer?" My grandfather was good at getting right to the point.

"I wish I could tell you. Normally I know the client and have met with them virtually or in person. Not this time, however. I was only told to purchase a large, historical collection."

"Interesting," I said, wondering who could be behind this acquisition. My grandfather paused as if he were pondering something of great importance.

"Andi says that I can trust you." He waited, thinking carefully about what he was about to say. "It's time I pass some information on to Andi, and it sounds like you might need to know it as well." He stood up, placed his mug on the table, and walked out of the room. We looked at one another puzzled.

"I'm not sure what he's talking about," I said to Theodora.

Her phone dinged, announcing a text. She flipped it over and quickly scanned the screen. "My boss," she said, flipping the phone back over. "I'll check in with her later."

My grandfather came back into the room carrying an old box. Setting it carefully on the table, he sat back in his chair, took a long breath and exhaled, resting quietly for a moment. "I've been waiting for you to ask me some questions, Andi. That's when I knew you would be ready."

"Ready for what, Pops?"

"Ready for me to tell you our family's history and finally pass it on. And I have to say, Andi, you're just in time." He opened the box and took out an old, large, leatherbound book with intricate designs pressed into the leather. A gold plate, finely polished, set embedded in the cover. The word *Jolnir* was fancifully written in beautiful script.

"What is that, Pops?" I asked, recognizing the name on the cover.

"It's our family history, Andi. It's everything you need to know." He carefully handed it to me. I looked at Theodora. She sat her drink down and moved closer so that we could look at it together.

"Where do I know that name from?" I asked out loud as I looked at the cover of the book.

"The research," Theodora reminded me. "Konrad Jolnir… He brought books that started the first library."

"Precisely," my grandfather said, joining us on the couch and motioning for me to open the book. In the middle of an intricately drawn tree diagram was Konrad Jolnir, 1822–1878. Several branches beneath his name was Pops's name connected to my grandmother. Underneath their names were Mom and her sisters. And there beneath my Mom's name was Sean's name and mine. I ran my finger over the ornate letters that spelled Andrea Thatcher. All the writing in the book, from the first name to the last, which happened to be mine, was written in the same script.

"Who wrote this?" Theodora asked, just as confused as I was. "It's beautiful," she said thoughtfully as she scanned the page, looking at all the names.

"No one knows," Pops said, shrugging his shoulders. "The names just appear. Look carefully, Andi." He was pointing to my name. I lifted the book and investigated the thick paper. A line appeared next to it and the beginning of another word, one solitary letter: T. The faint outline of an h was beginning to emerge. Slowly I looked at Theodora. She stared at the page in disbelief, watching a phantom write her name. The letters continued to emerge, darkening and then they would disappear, completely, leaving no sign that they existed. The cycle happened a few times as if the universe was unsure.

"Pops, what does this mean?"

I watched a warm smile appear on his face. "It means it's your time, Andi." He looked at Theodora, offering her the same warm smile. "And I think it means it may be your time too."

Theodora stood and walked behind the couch. Her hand slid along the back, clutching the worn leather. She let it guide her as she slowly walked behind me, staring at the floor, almost in a trance. She was obviously engulfed in thought, my grandfather's words racing through her head. She raised one finger as if to ask for a moment, turned, and walked out the front door.

"Give her a minute, Andi. This is a lot to take in. After all, the two of you did just meet." My grandfather sat down in his chair, facing the fireplace. He placed the book on the table and picked up his mug like it was a regular day, a normal visit. Like we didn't just see a ghost write our names in an old book. I waited a few more seconds but that was all I could do. I quickly followed her.

"Theodora!" She continued walking. "Theodora!" I said a bit louder. She continued on her path. "Teddy!" She stopped in her tracks.

She stood silently, staring straight ahead. I reached out to grab her hand. She resisted at first but held on with just one finger, not wanting to commit but not wanting to let go.

"I am just as surprised as you are. I have no idea what all of this means."

She reluctantly turned toward me after I tugged on her hand. Her eyes told me that she was in a knockdown match with her emotions, but on the outside, she was trying desperately to remain calm.

"Understand that this is incredibly difficult for me. You have the comfort of knowing that whatever this means, it's your family. It's your history. I came here to do a job. Just like I have done a hundred times before. Do the job and leave. It's all business. And then I met you. I knew the moment I saw you in the middle of that holly-jolly hell that I was screwed."

She was passionate and beautiful, her eyes filling with tears and her chin quivering. I knew she was exceptionally vulnerable. The weaknesses in her armor were showing. "Knew what?" I asked quietly. She dropped her hand and walked a few steps away. She used her finger to wipe the tears away. "Knew what?" I asked again, following her.

"I knew I was in trouble," she said, forcing a laugh. "I don't know how to do this. I wasn't expecting this in my life and then you crawl out from under a reindeer and change everything."

"It was actually *over* a reindeer and if it's any comfort, you did the same to me."

"It all seems too easy," she said as the snow began to fall. "And on cue, the gentle snow begins to fall in the perfect Christmas town."

I laughed at her as the large snowflakes dotted her hair and slowly melted. "This seems easy? A magical book, a strange collection, and the love of my life, all in one week." A long silence hung in the air.

"The love of your life?" Her eyes filled once again, as did my own. I guided her hands around my waist. We stood face-to-face. My confidence easily outweighed hers at this moment. I couldn't explain the certainty of my emotions or even what I felt for her, but I knew I would have to be sure enough for both of us.

"I'm not asking for you to say anything. I am just telling you how I feel." Our foreheads met as the snow continued to fall. A warm tear fell down my cheek as I closed my eyes, wanting to take in this moment and remember it forever.

"Andi." I heard my grandfather calling my name from the porch. "You need to come in, both of you." I opened my eyes to see Teddy looking at me.

"It's okay," I said, placing my hand on her face. I wiped the tear that hung on her lashes. She gave me a half-smile, running her hand over mine, and then she kissed my palm.

"I think I'm going to need more than that." I breathlessly kissed her softly. Her hands tightened around my waist as we pulled each other closer. Holding on tightly with a new understanding that things were about to change.

My grandfather sat at the table now with the book in front of him. He pushed it toward us and pointed to the page. Teddy's full name was beside mine, printed in the same script. I pulled out a chair and sat down.

"What does this mean?" I asked quietly.

"I think you know what it means, Andi-bug. I think you both know what it means." We watched her name flash like a lightbulb deciding if it wanted to go out or not.

"Has a name ever been erased from the book?" Teddy asked hesitantly.

My grandfather thought carefully for a few moments. "Not that I know of. As a matter-of-fact, I remember a story your grandmother told me about the night we met." He paused for a moment for dramatic effect. "The train still ran through town."

"This is a good story," I said to Teddy as I put my hand on her leg. She leaned into me, letting me know she was there.

"Andi knows that Kringle Falls isn't the first place I called home. I was coming back from being stationed out west. The train happened to run right through town. There was a terrible snow that night."

"That happens a lot around here doesn't it?" Teddy said with a smirk.

"Come to think of it we have had our share of dramatic snowstorms in the last few days. It is Kringle Falls. Apparently, anything is possible," I added with a nervous laugh.

My grandfather continued his story with a smile and a wink. "The train couldn't go any farther. The inn was nice enough to take care of all of us. Thank goodness there weren't many of us left on the train. Luckily, I had my dress uniform with me. The inn was beautiful that night. I had never seen anything like it and after being away from home for so long, I needed a little Christmas cheer. And this place, Kringle Falls, reminded me of the perfect Currier and Ives painting." A smile came across his face as he remembered the evening. "Andi's grandmother changed my plans."

"This is my favorite part," I said, nudging Teddy. "Go ahead, Pops..."

"Just as my foot hit the bottom step, I turned toward the study to have my breath taken away. My future wife stood beside the fireplace wearing a long red dress. Katherine was as glamorous as a Hollywood starlet." My grandfather was hesitantly walking through the past, remembering the moment. "And I knew," he said softly.

We all sat quietly as Pops relived the night in his head. Teddy broke the silence.

"This sounds remarkably familiar, right down to the red dress." I smiled, remembering Teddy sitting in that same study wearing a red dress and waiting for me.

"Your grandmother told me later that she went home that night and looked at the book. My name appeared beside hers."

Teddy appeared to be invested in the story. I think it gave her comfort. But we still didn't know what it meant. Why were our names in the book? Why did Teddy's name go in and out? There was a lot we needed to uncover.

CHAPTER TWENTY-FOUR

Pops made a new kettle of hot chocolate and a few sandwiches. I had a feeling we were going to be here a while. Teddy looked a little less stunned but she still seemed overwhelmed. After putting a few more logs on the fire, he brought the book over to the table. His house glowed with the sparkling lights of the tree and the festooned mantel.

"I wasn't sure if it would be you or Sean," he said, breaking the silence.

"Why not Sean?" I asked, surprised.

"It takes two of you. Two of you to protect the secret and ensure it stays safe here in Kringle Falls."

"Sean and I make two, and we're in the same family," I began.

"It doesn't work that way, Andi-bug." He opened the book again and ran his finger down the page. "Look at the sentinels listed here."

"Sentinels?" I asked.

"That's what we're called, sentinels. We watch over the Kringles. We keep them safe." I sat down, trying to put all the pieces together. "All of the sentinels found their true love, their lifelong mate. A serious job requires a pair of individuals who trust one another with everything they have and a love that runs deeper than most."

"And that's us now?" I asked hesitantly. I felt uneasiness building in Teddy.

"It appears so."

I looked down at our names, the black ink of the script looking as if it had dried on the page for decades. "Tell me what this means, Pops," I begged, wanting to understand. "This is a lot for us to take in right now." Teddy let go of my hand and was rubbing her forehead. "Teddy, we'll figure this out."

"It seems like we don't have a choice," she said, trying desperately to push down the anxiety that was building inside her. From what little I knew about her I could tell she had probably spent most of her life in control. All this information was racing through her head and she was trying to hold on to some thread of her former self as everything was changing before our eyes.

"I found out the night I asked your grandmother to marry me. She wanted me to know everything." You could see the memories replaying in his head. "It just made me love her more. You don't have that luxury right now. Things are changing fast, and I need to hand this responsibility over to the two of you." For the first time, he looked worried as he removed his beanie to reveal his ruffled salt-and-pepper hair sticking up in all directions.

"What's changing?" Teddy asked, looking more concerned than anxious.

"It's hard to explain, but you'll understand once you're a sentinel. It's a feeling, when you know things aren't right. And then there's this." He pointed to the Christmas clock that sat on the mantel. The clock had been there for as long as I could remember. My grandmother loved it dearly. She told me it had been crafted in the Black Forest. It was a delicate timepiece that kept perfect time. St. Nicholas would emerge from one of two doors on the hour, a tiny brass bell in his hand that would ring the hour. Beneath the clock face, another set of doors would open, revealing figures dressed from different cultures around the world. They walked through one set of doors and exited through another while St. Nicholas rang his bell.

"What time is it, Andi?"

"About ten past noon," Teddy said as she looked down at her smartwatch.

"Exactly. The clock should have gone off," Pops said as he moved toward the mantel.

"It didn't," I said, worried. I couldn't remember a time the clock had not worked properly.

"When things aren't right, the clock begins to slow down. The slower it gets, the more dire the circumstances."

"When did you notice it losing time?" Teddy asked, walking over to the clock.

"A few weeks ago. But it really slowed down a few days ago. The day Andi came back into town," he said quietly.

"The day I came into town," Teddy said as if she was putting something together in her head. We all paused for a moment, wondering which of us had caused the disruption, or was it both?

"What does a sentinel protect, Pops?" I asked, returning to the table.

"A collection. Probably one of the most important collections in the world."

"Does this have anything to do with the cases I found in the library's cellar?" I asked, knowing the two went together somehow.

"You found them," he said with a smile. "Your grandmother and I went to some pretty great lengths to hide them. I hope it took you a while," he said, half laughing.

"It did, Pops. You guys did a good job."

"What are they? The cases? What do they hold?" Teddy asked, wanting desperately to know more information.

"Honestly? Small statues of St. Nicholas."

"I'm sorry. What did you say?" I asked, wanting to make sure I heard correctly.

"Figures that represent St. Nicholas, from all over the world. Each dressed in traditional robes that epitomized the culture of that particular region. Expert craftsmen have painstakingly made them. Each meant to embody the true spirit of Christmas, peace, and unity."

"Sounds like a lovely collection, but what makes it so important? Why not just display them in a museum somewhere? Why keep them in a damp cellar, hidden from everyone?" Teddy asked, sounding a little frustrated but curious.

"It's not just a collection of statues. These figures hold the spirit of Christmas within them for the part of the world they represent," he said hesitantly, expecting us to find this unbelievable.

"I'm not sure I understand," I said, confused by his explanation.

"St. Nicholas knew that the world could certainly be an evil place. He wanted a way to ensure that no matter how ravaged a region might become from war, famine, or any other catastrophic event, the spirit of Christmas, unity, love, kindness, and helping one another, could still exist. He traveled the world finding the seeds of love, good deeds, comfort, and joy and he collected them, placing them in the figures he called 'Kringles.' When he could no longer do it, he enlisted the help of trusted allies, all combing the Earth looking for good and all given the power to collect and store that good. As long as the Kringles exist, no matter how dark it may become in a region, hope will never be lost. And that hope will always grow and overshadow the darkness." He was smiling as he finished his story, happy to pass the weight of this incredible job on to someone else.

"What if something happens to a Kringle or it gets into the wrong hands?" I had to ask, but I wasn't sure I wanted to know the answer.

"If a Kringle is lost, so is all that is good. The darkness will creep back in and spread its tentacles through the region. How do you think the Holocaust happened? An SS officer was able to acquire the German Kringle. Times were dark. The entire world plunged into war."

"How did you get it back?" Teddy asked.

"My great-grandfather," I said, remembering a story I heard years ago.

"That's right. Your great-grandfather was much more than a pilot in World War II. While flying mission after mission over enemy airspace, he was able to locate the Kringle outside of Berlin. No one knows all the details of the dangerous recovery mission. All we know is he brought it home. Soon after, the war ended."

"The Holocaust?" Teddy asked in disbelief.

My grandfather nodded. "But even in the darkest of those days, there were still sparks of hope, rays of light. Thank goodness they didn't destroy it. Even the slightest glimmer of hope would have been lost." His last sentence echoed through the room. The weight of it settled on all of us.

"There are people who know where the Kringles are located," I said, concerned.

"Where they *were* located. For hundreds of years they were in Finland. When Konrad Jolnir immigrated here, he brought the books and the information with him but kept the location of the Kringles a secret. He thought they were safe, concealed in the frozen wilderness of Lapland. He also thought if anyone were on the path of the Kringles, his immigration to the United States might complicate the situation."

"When were they moved?" Teddy asked.

"Right after the war. When the Germans found the Kringles, your great-grandfather knew they had to be relocated. He enlisted the help of the United States government and had them airlifted here to Kringle Falls."

"Am I to believe then that the United States government is aware of this collection and helped bring them here?" Teddy asked in disbelief.

"All countries that belong to the United Nations are well briefed in the existence of the Kringles. They understand their importance and work together to keep them safe."

"Why are the sentinels necessary then, Pops? If all the power of the world's armies is available to protect them, why are we here?"

"We are neutral, the Switzerland of Christmas spirit if you will. One country cannot be given the task of such a large undertaking."

"You mean one country cannot be trusted with such an undertaking," Teddy said, no longer looking confused. She was calculating, putting information together, and understanding the magnitude of what lay ahead.

"Exactly. Anyone who becomes a sentinel automatically becomes a steward of the entire collection, pledging always to treat the largest and the smallest territory with the same respect and significance. Understanding that they are dominoes. Knock one down, and they all could go."

The three of us sat at the round table, quietly reflecting. I began to wish this was an elaborate prank my grandparents had orchestrated.

"I know it's a lot, Andi. I also know you're ready for it. He paused and looked at Teddy. She no longer looked shaken. She looked as if she had been handed a mission, and indeed she had.

"I can't imagine what's going through your head," my grandfather said to Teddy. "I understand a little, but I had time, and I was invested. I knew that whatever we faced, we could do it together. And I loved that woman more than I could have ever imagined." I watched the tears fill his eyes as he pulled a handkerchief from his pocket and wiped them away. "You know she would be so proud to know that the two of you were next in line. I think she's looking down on us right now, comforted in the knowledge that you and Teddy will be carrying on our family's duty." He reached out and put his hand over Teddy's. She smiled and placed her hand on his.

"Honestly, I'm not sure what to think," Teddy said as she patted my grandfather's hand and stood up. "I'm terrified, excited, and dumbfounded. I don't even know your favorite color." She shrugged her arms, motioning in my direction.

"Green," I said with a smile.

"Red," she returned quickly.

"I hate to say it, but sounds like a perfect match." My grandfather chuckled as he reached into the box. "There's one more thing."

"You're Santa Claus?" Teddy quipped as she placed her mug in the sink.

"Of course not. He lives in Finland. I think he's calling Rovaniemi his home now." Teddy threw a side-eye at me as my grandfather talked about where Santa was currently calling home.

"But I digress, we can talk about that later." He laughed, enjoying the look of surprise on both of our faces. He moved to the box, removing what looked to be a metal container. Intricate designs were engraved throughout the edges of it. Large medallions were pressed into the sidewalls, each elegantly carved. One was missing on the lid. He set the box down on the table. I expected a large beam of light to be cast upon it while a choir sang. Instead, it sat quietly on the table, waiting. My grandfather went to the clock on the mantel, turned it upside down, and removed something. He returned to the table and placed it in the missing spot. It began to spin and then locked in place. The gears inside moved and dislodged slowly while the sides opened up. A red velvet interior was exposed. Two bright silver pieces sat neatly in the velvet. The first was a silver wreath that formed a ring. The second was a small silver Christmas tree attached to a silver chain. He took them both from the box and handed the ring to me and the tree to Teddy.

"They fit together perfectly," he said. We moved toward each other to test the theory. "But never put them together unless it's absolutely necessary." We stopped in our tracks and looked at him. "It's a doomsday signal. The last resort. If the two of you join them together, you are asking for help from the world."

"Whoa," I said, stepping away from Teddy.

"Your grandmother wore that ring all the time. I know you've seen it before."

"I have. I recognized it as soon as you handed it to me. I never realized…"

"I have to say, I'm relieved to pass this on. I feel like the collection has not been fully protected since your grandmother passed. I'm so happy you're home, Andi."

I helped Teddy put the necklace on. Her strength and resilience were returning as the information from the afternoon was beginning to sink in. I admired the fact that she was still here. What could possibly be going through her head? I knew how I felt. I knew how she made me feel. It was both comforting and unnerving at the same time. It was a feeling of being at home, but even with my idyllic life, it was like no feeling I had ever known.

She stood looking at Pops, holding the necklace against her chest. Teddy was well aware of the responsibility we possessed. It was an impossible challenge she was willing to accept, at least I hope she would. The emotional side, the connection I hoped we shared, was more of an obstacle for her. I wanted her to feel the same way about me, since so much depended on it.

My grandfather neatly packed everything for us in the old wooden box. Ironically, it was a handcrafted Christmas ornament crate from Italy. The items in the old crate had been passed on to my grandparents many years ago, and now they were ours.

I hugged my grandfather. He hugged Teddy, his face wrinkled with worry, even so, he held on to show his support and maybe just to reassure himself a little. Her body relaxed in his arms. She even allowed her head to rest on his shoulder. The image of the two of them helped my anxiety, even though I could still see a bit of apprehension on my grandfather's face.

We sat in my truck silently for several minutes. The snow fell on the windshield, melting and sliding down the glass.

"I'm afraid to ask you what you're thinking," I said, running my hand over the ring that rested on my finger. It was a perfect fit. She took a long, deep breath and exhaled slowly, her hand still holding the necklace.

"Honestly, I don't know what to think. I don't know what to say. This is the last thing I expected." She paused for a moment, looking out the window. "I've been alone the majority of my life, Andi. I like it that way." She turned to look at me. "I don't have to depend on anyone. There is no one to disappoint me. I take care of myself." Those words hung in the air.

"Teddy, this is an impossible situation. I know that."

"That's what I mean. Why do you call me Teddy? No one, absolutely *no* one, has ever called me that."

"It feels right. You feel right. I can't explain it. I've never experienced anything like this, but I feel like, right now, I need to be sure enough for both of us."

"Maybe you do, at least until I understand this." She looked out the window again. I slid my hand into hers. A smile lifted the corners of her mouth. It wasn't for me. It was a direct reflection of what she was feeling. She knew she was feeling the same thing I did, and she was wrestling with those feelings, not wanting to let them win. She had built her life around being alone.

CHAPTER TWENTY-FIVE

The drive to the inn was quiet. We both had a great deal to process. Nat King Cole gently sang to us, offering me a bit of comfort. I knew it wasn't the same for her. I wanted to reassure Teddy and tell her that I knew everything would be okay. It had to be. But she needed time. In just a few days, her life, and mine, had changed more than either one of us could have imagined.

I pulled into the circular driveway of the inn and stopped just before the stairs. We sat quietly for a moment. I didn't want her to get out.

"You need to get some rest," I said. "We both do. I'm a phone call away."

She paused for a moment. *Please don't get out of the car. Stay with me.* I wanted to talk about everything. I wanted to hold her and let her know we were going to be okay, but *I* didn't even know that. Teddy wasn't the kind of person you hold on to. I had to give her space. She needed to process it and then come back to me when she was ready. She hesitated and held on to my hand, looking as if she were searching for the right words to say. *Say anything! Let me in.*

"I am a bit tired. I think I'll rest a little and then I'll call you."
She still lingered, maybe she was waiting for my reassurance. I
didn't let go of her hand. I pulled her toward me, letting her rest
on my shoulder. I kissed the top of her head, holding her against
me. I was sure that Teddy did not show weakness. Her strength
was who she was and how she identified. She was letting me see
her exposed, worried, filled with questions, unsure of what the
future held.

"I'm not going anywhere," she said softly as if she thought I
questioned her sticking around.

"I know." I pulled her in tighter. Her eyes were filled with
questions and uncertainty. I tried to push it away with a soft,
reassuring kiss, a gentle reminder that I was not going anywhere
either. My hand moved to her face, lifting her chin, our lips so
close. My eyes met hers and they became transfixed. Images of
centuries that preceded us flooded my head as our lips touched.
The white heat of our kiss rose between us, our hands searching
for each other if only to hold on. It touched off a sea of emotions
inside me. Suddenly, I felt as if I couldn't breathe if she were not
with me. We both looked at one another, breathless. Teddy's
eyebrows became furrowed, her confusion becoming obvious
as she processed what was happening. Whatever switch had
just been flipped was evident to both of us but her reaction
wasn't what I expected. Was this part of becoming a sentinel?
The feeling washed over me, easing my apprehension and
comforting me. It felt like the cornerstone of the foundation of
whatever this was had just been laid. Anything was possible now.

Teddy did not feel the same way. She backed out of the
truck, standing beside it, her fingers on her lips, looking at me
in confusion. "What...what was that?" she asked, staring at me.

"I don't know. You felt it too?"

She looked lost as she continued to take a few steps back,
and turned toward the inn. "I'll call you."

I barely heard what she said as she was walking away. I wanted
to call after her but she wasn't capable of hearing me right now.
She needed time and giving her that time was one of the hardest
things I would ever have to do. I sat in the truck, desperately

missing her. Her scent still lingered. I tried to breathe it all in. The trajectory of my life was changing. It appeared quiet, small-town librarian was merely a side hustle now.

I pulled forward, looking in the rearview mirror. A woman walked out of the inn, meeting Teddy at the top of the stairs. She was just as flawlessly dressed as Teddy but was impatient and filled with anger. Teddy quickly reacted and returned the anger. She knew this woman. And then I realized I had no idea who this could be. Was she a girlfriend? Certainly not her wife. There were so many unanswered questions. I waited a moment, watching. They continued their argument into the inn. I wanted to stop and follow them, but I had a feeling that whatever Teddy was facing, she needed to do so on her own, and I needed to trust what was happening. Still, I worried as I pulled onto the road that led to my parents' house, feeling as though I left behind half of myself.

CHAPTER TWENTY-SIX

We were five days from Christmas. As the competition was quickly approaching, I knew my parents' house would be a swarm of activity. I was surprised to pull into an empty driveway and a quiet house. The back door was unlocked.

"Mom? Dad? Sean?" I yelled as I walked through the kitchen, avoiding piles of gingerbread. Gris didn't even bother to bark as he rested on the fireplace hearth, a giant candy cane between his paws, gnawing it down with his back teeth. His tail wagged slightly in acknowledgment, but he was too busy to bark at me. He wore his Christmas sweater and collar filled with bells. Each time his head moved, the bells jingled slightly. He would have been furious at the outfit if he had not had a candy cane. That dog's stomach was made of steel. He ate everything and never managed to gain a pound and rarely threw anything up.

My mother had set up a small office in her kitchen when she realized that she needed space to construct her drawings. She had ordered an oversize spinning chair that commanded the room. It made her feel like she was the captain of her ship. I was surprised when the chair slowly turned to reveal my mother, legs crossed, hands resting on the armrests in her best *Godfather* stance.

"Mom!" I screamed, grabbing another giant candy cane lying on the counter. It was the closest thing I could find to a weapon. My mom looked at it and snickered.

"Planning on decking my halls, dear?" she said, laughing. "If you're going to be a sentinel, you'll need to be much sharper than that, honey."

"You talked to Pops?" I said, slowly lowering my weapon as Gris whined, moving his eyes with my candy cane baton as his tail methodically wagged like a sarcastic slow clap.

"I did talk to him, Andrea, and you have some explaining to do." My full name, she meant business.

"I could say the same thing, Mom. How long have you known?"

"They're my parents. My sisters and I have known for some time. They waited, of course, until we were older, but they wanted us to know what it meant to be part of our family." She thoughtfully reexamined her childhood. "We all waited to see if we would be next. Which one of our names would appear in the book? Nothing, until today." The pause was dramatic. Her eyebrow rose slightly as her fingers began to drum on the arm of the chair. "Your name appears, and then someone named Theodora? I don't believe I've met anyone in your life named Theodora." She said the last two sentences very slowly for emphasis. A younger me would have been shaking at this point.

She was mad because there was someone in my life she didn't know. Not that this family calling, which involved world peace, had skipped a generation, leaving her out, but that I had not introduced her to Teddy. My mom had priorities.

"Mom, I just met her. I might have said something at breakfast the other morning, but *you* invited Jules. Things are happening so quickly."

"I would say they are escalating, but not too quickly to tell your mother."

"You've been a little preoccupied," I said, motioning to the absolute wreck that was the kitchen. She came over and put her arms around me.

"Andi, all I ever want for you is your happiness. If this Teddy makes you happy instead of Jules, I am totally on board. I am always on your side." She tucked my hair behind my ear and kissed me on the cheek. "So, Teddy comes to dinner tonight. We'll have to order out because, as you know, the competition is very close!" She gave me one last squeeze, walking past me and gathering her tools to go back to work. She paused for a second and turned to look at me. "I know you'll have questions, Andi, both of you will. The book has never been wrong. We're here to help you and support you. We love you, and I am sure that we will love Teddy. Now, call her and ask her to come to dinner tonight. I won't take no for an answer. I love you, Andi. I can't wait to meet her." And with that, she was back at work. Gris was vigorously wagging his tail as if agreeing with what my mom was saying. After that candy cane, he would have fresh breath well into the new year.

I texted Teddy about dinner but she didn't respond. I wondered whom she had met outside the inn. I saw her arguing. Should I have stayed? This was important. I needed to let Teddy work through this on her own. I sat on my bed watching the phone, waiting for the three dots to appear telling me she was answering, but they didn't come. Instead, Gris walked through my door, candy cane glued to the scruffy fur around his mouth, tail wagging. He jumped up on my bed, leaned against me, crossed his paws around the candy cane, and continued eating. Dogs always know when you need a little something extra. To tell him thank you, I took the jingle-bell collar off and kissed him on top of his scruffy little head.

The familiar ding of my phone brought my attention back to the problem at hand. It was Teddy. She was telling me that she couldn't make it to dinner. No explanation, just an apology. I waited for another text, anything to explain what she meant. Three dots appeared and vanished, and then nothing. My heart sank, and I felt utterly alone, the weight of the world resting on my shoulders.

I sat on my bed, hands resting on my knees, moving the new ring up and down on my finger, wishing I could feel a connection to her. Nothing.

I jumped when my phone rang. My heart raced as I fumbled to answer it. It wasn't the voice I expected. Pops was on the other end.

"Andi, I don't know how to say this."

"What, Pops, what's wrong?" He was scaring me.

"The book, Andi. Teddy's name is gone."

CHAPTER TWENTY-SEVEN

Teddy

The small café in New Hope was nice but nothing compared to Nick's in Kringle Falls. Andi would like the ski motif. There was a nostalgic nod to the Olympic Games in nearby Lake Placid. It was near the train station, and I desperately needed somewhere to escape to. The day had been much more than I ever could have expected. I needed a second to retreat into some place that could give me a moment of peace and stillness and hopefully allow me to figure this out.

I left Andi confused and overwhelmed, feeling as if I had lost control over my own life. Still reeling from that, I stumbled onto a very angry Becks who was furious with me for not returning her calls or texts. We had been friends for some time, working together as colleagues, never letting the fact that she was my superior influence our relationship. We had briefly dated when we both started working at Whitby's but nothing serious.

The problem was that she knew me well and she knew something was going on that was influencing how I did this job. After listening to what could only be described as a lengthy lecture, I managed to console her enough to put her on a train back to New York. She reiterated—repeatedly—the importance of this collection. Her urgency was out of character for Becks. It was her attitude that our clients worked on our time, trusting our process. She never rushed or seemed impatient when it came to a client or job. And now she had traveled from the city to chastise me for not doing my job correctly. There had to be other forces at play but she wasn't willing to give up that information. Becks reluctantly left. Her last words were, "Get it done, Declan."

I had sat at this table for so long my coffee had gone cold. The new barista had started making drinks. There had obviously been a shift change. How long would they let me sit here? I wanted to talk to Andi. Her texts slid across my phone. Why couldn't I answer her? Because answering her meant I was acknowledging this new reality. I would rather sit here in this café, watching the world go by and keeping my reality as it was. I could easily get on a train and leave here, leave everything. The idea that I was half of a team responsible for world peace was rich. I rarely found moments of peace in my own life and now I was responsible for the world?

I had managed to keep everyone in my life at bay, forming relationships that lacked any depth, and building defenses around me, brick by brick, year by year. I chose the lack of feeling anything over the pain of disappointment or heartbreak. Returning to Kringle Falls would destroy every wall I had ever painstakingly built. Leaving on the next train to New York would give me my life back. Sure, Becks would be disappointed, but she would get over it and my life would go back to normal. I welcomed the thought of that right now. Even so, there was a growing feeling in the pit of my stomach—my conscience. Normally she was easy to control but not this time. She was rearing her ugly head in a violent battle to survive.

I took my glasses off and closed my eyes, rubbing my forehead, feeling the beast within growing the longer I sat there.

"Are you okay, dear?" I heard a sweet voice near me. A small woman sat at the table behind me. She wore an elf's hat complete with attached ears. Her Christmas sweater jingled with her slightest movement. Her smile matched the jolliness of her outfit.

"Yes, I'm fine," I said, putting my glasses back on.

"You seem upset. It makes me so sad to see someone upset at Christmas. Are you worried about something?"

I thought for a moment about everything that had taken place, fully feeling the weight of it. "Yes, world peace. I'm worried about world peace."

"Honey, that's a lot to put on your shoulders don't you think? You look as if your heart is heavy enough right now."

For my entire life, I had hidden almost everything about myself from the world and here I was showing a stranger in elf ears how I felt.

"Is it that obvious?" I asked, not really wanting to know the answer.

"I'm a bit more observant than most people," she said, cleaning up her table. "Would it help to talk to a stranger? I will do a good job of being impartial." I turned to face the woman. Was I feeling so overwhelmed that I would find comfort in a complete stranger? I could just add this to the list of new things for Teddy today. Great, now I was calling myself "Teddy." I let out an audible sigh, annoyed with who I was becoming. "Come over here and sit, dear. I'll get us something to drink. Black coffee?"

"Yes, thank you." I gathered my coat and purse and sat down at the stranger's table. My phone buzzed again. It was Andi.

"Andi, huh? Is he the reason you're sitting here contemplating world peace?" she asked as she sat down, looking at my phone.

"Yes, *she* is."

"Oh, good for you, honey. I don't judge. Love is hard enough to find in this world. When you find the right person, you have to snap them up. Am I right?" She poured some milk into her coffee, three heaping teaspoons of sugar, and then she pulled a candy cane from her purse that she used to stir it all together.

"You really like Christmas don't you?"

"It's a big deal in my family. Lots of traditions. You might say it's like a family business." She pulled a little container from her purse. There were two pastries, shaped like figure-eights. "Kringlas. The Norwegian version of a sweet pretzel. They are quite lovely. May I interest you in one?" She cracked the lid to let the sweet doughy smell of the Kringla escape.

"Thank you. Anything else in there?" I asked, looking at her purse. "Perhaps the key to world peace?"

"I think you're going to have to find that one on your own. I do think the answer is closer than you think."

"I'm not even sure what the question is," I said, twisting the soft dough to tear off a small piece. The cookie melted in my mouth, a sweet pretzel, unlike any other cookie I had ever tasted. "Holy shit!" The words left my mouth before I could stop them.

"They are good aren't they, dear?"

"Fantastic. Where did you get these?" I would have gladly paid for these cookies. Andi would love them.

"Oh, I made these. I've been making them for years. The recipe was passed down through my family, generation after generation. I will say, I add a little bit of nutmeg to mine but don't tell anyone."

"Your secret is safe with me. Andi would love these."

She snapped the cookie container shut, leaving the last cookie. "Take this one to your Andi. I guarantee she will love it." She pushed the container across the table toward me.

"My Andi," I said, thinking that it sounded so strange but then again it sounded right.

"Can I give you a piece of advice?"

"Yes, please." At this point, it could only help.

"I was never one to believe in soulmates or true loves. That is until I met my husband. Chance didn't bring us together, fate did. I knew the minute I saw him. I'm guessing you're wrestling with other demons not related to your Andi and that's why this is so hard for you. Listen to your heart. I would bet it already knows what to do. It's not always easy, but it is always worth it."

I thanked the sweet woman and excused myself to the restroom. I stood looking at myself in the mirror, knowing that

CHAPTER TWENTY-EIGHT

With Teddy unable to make dinner, my family and I went our separate ways. Choosing to eat leftover mac and cheese in my room, I watched *It's a Wonderful Life* and fell asleep thinking about Teddy, wondering where she was, what she was doing, would I see her again. Nothing was as clear as it was just a few hours ago. I drifted off, cradling the bowl in my lap. I woke up the following morning with a bowl that was licked clean and Gris lying next to me with cheese smeared all over his whiskers, his three paws in the air and one in his mouth, not a care in the world.

I sent Sean a text and asked him to meet me at the library. Not only did I want his perspective, but I also needed a backup in case the intruder returned. After apologizing profusely, again, to my mom about dinner, I stopped by Pops's to pick up the crate and headed to the library. Of course, I had to drive by the inn. This in no way helped the situation, as her BMW was no longer in the parking lot. Should I stop and see if she checked out? Should I trust in the unwavering faith I felt in her just a few hours ago? Pops told me her name had disappeared. How strong was my faith?

Sean was waiting for me on the steps. Due to the time constraints of the competition, our mom had given him the CliffsNotes version of what happened.

"I'm going to need you to fill in some holes for me," Sean said, taking the crate from my hands as I walked up the stairs.

"I can only imagine what she told you," I said, unlocking the door and using the flashlight on my phone to see through the darkness. I had contacted the power company but needed an electrician to reinstall the power to the library. We had a few in town, but one wouldn't be available until tomorrow. I took the two lanterns out of the crate, handed one to Sean, and began lighting the fireplace.

"You're right about the electricity, Andi. After we talked, I came down to make sure everything was okay. Someone disconnected it."

"I don't know if they knew if we were here or not. I'm not sure it mattered."

Sean sat on the couch, the lantern casting a warm glow on his stubbled face. "Tell me more about your conversation with Pops."

I spent the next half hour telling Sean the entire story. I shared the book with him, wary about opening it to the family tree. He ran his fingers down the page until he found our grandmother and grandfather. His mouth curled into a smile I'd seen so many times when our grandmother called his name from the front porch. We all missed her so much. After a heavy sigh, he continued down the page.

"Whoa, look at that!" I was terrified to look. Had someone else's name appeared? Was Teddy gone for good? I could feel my heart sinking.

"Our names...are they still there?"

"Well, the beginning of your name is here. But there is only one name on the line connected to yours: Tereshchenko. Does that sound familiar?" We both looked at each other.

"No, not at all. Is that a Russian name? I don't even know—"

"Is that Teddy's real name?" Sean asked, just as confused as I was. "It has to be connected to her somehow, right? Didn't you say that Pops told you that the two people chosen had to be soulmates? Have you met anyone else?"

"No! I haven't met anyone else. What's wrong with you?" My temper was growing short.

"Hey, just looking at all the possibilities."

"Why can't this book just make up its mind and commit already?"

"It's not the book, Andi. It's you and Teddy. You two must decide. Where is she anyway? Why isn't she with you?" He softened his tone, waiting for my answer.

"I don't know where she is. I asked her to come to dinner. She told me she couldn't make it. I drove by the inn this morning and she wasn't there. Her car was gone."

"Does she have like a James Bond kind of car?"

"Sean, focus."

"I'm sorry, Andi, that has to hurt." He dropped his giggle when he realized I wasn't there for it. "I don't envy the position you guys are in right now. I can't believe her name appeared next to yours and then disappeared. You two must have had some kind of night here in the library." He laughed again and shook his head. "Who knew my little sister was such a..."

"Such a what, Sean? You should think carefully before you finish that statement."

"I'm just kidding, Andi. Honestly, it's ironic that this happened to you. You're the steadiest, most straightforward person I know. You dated Jules for years. I thought the two of you would get married. Very glad you're not, but still. And then this woman comes into town, and the two of you are saddled with this job that could impact the entire world. That's a lot for two people who just met. Man, talk about packing the U-Haul."

"Tell me about it. I haven't even had time to sit down and talk to her. I shouldn't have left her at the inn, but I felt like I had to. I felt like she needed some space. And then I see her arguing with this woman on the front porch as I was driving away."

"Arguing with a woman?"

"Yes, as I was pulling away, a woman came out of the inn and immediately started arguing with Teddy. She knew her because Teddy gave it right back to her."

"Why didn't you go back?"

"I don't know. They went inside. I didn't feel like it was my place. Teddy is perfectly capable of handling things herself. Did I tell you she jumped out of the window and chased the person that tried to break in? Trust me. She doesn't need any help."

"Nice!" Sean was very impressed with Teddy's prowess. "Andi, you guys are a team now…maybe. And if you are, I don't think the world has time for you to give her some space."

The scope of everything settled on me like a thousand pounds. I felt as though I could barely stand, let alone breathe. The world was counting on the sentinels, whatever form they may take, and here I was giving her some space. Granted this wasn't the ideal situation for any fledgling relationship, but there wasn't time for this. I had to muster enough faith for both of us. I had to find her. We had work to do.

CHAPTER TWENTY-NINE

Sean was right. There wasn't any time for me to worry about either one of our feelings. We were now the sole recipients of an obligation that affected the entire world. I grabbed my keys, leaving Sean as the caretaker of the book, and quickly dashed through the front door, only to be met by Jessica. Great. Perfect timing.

"You're off to somewhere in a hurry."

"I am. I can't explain now, but maybe we can talk later."

She was in a very persistent mood as she stepped in front of me, blocking me from going any farther. "This will just take a second. I need you to come over tonight. Jules came home pretty upset from your house the other morning, and she's been a little down in the dumps since then. Can you just drop by for a few minutes?" Jessica had terrible timing and could not read a room to save her life.

"I don't think that's a good idea right now. I told you, Jess, we're just friends. We'll always be friends." Unless our families destroy that for us, which lately, seemed more and more likely.

"I heard there's someone else?" she asked with a mix of curiosity and anger.

"Jess, I really, really don't have time right now."

"You must be going to meet her. She must have really done a number on you."

"Stop. Before you say something you'll regret." I moved past her and straight to my truck, parked in front of the library. As I drove away, I caught a glimpse of her face. She was furious. There was a time I would have been more concerned. I had bigger issues at hand.

Teddy's car was not in the inn's parking lot. I had tried texting her but still no reply. Rushing in the door, I surprised Nate, standing behind the counter adjusting plastic gingerbread men in a pine centerpiece.

"Everything has to be perfect for the competition." He smirked as he unwrapped another gingerbread man and arranged it.

"I think those gingerbread guys are supposed to stay wrapped."

"What? Why?" He looked panicked.

I hesitantly pointed to the top of the decoration. "The ribbon, it's a little much for packaging. I think it's part of the decoration."

"Damn it! How am I supposed to know these things?" This might have been entertaining if I had not been in such a hurry. He slumped over out of sheer exhaustion. All the little plastic gingerbread wrappers were strewn about.

"Did Teddy check out?" My direct and loud question startled him. The poor kid jumped back, dumping his arrangement.

"Jeez, Andi," he said, straightening his vest and picking up the scattered centerpiece.

"You're really jumpy, Nate."

"I'm sorry, there's a lot going on around here." This poor kid was really overworked.

"I don't mean to add to your stress. I just need to know if she is still here. It's important or I wouldn't ask."

"Um, yeah, she left a few hours ago. A woman was here waiting for her, and they left together."

My heart sank, and I felt like I needed to sit down. I braced myself against the desk, feeling the weight of the ring on my finger. "What do you mean she left? Did she say where she was going?" My heart breaking was the least of the problems arising from Teddy leaving Kringle Falls.

"Andi, are you okay? You don't look so great."

"I wasn't expecting you to say she checked out." I heard the words leave my mouth, but they didn't seem real.

"Oh, I'm sorry, Andi, she didn't check out. You asked me if I saw her and yes, I saw her a few hours ago when she left."

I stood staring at Nate, biting my lip, wondering if I should hug him or punch him. "So she hasn't checked out? She is still a guest here at the inn?"

"Let me double-check, but yeah, I think so." He tapped on the keyboard a few times as his eyes scanned the screen. "Yeah, she's still a guest here. You guys seemed like you had a great time the other night," he said with a goofy grin.

"The other night? Oh, dinner. Yes, we had a really good time." It seemed like years ago.

"I thought so. After you left, she came back downstairs and sat by the fire for a while. I think she was having a hard time sleeping. I asked her if she needed anything. She asked a lot of questions about you."

"Really?" I said, wanting to know more.

"Of course, I told her how much you used to make us run for absolutely no reason." He snickered to himself. "Don't worry. I made you look good. I told her what a great coach you were and about all the community stuff you made us do, the animal shelter, and cleaning up after the parade every year. I think she likes you." He leaned over the desk, whispering to me.

The relief I felt was indescribable. I still needed to find her. The biggest question was, who was the woman she left with?

"Nate, would there be a way I could check out her room for a second? She had my jacket, and I think I left a set of my keys in the pocket. I need them for the library." It was a total lie but pretty good for thinking on my feet. If anything, looking in her room might give me a clue as to where I could find her.

"I don't know, Andi. I shouldn't let anyone upstairs who isn't a guest, especially not into someone else's room."

"I know and I hate to ask, but it will just take a second. I really need those keys. You can wait out in the hallway."

Nate looked around. I could see his wheels spinning. "I can't leave the desk, but you can go up. Just be super quick, please. My parents would kill me if they knew I let you go up there. They would kill me if I let you go in anyone's room, but they seem to think Ms. Declan is a big deal and want to keep her happy."

"Why do they think that?" I asked, rooting for information.

"Her room was paid for by a wire transfer from out of the country, somewhere in Russia, I think. My mom thinks she's some kind of royalty." He laughed, handing me the card to open her door. "Seriously, Andi, please don't get caught, and remember, you told me two minutes. Her room is up the stairs at the end of the hall on the right."

"The Nutcracker Suite?" I asked, remembering the upstairs layout from the time Sean almost burnt the house down, drying his boots in the oven. We had to spend two nights at the inn while our house aired out. There is no way we could have afforded The Nutcracker Suite. "Thanks, Nate. I really appreciate it."

I thankfully took the card and headed up the stairs. I had two minutes to find anything that might help me locate Teddy.

Two life-size nutcrackers stood guard beside the double doors of the Nutcracker Suite. I knocked first to ensure the room was empty, swiped the card, and opened the door. The room was a mess. There is no way Teddy's precision would allow her room to look like this. It was a large space lit by the warm glowing lights of a Christmas tree tucked into a corner next to a fireplace that had seen its share of history but still looked very elegant. It was decorated with pine and a small collection of nutcrackers. A large leather sofa sat in front of the fireplace, covered in large pillows and a cozy throw speckled with nutcrackers. A king-size, four-poster bed filled out the rest of the room. Two large double doors led to a balcony, one of which was slightly open, the cold air squeezing through the gap as the door shuddered on its hinges.

Her suitcase sat on a long, upholstered bench at the end of the bed. It was ajar, with items hanging out. An open laptop sat on the desk, papers haphazardly lying around. I touched a key to awaken the computer, but it was locked. Too many attempts had been made to log in. The furniture was disheveled, the mattress askew. Someone was looking for something. Had they found it? My time was running out. Nate would be up here soon wondering what I was doing. I scanned the room, looking for anything that I might have missed.

There were a few items on the coffee table, a half-filled glass of water, a pair of glasses, silver hoop earrings, and a very old copy of *The Snow Maiden*. This couldn't possibly be a first edition. I sat on the soft couch, not wanting to touch it. The gray cover was embossed with a golden wreath. The title sat within the wreath. I carefully opened it to find that it was indeed a first edition. A small envelope fell to the floor. The envelope was old but not as old as the book. Across the front of it, Teddy's name was written in a script from another time. And then I saw it, *Theodora Declan Tereshchenko*. My mind went back to the book. It was her name. Declan was her middle name. A small sigh of relief left my body.

Beneath her name was scribbled the word *Snegurochka*. I wanted to open it, but I felt as if I were going too far, already feeling bad enough being in her room. I just needed to know where I could find her. I placed the envelope back in the book and carefully sat it on the table, in awe of the first edition of my favorite volume.

Taking one last look around, I noticed smoldering embers in the fireplace. There were small pieces of paper, almost entirely black. I grabbed the fire iron to sift through the ashes, looking for anything that may not have burnt. There beneath the carved remains of a log was a piece of white paper, slightly burnt on the edges but intact and covered with an illustration. It was a figure in long blue robes lined with white fur. Golden braided ropes hung from the figure's waist. Designs of gold were embroidered into the blue coat. The figure was holding a staff, his white beard flowing down below his waist. It wasn't an illustration but a picture of a carved figure.

Footsteps approached in the hallway. I shoved the charred paper into my pocket and headed for the open terrace door.

"Andi!" A hushed voice came from the opening in the door. It was Nate. I knew my time was up. "My dad is downstairs. He's headed this way."

"Thanks, Nate." The door clicked as I slipped out onto the terrace, knowing that a trellis ran down the side of the inn to the garden. While I considered myself athletic, I certainly was not graceful. Steadily I lowered myself off the balcony, carefully reaching for new footholds as I gingerly made my way down the side of the wall. The abundant ivy was worse than Sean's Christmas tree. I felt consumed with each step. The cold and the ice only added to the treacherous journey. The whole world would know I was in Teddy's room if I ended up dead.

My first step onto solid ground brought relief. This was a fleeting moment, however, when my feet and head quickly changed positions, and I found myself lying on my back like a turtle, smack in the center of a thin patch of ice. It was the kind of fall that took the wind right out of your sails. The audible thud must have startled the few guests left in the dining room as it suddenly went silent. I lay on the ground for a moment in the event anyone investigated. Actually, I just couldn't get up. Once the air seeped back into my lungs, I slithered off to the sidewalk, licking my wounds and pulling sprigs of ivy out of my hair. I did not possess one ounce of grace.

I couldn't hang around here and wait. I needed to start doing my new job. The Christmas clock was slowing down, someone had broken into the library, and everything felt wrong. Things couldn't possibly get any worse. I heard somewhere that those were famous last words.

CHAPTER THIRTY

I sat in my truck for a moment, waiting for the sting of my recent fall to go away. When I grabbed the blanket from the back seat to wrap around my wet legs, Teddy's scent lifted from the wool and filled the cabin. It was a gut punch. A reminder of where we had been just a short time ago and a reminder of how much I already felt like I needed her. I had no idea what to do or where to go. I needed some divine intervention from my grandmother...and then I heard the song on the radio, Doris Day singing "Let It Snow."

The tavern flashed through my mind. Randi's parting words: "We're here if you need us." My truck made a horrible grinding sound as I pushed it into gear too quickly and headed toward Hogmadog Pass. The afternoon sun beat down on the pavement, erasing the snow at the edges of the road.

The area where we'd pulled off to ride the weather out came upon me quickly. I slid to a stop and pulled off the road. There was no tavern in sight. The pass was normally windy but today, the driving gusts pushed the truck back and forth. The snow blew up, whirling in tiny tornadoes around me. A few clouds came across the mountain, climbing up the far side to the crest and sliding into the valley, settling on the pass. Dark shadows, from above, passed over the ground, a few to start and then filling in to darken the sky. The sun had been eclipsed. Large flakes began to fall, adding to the whirlwinds of snow that were already wreaking havoc around me. The storm came from nowhere and within a few minutes it was raging once again.

It was easier being in this situation with Teddy. I could do anything with her. Sitting here by myself, I felt my anxiety begin to peak. And then, in the distance, I saw the glow of the warm light, first from one window and then from another. Once again, I put my truck in gear and moved forward toward the lights. Within no time, I found myself at the entrance. The old cabin opened for me as the familiar scent of a wood-burning fire infused with cinnamon pulled me inside. The wood door carefully moved behind me, ushering me into the warm space, a place of welcoming repose. The fire was low in the grate and only a few candles were lit on the tables while Christmas lights twinkled on their strings, always on duty. I walked to the bar looking for Randi and I heard someone behind me.

"Andi?" the soft male voice said. I turned to see Thomas walking toward me. "We thought we might see you sooner than later."

"You know who we are, who I am, don't you?" I heard the words escape my mouth. I had yet to vocalize what was happening to me, hopefully to us.

"Yes, we know. We were waiting for you," he said, walking past me to sit at the seat he claimed at the end of the bar.

"Who are you then?" I asked, hoping Thomas could fill in some blanks for me.

"Who do you need us to be?" He leaned over the bar, reaching for something that sat just beyond his reach—a bottle. He poured a rich amber liquid that landed with a heavy splash in the glass. He took a small sip, reacting as it ran slowly down his throat. "Even after a couple of hundred years, this only gets better."

I certainly wasn't surprised by what he said. I should have been, but nothing was surprising anymore.

"Back for more cider?" Randi asked as she pushed the door open behind the bar and entered the conversation. She looked at Thomas with a raised eyebrow as she took the bottle from him. He acknowledged her with a roll of his eyes. Their relationship obviously spanned a great deal of time.

"Honestly, I'm not sure why I'm here, some help maybe?"

Randi laughed as she poured herself a drink from the same bottle as Thomas who scoffed at her choice. "Where's Theodora?" Randi asked, even though I had a feeling she knew.

"I'm not sure. We received some news and I don't think she's dealing with it all that well. I dropped her off at the inn, saw her argue with a woman she knew, and now she's gone."

Randi and Thomas looked at each other. Their eyes were carrying on a conversation I was not privy to. "The two of you had quite a bomb dropped on you, didn't you?" Randi's words were comforting in their recognition of how I felt. "This isn't unusual. You have been gifted with extraordinary responsibility. Who among us would not feel overwhelmed and intimidated?"

"How do you know all this?" I said, taking the warm drink that Randi offered me.

"Don't worry, dear, it's hot chocolate. You need your wits about you." I smiled, touching the cup to my lips and smelling the delicious drink. I took a deep breath, letting my shoulders relax, and letting in a moment of peace.

"You must have talked to your grandfather," Thomas said.

"He talked to Teddy and me both. Wait a minute, do you know my grandfather?" My mind raced back to the framed image on the wall. My grandparents standing in this very tavern, decorating a Christmas tree. The wood floors creaked as I rushed across the old planks to inspect the image once again. Flashing Christmas lights splashed color across the glass that protected the picture. Scribbled on the bottom of the image was *Christmas 1961*. And just as I remembered, Randi stood behind the bar, smiling and timeless, over sixty years ago, looking like it was yesterday.

"You found it. Your grandparents were here quite a bit when they first became sentinels." Randi walked up behind me, looking fondly at the picture. "Your grandfather is still one of the funniest people I know. And that is saying something."

"Considering how long you've been around, it certainly is." Thomas chuckled.

"I have so many questions." I sat down in the booth where Teddy and I had sat not too long ago. Randi took the seat across from me. "You haven't aged at all. You know my grandparents and you called them sentinels." My heart began to race as the adrenaline rushed through my body. The weight of the last few days landed heavily in my gut. I had come back to town to be a librarian. A simple, small-town librarian. My plan was to live with my parents, maybe buy a little house, meet some nice girl, get married, and live happily ever after. I should have known I was going off the rails when I decapitated Santa and met a woman who was obviously some kind of CIA operative, and now I was in a phantom tavern telling my problems to a bartender who was probably Mrs. Claus.

"Your life has been turned upside down in a matter of hours. We're here to help any way we can. Thomas and I are wardens, in old Norse, *vorors*. We are the watchers of the sentinels. We offer respite and guidance but that's only the beginning really. We have seen so much and lived through so much. Our weapons are what we know."

"Then please, tell me where she is, where is Teddy?"

"We don't have visions," Randi said as she reached for me. Her hands encircled mine. They were colder than the storm outside, even so, I still felt comforted.

"We have the knowledge given by centuries of being a warden." Thomas joined us at the table. "We know the events of the past, the evils that you will face, and the powers that you're growing into. We're here to help."

"I want to know everything. I need to know everything. But none of it matters if I can't find her."

"Being chosen as a sentinel is like hitting the lottery. Everything aligns, events, time, and space, and you are the chosen ones. It doesn't happen on a whim. The universe has picked you and Teddy. This has gone on for over a thousand years. The two of you have something or your names would never have been written in the book. Trust in that. Trust in her." Randi gripped my hands.

"Her name disappeared," I said reluctantly. Randi and Thomas looked at one another. They were both surprised but were trying to hide it. "It's never happened before has it?"

"I wouldn't say that," Thomas said. There was an awkward silence. I knew that Thomas and Randi were both choosing their words carefully.

Randi offered a smile, trying to comfort me. "While it is true the universe aligns when two people are meant to be together, both people must make the choice to be a sentinel. The job takes a dedicated and loyal heart. Her name will not fully appear until she has accepted who she is and what it means."

"I'm not sure of any of this and my name was practically etched into the paper."

"Your heart knows," Thomas said. "Your heart has already made the decision that you will follow in the footsteps of your grandparents. Loyalty is everything to you." He was right even though I didn't want to admit it. "Understand that circumstances in the world are changing and sentinels who had been at their post for years would be on high alert right now, preparing. The two of you are at a clear disadvantage. We believe that whoever is causing this instability knows that there has been a changing of the guard. They are looking for a weakness and hoping to find it in you."

"It's not fair to either one of you. But this job was never intended to be easy. Have faith. Most importantly, have faith in Teddy. She needs you." Randi looked so certain of what she was saying.

"Has the clock slowed down?" Thomas asked.

"Yes, I'm sure by now it has stopped," I said reluctantly.

"Let's hope not. If so, things are much more serious than we realize." Randi gently squeezed my hands and pulled away. I knew it was time for me to go. I still didn't know where

CHAPTER THIRTY-ONE

I drove back to town letting my mind wander through the events of the last few days. The family book, Pops' stories, Teddy's room, the hidden underground vault, all of it racing through my head. My chest began to pound with my heart, loudly echoing in my ears. I was a sentinel now. Surely that came with some kind of calming superpower, some tool that acted like a super dose of Xanax. If so, it wasn't kicking in. I needed a place to think and sort everything out. The only place that came to mind was the library.

The old building was dark. It looked out of place amongst the other houses twinkling with the lights of the season. I thought Sean had left, and then I remembered the electricity had yet to be repaired. I tried the door, but it was locked. I had left everything with Sean, the book, the key, all of it. Quietly rapping on the glass, I peered through the window, hoping to catch a glimpse of him coming toward the entrance. It was quiet and empty. The doorframe offered stability as I leaned into it, letting the cold wind blow across my back. My phone buzzed and vibrated in my pocket. While I wanted to quickly pull it out and see who had texted me, my hand rested on the phone, feeling the vibrations as they buzzed through the denim of my pants. I didn't want to be disappointed. I wanted it to be her. It had to be her.

Sean's name flashed across the screen of my phone. I didn't read the messages because it wasn't Teddy. My heart sank a little as I rested my forehead against the glass like a little kid waiting for the candy store to open. And then I felt someone behind me. Immediately I thought of the intruder. If sentinel powers were going to be bestowed upon me, now would be a great time. Maybe they had to be activated by some event. This was as good a time as any. My senses were keenly aware of the person moving closer, their soft footsteps on the stairs behind me. My keys were the only weapon I possessed at the time. I cupped them in my hand, letting the truck key protrude through my fingers. That self-defense class in college was finally paying off. I planted my foot and spun around, arm extended, waiting to make contact. And then I was across the banister, through the bushes, lying on the ground. Second time today.

The force of the ground pushed the air out of my lungs with a thud. And there, leaning over the railing was Teddy looking very surprised.

"Are you okay?"

"I think so, just a little stunned." I sat up on my elbows, feeling the cold ground begin to seep through my clothes.

"What were you trying to do?"

"I thought you were the intruder." She quickly and easily jumped the banister to help me up. "Show off," I said, scrambling on the ground.

"Were you trying to attack me?" I was sure she didn't mean it as condescending as it sounded.

"I think the better question is what did you do to me?"

She helped me up and dusted the snow off me. "I don't really know, a gut reaction, instinct I guess."

"Well at least one of us has superpowers."

I continued to clean myself up, disgusted with my lack of game when it came to sentinel prowess. We faced one another. Even in just the short time we had been separated, I missed her face. I wasn't sure if I would see it again but here she stood in front of me. There was so much to say but nothing would come out.

"I'm sorry," she said, quietly enough that the wind almost carried it away. Her gray eyes were filled with sincerity. A smile lifted the corners of my mouth and it was enough for her. She stepped toward me and I found myself in her arms. She held me tightly. I pulled her into me, not wanting to let go. Our bodies clung together, our energies syncing. We slowly let air invade the space between us, her scent filling my senses. With our foreheads still touching, we looked at each other as if we had been separated forever.

"I'm sorry," she said again, our faces close enough for me to feel her warm breath. "I should have told you more, given you more information. I realized how my texts must have sounded. I left you with very little explanation."

"So much has happened, so quickly, and then I didn't hear from you." I closed my eyes, taking in everything—her smell, her touch, the sound of her voice. We both knew letting go meant acknowledging a new reality.

"Ladies, I hate to break this up, but I think the world might need the dynamic duo." Sean stuck his head out of the front door and brought us back to reality.

"We're not superheroes, Sean," I said, reluctantly letting go of Teddy and climbing back onto the stairs.

"We don't even know what we're doing." I heard Teddy's words behind me. I turned quickly.

"*We* don't know what we're doing?" I asked hopefully.

"My understanding is that it takes two sentinels which means we're a package deal. So no, *we* don't know what we're doing," she said as she hopped over the railing, landing beside me on the stairs. The comfort her words brought was quickly interrupted by the stark reality of the fact that we didn't know what we were doing. Would there be a bolt of lightning that would empower us with superhero strength, stunning boots, and long, flowing capes? Or were we left on our own with a book and a Christmas clock that seemed to work when it wanted to? At least we had our wardens. I had so much to tell Teddy.

I went into the study and sat on the couch. Sean had placed lanterns on the mantel and the tables. The fireplace had not seen this much use in years. The flames danced between the logs, tossing shadows around the room. Had I not known the darkness was a result of someone cutting the power, it would have been very romantic, even cozy. Teddy joined me on the couch. Sean followed us in, pointing to something on the table, the Christmas clock.

"It's stopped, Andi. Pops brought it by while you were gone. He said the two of you needed it." We all looked at the clock, silently wanting it to start ticking. Instead, it sat motionless.

"Did he say anything else?" I asked, hoping Pops had left us with some words of wisdom or a salty old tale of what to do next.

"He didn't. He said he had to go home. He didn't want to miss *Jeopardy* but call him if we needed him."

I sighed heavily and closed my eyes, resting my head in my hands. I felt Teddy's hand on my back, giving me all the reassurance I needed, at least until Sean's phone rang. I heard my mother's voice very clearly and very loudly listing off ingredients *she* needed, followed by strict instructions to get home as quickly as possible. Sean shrugged his shoulders. Was this situation not as dire as we suspected? My family was carrying on with everyday life as if the Christmas clock was running like a finely tuned machine. Maybe that's what Teddy and I needed to do, relax a little bit.

Sean left the library under the guise that he was keeping my mom off our backs. I was sure he was much more scared of her than anything that threatened world peace.

I locked the door behind him and joined Teddy back in the study. "I don't think it's safe to stay here tonight," I said, thinking about the intruder Teddy had chased out just a few days ago.

"I agree." She paused for a moment as if she were looking for the right words. "I don't want to be without you." My heart began to beat quickly. "We can't go to the inn. It's a long story. I'll tell you everything."

"I look forward to hearing it," I said, wanting to know more about the woman I saw. I also needed to explain to Teddy why I broke into her room. "That leaves us with my parents' place."

Teddy laughed and shook her head. "Please tell me your room is exactly like it was in high school."

"Not exactly," I stammered. "There is a treadmill they use as a clothes rack now."

We sat for a moment in silence, our legs touching. I wanted to hold her hand but didn't want to seem needy.

"It was weird without you," I said, not sure how to tell her what I was feeling. She hesitated longer than I wanted her to.

"I know. Me too."

"We have help," I said, turning to her.

"I know, your family is great. I am so glad we have them."

"No, I mean yes, they are wonderful, but...do you remember the tavern at the pass? Maybe you don't because that cider hit you hard." I let a little laugh escape.

"Of course, I remember the tavern. And Randi, right?"

"Right, Randi and Thomas. They are our wardens, our watchers. They are here to help us. They know my grandparents. They were their wardens as well."

"How is that..."

"Possible?" I finished Teddy's question without hesitation. "No idea but it seems as if they haven't aged in quite a while. That or they have an exceptional skincare routine."

"We have so much to do..." Teddy's voice turned into a yawn before she could finish her sentence.

"You're exhausted. To tell you the truth, I'm a little tired myself. Let's get you to my parents' house so you can rest." I wanted to believe she was back and everything was perfect. We were the dynamic duo, ready to take on the world. Something pulled at my gut. I chose to ignore it because I was so happy to have her back.

We closed the library and drove to the house. There was a general commotion coming from the kitchen, nothing serious, just my family in the throes of last-minute prep. Teddy walked up the stairs. I grabbed her hand and pulled her away.

"Oh, no, we're not going into that hot mess. My mom will lose her mind because she finally gets to meet you, my dad will try to impress you, and Sean, well you know Sean." Teddy looked puzzled as I led her to the back of the house. I stood beneath a large maple tree, placing one foot on the old board that had been nailed to it years ago.

"Wait a minute, what are you doing?" she asked, watching me begin to climb.

"Shhh, I'm sneaking my girlfriend into my room."

"Hmm, girlfriend? I like the sound of that. Is this something you are used to doing?"

"Absolutely...not." I winked at her. "I'm a rule follower through and through. When Helen is your mom, you toe the line."

She followed me up the makeshift ladder. Teddy was exceptionally athletic and quickly made her way up the trunk. "If you're a rule follower, then why the ladder?" she asked, pushing herself to the bend in the tree.

"I didn't say I was perfect. Sean attached these years ago. He's a little looser with authority than I am."

"You wouldn't know that by the way he left the library. I think your mom scared the hell out of him."

I slowly scooted my way toward the roof, balancing along a branch that would support my weight, edging toward the gutters.

"It's gingerbread season. You don't cross serious competitors in this town." I made the jump, landing with a thud. The house quieted down for a moment. I lifted my finger to tell Teddy to freeze. The house began to hum again. I motioned for her to make the jump. She landed like an elegant cat to my clumsy dog.

"I never thought, at my age, I would be sneaking into my girlfriend's room at her parents' house."

"Hmm, girlfriend? I like the sound of that." We smiled at each other. I pulled my window open and stepped down into my room, holding my hand out for Teddy. She was already through the window, missing the trunk I had used for a step and falling toward me. We both tumbled backward, landing on my floor.

"Are you okay?" I asked.

"Are you?" She began to get up.

"Not so fast. I'm taking advantage of this opportunity." I wrapped my arms around her waist and held her against me. She smiled and lowered herself back down again. Her hair, which now fell in blond curls, tickled my face. She slowly rested all her weight on the palm of her hands. Her eyes were playful as her knee separated my legs. The slightest groan escaped me as I closed my eyes.

"Look at me," she said, pressing against me. I opened my eyes. She slowly moved toward me. Her playful eyes turned intense as they were drawn to my mouth. She hesitated, just enough to make me want her even more. I lifted my head to end the intense pain I was feeling. With a slight smile, she backed away just a little.

"You're a tease," I said.

"Is it working?"

Catching her off guard, I quickly wrapped my legs around her and changed our positions, my weight pinning her down. "What were you saying?" I laughed, seeing the look of surprise on her face.

"I underestimated you."

"Many people do," I said as I lowered myself down, placing my lips close to hers. I lightly bit her lip.

She let out a controlled groan. "I won't do it again," she said, kissing me.

"Ladies, I hate to break this up but...the floor? Really?" Sean said as he leaned into my room from the door. I let my head fall on Teddy's chest. We both sighed heavily.

"Your brother absolutely has the worst timing," she whispered.

"I'll say it again, or the best timing. You two could have hurt yourselves down there," he said, giggling. "I heard Andi jump on the roof. I thought I would come up here and unlock the window for you. I told Mom and Dad it was probably one of her squirrels. You know she feeds them."

"That would have been one hell of a squirrel," I said, laughing.

"Some of them are bigger than raccoons. They get all her gingerbread mistakes," he said to Teddy, chuckling.

"Sean, please don't tell Mom we're here. We need a few minutes."

"I'll say you do." Sean cocked his head, gesturing to the floor he'd just found us on.

"Sean!" I said, louder than I intended, hoping he would stop talking.

"Why don't you just take my place out back? No one will bother you there."

"There is no way I'm going back down that tree. We're here, and we're staying put. And trust me, we could stay up here for days and no one would know. Mom and Dad are too busy trying to wrap everything up." Sean agreed shaking his head as he grabbed the door handle. "Can you bring us up some food? I don't know about you, Teddy, but I'm starving."

"That would be great. Thanks, Sean," Teddy said as we pulled ourselves from the floor.

"Anything for you, Teddy." Sean winked at her and looked at me. "I like her, Andi. Nice job."

Sighing deeply, I pushed him out the door and quietly latched it. "Sorry about that," I said, turning on a small lamp.

"Sean? He's great. I always imagined if I had a brother, he would be a lot like him."

I smiled, realizing that he really was a fantastic ally. He had been my entire life.

"Thank goodness I have my own bathroom. Would you like to change your clothes? I'm sure I have something that will work." I looked at her jeans, which were now wet and covered with the outside from climbing up the ladder and scampering across the roof.

"Yeah, that would be great."

"I have sweats or these lovely Christmas onesies my mom gets us every year." I held up the green-and-white-striped pajamas with the attached feet. She smiled and rolled her eyes.

"Why not? Seems appropriate for the last few days. But only if you'll wear one too."

I laughed and threw it at her as she headed to the bathroom. Being here with Teddy was surreal. Just a few hours ago I wondered if I would ever see her again. And now she was putting on last year's Christmas pajamas and spending the night with me. My middle school self would have been very proud of me. My euphoric feeling, however, was interrupted by a knock at my bedroom door. Sean stuck his head in and waved a bag at me. He set it down on the desk with a bottle of wine and quickly ducked out. Before he left, he lifted the bottle and winked at me, snickering.

I changed my clothes, shoving my feet into the footies of the red-and-white-striped pajamas. Turning around, I caught a glimpse of myself in the mirror—disheveled hair, Christmas pajamas, who wouldn't run screaming from this? I quickly tucked my hair on top of my head, pulled a few strands down around my face, and added a little bit of lip gloss just before the bathroom door opened. Teddy stood in the doorway. I never knew Christmas onesies could be sexy. I was pretty sure, however, that Teddy could make a burlap bag look good.

Even though they were filthy, she had neatly folded her clothes and set them down on the desk. She lifted the bag that sat next to her clothes.

"Sean?" she asked, looking into the bag.

"Yes, what did he get us?"

"Hmm, you'll find this surprising, a large gingerbread man, probably a prototype, half a cheeseball, a container of marshmallow fluff, and a few crackers, oh, and a candy cane."

She brought the bag over to my bed and plopped down. "That seems about right."

"You're adorable, by the way," I said, looking at this woman who had completely surprised me in the last few days. I would have never guessed this elegant, breathtaking woman would be sitting in front of me wearing Christmas pajamas, with feet in them no less, eating marshmallow fluff out of a container with a headless gingerbread man. I think I might just love her.

"What?" she asked, pausing to look at me.

"You have fluff on your face."

She laughed, closing her eyes in embarrassment. "I've fallen so far, so fast."

"It's just fluff, you'll recover." I leaned over and kissed her cheek, taking care of the fluff.

"Maybe it was on purpose." She threw me a sly smile, smearing some on her lips with an amputated gingerbread arm.

"Let me get that for you." The sticky fluff stuck between our lips. I removed it with my tongue, once again biting her lip. I felt her warm fingertips on my waist as she rose to meet me, my hand sliding behind her neck and pulling her toward me. Our tongues intertwined as our bodies met, the heat between us intensifying. I slid down her neck, kissing every inch of her soft skin as she leaned back, quietly moaning. My tongue traced the outline of her open top, my hand sliding up her tight body. She grabbed my wrist just before it found what it was searching for.

"We can't," she said exasperated.

"Yes, we can," I assured her.

"I don't want to do this in your parents' house while I'm wearing pajamas with feet in them. I pictured something a little more...adult?" We looked at each other and realized how much this seemed like a sleepover and burst into laughter. Reluctantly we retreated to our sides of the bed, surprised we let things get that far.

"Are you going to share any of that?"

She pulled off a gingerbread leg and dunked it in the fluff. "What do we have to drink?" she asked, looking at the bottle.

"Aw, this would be one of my mom's finest screw-top Moscatos. She goes through cases of it this time of year, claiming it's the fuel that keeps the machine running. She also swears it helps with her creativity. We don't stand in the way of creative genius."

"I love your family. I can't wait to meet your parents."

"You do realize what you're saying, right?" I asked as I unscrewed the bottle.

Teddy went to the bathroom and got two little cups from the dispenser on the sink. "Anyone who puts little Dixie cups with sporting equipment on them, in her grown daughter's bathroom, is someone I need to meet."

"You saw those, huh? I appreciate her support even in my Dixie cups. She never once tried to sneak a princess cup in there."

"They're a little hard to miss, Andi." I poured the wine into cups decorated with baseballs, soccer balls, and footballs. Truthfully, more balls than any self-respecting lesbian needed. We toasted to a new beginning and finished off the cheeseball.

"I like your room." The dim lamp partially lit the room decorated with soccer and rowing team pictures. Rugby stripes ran along the walls, ending behind the mounted television. A large desk sat to the right of the door. The opposite wall was home to a worn, overstuffed chair, completely covered with clothes. Large windows flanked my bed, leading to a roof where I often sat on sunny days and warm nights, watching the stars, never thinking, in my wildest dreams, that my life would lead me here.

"It's definitely a blast from the past."

"An athletic librarian. I like it," Teddy said with a flirty smile.

"Well, this is me more than a decade ago."

"Your parents must really love you."

"As much as I make fun of them, lovingly of course, they are amazing. I mean, look around. My mom knew way before me that I was gay. It was never a thing with them. My mom knew that Amy, the girl that sat behind me in sixth grade, was my first crush. They never raised an eyebrow. I never had to say, 'I'm gay' to them. It's just who I am."

"That must have made for an incredible childhood." She paused for a moment before she continued, "I came home for Christmas after my first prep year in Switzerland. Let's just say my roommate and I hit it off. I, of course, thought I was in love."

"First loves are the hardest," I said, sympathizing. She drank the rest of the wine in her cup and filled it again.

"They certainly can be. I came home and told my father all about Anne-Laure. I'm not sure why. He and I never had a relationship where we shared...anything. He sent me to Switzerland so he wouldn't have to raise me. He couldn't be bothered with me. And why I wanted his approval is beyond me."

"He is your father. Everyone wants their parents' approval. If you don't mind me asking, what happened to your mom?"

"She was killed in a car accident. He didn't even take the time to mourn her. One day she was here and the next she was gone."

"That's incredibly harsh. That must have been horrible for you. It doesn't sound like he ever worried about your feelings."

"In his eyes, he had no reason to be concerned about my feelings. He told me I needed to learn how the world worked and that he would be doing me a disservice if he protected me from it."

Teddy was maneuvering her way through this conversation steadily like she was telling this narrative as if it were someone else's story. My heart broke for how normal this was for her. I reached for her hand. She squeezed it gently and returned to the bottle for another cup. She was compartmentalizing, putting everything in neat little boxes, and she didn't need me edging in and offering support. She was fully aware of her past and how it shaped her as an adult. Her armor was thick and crafted by her very own hands. Still, she had to be tired of carrying it around.

"So, how did that go? Telling him about your roommate?"

"You can imagine. He hoped I didn't embarrass him. That I wasn't showing myself with this *girl*. He pulled me out of the Swiss school and sent me to a school in London. He took my phone and destroyed it, destroyed my computer. I was so scared I never tried to contact Anne-Laure. I never saw her again."

"I don't even know what to say. That's terrible."

"So, needless to say, all relationships after that, I kept to myself. I didn't go home as much. I tried to travel on breaks at school. I figured he could keep throwing money at the problem, and I would take advantage of it and travel."

"The problem?" I asked.

"Me. I'm the problem." She poured another cup of wine.

"Problem is not a word I would ever use to describe you. You…you're…amazing. You are incredible in every way. I mean, obviously, you're beautiful, but the most attractive quality you have, by far, is your intelligence. You are funny, adorable, confident, and charming. Do you want me to go on?"

"Please, go right ahead," she said with the slightest laugh.

"You really don't see any of that do you?" I asked, surprised.

"I know what I need to do to be successful, a force to be reckoned with. I swore I would never let anyone make me feel the way he did. So no, anything else is not necessary."

"Oh, it's necessary," I said, taking the small cup out of her hand and putting it on the nightstand. "Everything about you that you have let me see in the past few days is everything that is amazing about you." I placed my hands on either side of her folded legs, moving to make her look at me. "This makes you uncomfortable, doesn't it?"

"It does," she said, looking at me.

"Why?"

"Because with you, I'm not in complete control. I'm not hiding. And who I am just naturally comes out. And that person, she's someone I've worked hard to keep hidden away."

"You can trust me. That version of Teddy that you've locked away is safe with me."

"I don't trust anyone," she said, looking directly into my eyes as if this declaration was final.

"You can trust me," I said again, returning the gaze. Her chest rose with a long, deep sigh. I saw a battle raging inside her. She was comfortable with her life the way it had been. Building up walls this strong took some time. They weren't going to come down overnight.

Teddy sat before me in Christmas pajamas that were ridiculously too big. Her hair was casual, not meticulously put into place. She was vulnerable, and she was letting me see that.

She was also exhausted. I pulled the blankets back, lifted her feet, and tucked her into bed. The small lamp was the only light in the room. I added a blanket to her side of the bed and kissed her on the cheek.

"I'm not used to this," she said as I pulled the blankets over her shoulders.

"What's that?" I asked, sliding into the bed beside her.

"Someone taking care of me."

"I think it's probably about time." I slid my arm under her pillow as she pulled herself close to me, laying her head on my shoulder and tucking her arms between us. I pulled her toward me, reassuring her.

"Can I tell you something?" I asked, waiting for her to answer. Nothing. "Teddy?"

In a split second, she'd fallen asleep. I laughed, wondering how on Earth anyone could fall asleep that fast. I wanted to tell her that this was beginning to feel right. I pushed back anything in my head that said otherwise. I kissed the top of her head and pulled the blankets around us, fiercely protective of this woman I had just met.

CHAPTER THIRTY-TWO

The sun shone through my window just enough for a thin strip to fall across my eyes and wake me up. Last night flooded into my head. I couldn't help but smile. I turned over to see Teddy sleeping peacefully. Could we lay here forever? Everything felt right and good. Why let the world in? And then the loud knocking on my door started. Teddy's eyes popped open as if someone was shooting. I put my hand across her mouth and motioned to the door.

"I'm sure it's Sean." Her eyes closed slowly as she rested her head on the pillow. From the other side of the door, we heard a voice.

"Honey, it's Mom. Can I come in?"

Teddy's eyes were wide again as she jumped up. We were teenagers getting caught by my mom. She grabbed the blanket, wrapped it around herself, and hit the floor just as my mom opened the door.

"Hi, honey. Did you get in late last night? I didn't hear you come in." She continued walking around the room, picking up clothes, not realizing that she had picked up Teddy's shirt and pants.

"It was late. I'm sorry, I should have said something."

"Oh, dear, it's fine. We're so busy with the competition, you know. Why don't you come down to breakfast? I can make some pancakes." She started to walk out of the room. I felt a great sense of relief. Teddy was half under the bed. She let out a long breath. And then my mom turned around. "And tell Teddy to come with you. She's family now. Why on Earth you let her lay on that cold floor, I will never know. I'll see you girls in a few minutes. Looking forward to meeting you, Teddy." And with that, the door clicked, and she left us wondering what had just happened.

"She's like an assault weapon," I whispered.

"Well, that was humiliating," Teddy said as she sat up on her elbows, her blond hair hanging in her face.

"This should help. I think she took your clothes."

"Yes, that helps a great deal. Thank you."

We both laughed, knowing that Helen would not give us much time before she was up here knocking again.

"I have something for you to wear, I'm sure. We just need to get moving," I said, pulling some clothes out for Teddy, handing them to her, and kissing her for the first time today.

We sheepishly walked down the back stairs and into a busy kitchen. My family was already sitting down to breakfast, including Pops. We both felt a tremendous sense of relief seeing him sitting at the head of the table.

"There she is!" my grandfather said, standing to meet us. I walked toward him, waiting for his warm hug, when he passed me and embraced Teddy. She welcomed it like she had known him for years. With his arm around her, he walked her to the table, passing me in the process. I knew Pops was still very indecisive about Teddy but making her feel like she belonged was what he did. "You really should introduce her, Andi." I laughed at both of them.

"Everyone, this is Teddy. Teddy, this is…" I didn't get the rest of it out before my parents got up to meet her.

"Teddy, it's so good to meet you," my mother said, wrapping her arms around her. "I haven't heard enough about you," she said, pulling her toward the table. My dad stood back a little bit, feeling that Teddy might be overwhelmed. My mom continued, "This jewel of a man is my husband, Henry."

"Nice to meet you all," Teddy said as she took a seat next to Sean.

"Dear, we're a lot, you'll have to forgive us. We're just so happy to meet you finally." She didn't like awkward silence, so my mom tended to talk nonstop.

The fire was dancing in the hearth. Gris was sitting in his usual place gnawing on what appeared to be a gingerbread man. The kitchen was warm and inviting. Everything that meant anything to me was in this room and I felt whole.

My family was surprisingly reserved when it came to grilling Teddy. They treated her like she had been part of the family forever. I watched the tension ease in her body as her laugh changed from nervous to natural. My mom scolded Sean for feeding us half a cheeseball and marshmallow fluff. My dad tried his best to impress Teddy with tales of everything he had recently fixed. Sean was his normal goofy self. I think he might have even had a little crush on Teddy.

While I loved this first introduction of Teddy to my family, we needed to discuss the clock.

"Pops, what's happening with the clock?" I finally asked, needing more information.

"It just stopped last night."

The blood drained from my parents' faces. They looked at my grandfather, shocked and slightly terrified.

"What?" The word erupted from my mother's mouth. My father got up and left the room.

"Calm down, Helen. Andi and Teddy will know what to do."

My mom stood, took the tea towel off her lap, and started wringing it. She began pacing in the kitchen. Gris dropped the gingerbread man and watched my mom, following her movement back and forth.

"Dad!" Sean screamed. My father had walked back into the kitchen with a loaded pump-action shotgun.

"Henry!" my mom yelled at my dad. I thought she was as surprised as the rest of us, and then he tossed another shotgun to my mom, who readily took it, making sure it was loaded. Gris started howling, becoming the siren to this ridiculous scene.

"What are you doing?" I asked, shocked. "I didn't even know we had guns in the house." Teddy and I walked toward my parents, slowly, as if we were trying to disarm two raging lunatics.

"Oh, your dad and I have been practicing for this. We run drills when you kids aren't here. We're ready."

Pops sat at the table, eating his pancakes and shaking his head. "Helen, while I appreciate your enthusiasm, I don't think the two of you and your shotguns will cure the problems of the world. Why don't you put those down before someone gets shot."

Teddy gently took the gun from my dad and quickly disarmed it, pumping three shells onto the table. My mom also relinquished her weapon.

"You wouldn't get this if I didn't want you to have it." My mom winked at Teddy as she handed her the gun.

"I know, Mrs. Thatcher. You seem very skilled." Teddy popped out the shells and set them on the table. It was impressive, and to my surprise, the butterflies in my stomach, reared their tiny little heads. She knew her way around a gun.

I took a deep breath and sized up the room. Teddy was holding two shotguns, Sean was cleaning up the milk that had shot out of his nose, Gris was settled back into eating the gingerbread man, and Pops hadn't moved a muscle and had managed to keep eating. My parents were high-fiving each other in the kitchen and my new girlfriend was picking up shotgun shells from our family table. Not what I expected for my first family meal with Teddy but here we were.

"Can we all sit back down?" I asked, walking back toward my chair. And then I heard the door click. Jules was standing in the kitchen. "Why not?" I thought out loud to myself.

"Am I interrupting?" she asked, inching her way into the kitchen. She immediately looked at Teddy and then at me.

"Hi, Julie!" my mom overenthusiastically welcomed her, stepping toward her to offer a hug. "It's good to see you, dear."

"I think I may have come at the wrong time. I was just taking you up on your invitation to breakfast, Mrs. T," Jules said awkwardly as the rest of us made our way back to the table. Teddy tried to inconspicuously place the guns in the hallway, out of sight, but being the most noticeable person in the room and carrying two shotguns made that a little tricky.

"And I'm glad you did. Come on over and have a seat, honey." My mom led her to the table. I looked at my mom, puzzled as to what she was doing. My pronounced, what-the-hell look said it all while she hung behind Jules, shrugging her shoulders and mouthing something along the lines of *What could I do?*

"Jules, this is Teddy. Andi's new friend," my mom said, hooking her arm in Teddy's and leading her to the table as well.

"Nice to meet you." Teddy held her hand out to Jules, who didn't move.

"Same," Jules said as she ignored Teddy's hand and pulled the chair out, sitting down and grabbing herself a plate.

"Make yourself at home," I said under my breath as I sat back down. Jules had taken Teddy's seat. Sean quickly grabbed another chair for Teddy, obviously choosing sides. He winked at her as he pushed the chair in behind her and patted her on the shoulders. He looked like a trainer at a boxing match, preparing Teddy for the knockout.

"Thanks again for inviting me over, Mrs. T." She collected pancakes and a few strips of bacon. The silence at the table was deafening. I couldn't believe my mother was allowing it. We all continued eating. The forks clanged against the plates as the intermittent sounds of crunching could be heard.

Jules finally broke the silence. "What is everyone up to today?"

"Oh, you know, just trying to save the world." My grandfather chuckled as he slurped his coffee. Nervous laughter spread across the table as one of the shotguns slid down the wall and into view in the middle of the hallway. Everyone fell silent.

"Good thing it wasn't loaded," Teddy said. We all laughed except Jules.

The dislodged gun caused a domino effect, the second gun slid into view, and then a third fell into sight and on top of the other two. A deafening boom shot through the room as a large piece of plaster dropped from the kitchen ceiling, falling onto my mother's gingerbread construction site. Gris jumped up, coughing and choking as his howls dislodged the legless gingerbread man he had been working on. My mom let out a guttural scream from the depths of her toes as if one of her children had just been shot. Sean was already sheltering beneath the table, pulling on one of Teddy's legs to get her to join him. My father had unhooked some sort of weapon from the underside of the table and stood in a combat-ready stance. Pops continued sipping his coffee as I sat stunned at the tableau posed before me. The room was quiet except for the low sobs that escaped my mom's heaving body. Pieces of plaster crumbled from the ceiling, snowing on the village my mom had spent weeks working on.

Jules stood up from the table, wiped her mouth, pushed her chair in, and walked toward the door. "I think I'm interrupting. I'll just see myself out. Thanks again, Mrs. T." Jules headed for the door, dodging the pieces of the ceiling that littered the kitchen.

I looked at my dad, still standing like a ninja holding a long knife.

"Dad, what happened?" I asked, looking at the mess.

"You should always be prepared, Andi-bug. I was keeping a backup in the hallway. I guess I should have told you about that one too." I took the knife from my dad and sat it on the table and then I heard Sean's muffled voice.

"There's a whole arsenal under here!"

Teddy was on her knees, head just above the table. Sean had almost succeeded in pulling her down. She disappeared for a moment and returned with a look that could only be described as surprised and terrified.

"He's right. There's a full armory under there." Pops sat his coffee down and slowly pushed his chair out like he was avoiding a ticking bomb.

"How long has that been there?" I asked, surprised at my parents.

My mom had calmed herself a bit. She turned to me, wiping her tearstained face. "Oh, quite a while, dear. As I said, we must be prepared."

"Do you know how many meals we have here?" Sean asked, crawling out from under the table. "Thanksgiving, Christmas, birthdays…One wrong move and it could've been our last."

"Sean, don't be so dramatic," my mother said, fumbling under the table and coming back with a .357 Magnum.

"Lord, Mom! Put that thing down."

Teddy had ducked back under the table as my mom waved it around freely. "Your mom knows how to use that."

My grandfather refilled his mug and said, "When they were old enough to go on a date, I taught her and her sisters."

"Are we the equivalent of a Kringle mafia family? Is this who we are?" I said, sitting down and very slowly pushing myself away from the arsenal.

My mom sat in her chair and crossed her legs. She sat the gun on her lap and went into her best Don Corleone impression. "You don't mess with the family," she said, brushing her jaw with her hand. My dad laughed. I looked at Teddy, who was still kneeling on the floor.

"I swear I don't know who these people are and I apologize. I thought we were normal. No wonder my being gay wasn't a big deal. It was the least of their problems."

Teddy snickered.

There was a significant amount of cleanup as well as a lot of disarming of the furniture. We had to refocus on the problem. I had a distinct feeling that time was running out.

CHAPTER THIRTY-THREE

Teddy

"If we can all act like we have some sense, please, maybe we can talk about the clock and what we should do moving forward," Andi said, dropping between Sean and me on the couch.

I was experiencing an odd mix of feelings. On the one hand, I felt totally at home, but on the other hand, I was terrified. This family was accepting me as one of their own, at least they were making me feel that way regardless of how they really felt. I wasn't terrified because this family was equipped for the apocalypse. I was terrified because this was the first time I felt a part of something. The very few times I had felt like this in the past, I didn't stick around long enough to enjoy it. I knew I wouldn't survive the pain of disappointment and loss if anything happened. So here I sat in the middle of this group of people who were welcoming me into their lives, believing they were the definition of *home*. Terrified was an understatement.

"Pops, what can you tell us about the last time the clock slowed down?" Andi asked, trying to refocus everyone.

"Well, it was November 1989. The Berlin Wall had just fallen. Goodwill around the world was at an all-time high. Your grandmother had me pull down the Christmas decorations from the attic. She said it was a good time to celebrate."

"I remember that Christmas," Helen interrupted. "I had come home from college for Thanksgiving, and you guys already had everything decorated."

"By the time you got home, your mother and I had decorated everything and averted a global crisis," Pops said, reaching down to pet Gris behind his ear. He wagged his tail, leaned his head into Pops's hand, and whimpered.

"That's quite a statement, Pops," Sean said, leaning forward to grab a peppermint from the candy dish on the table.

"It's quite a story, Sean. We were decorating when we noticed the Christmas clock was losing time. As you all know, it never loses time. Katherine and I were immediately on alert. Our tenure as sentinels had been uneventful. Since the Kringles had been exported and were now housed at the library, in a sealed vault no less, we felt they were safer than they had ever been. Who could possibly know where they were located? The move had been top secret. Very few people knew anything about them. We felt like our job was pretty easy. But something was wrong. A few days went by and the clock continued to slow. That's when we spotted a stranger in town. Katie and I noticed him right away. He had a beautiful little girl with him. She had the blondest hair you'd ever seen. The man's accent was thick, Eastern European, I think.

The first time we met him was at Nick's. Katie and I were having lunch and noticed the two of them. She was always a sucker for little kids and struck up a conversation with the little girl. The gentleman, who we later learned was her father, was gruff and not very pleasant at all. Your grandmother felt sorry for the little girl and she worried about her. Katie told her that she had the perfect book for her if she would come by the library the next day. The next day came and went, and the little girl never showed. My Kate worried so much about her."

It was easy to tell that Andi's grandparents loved each other a great deal. Her grandfather paused, finding it difficult to continue the story. I knew that he had recently lost the love of his life and you could see him struggling. Andi told me that he painfully missed her every day. He wiped his eyes and took a drink of his coffee.

"Do you need a minute, Dad?" Helen asked, reaching out to him.

"No, it's okay. Where was I?" he asked, setting his mug down.

"The little girl," I said, intrigued by the story. There was something familiar about what Pops was saying. Something inside me was triggered.

"That's right, the little girl. Kate was desperate to find her. She wanted to know that she was okay. She kept saying it was just a feeling she had."

"What did you do?" I asked.

"We went to the inn, of course. The Driscolls would always know any comings and goings."

"What did you find out?" Sean asked, moving to the edge of the couch.

"No one was staying at the inn that met their description."

"Maybe they were just driving through. People do that all the time," Henry said, adding his two cents.

"We had seen them on several different days around town. It wasn't just a one-day trip they were on."

I had been sitting here listening to this story, images of my childhood racing in and out of my head and I didn't know why. "Why were you so worried about her...the girl?" I asked.

"When you're a sentinel, you acquire the ability to see good and evil. It's not just a feeling but something you can almost see in a person. This man had black all around him. It was like a mist that swirled, its tentacles reaching out to pull in anyone within reach. On the other hand, the little girl had this white cloud around her. The edges were gray and frazzled like a worn sweater, from fighting off her father's influence."

"You can see that?" Andi asked.

"Yes, I've seen it most of my life." It spilled out of my mouth before I realized what I was saying. Andi looked at me, waiting for me to say more. "I noticed it when I was five. I could see shapes and colors around people like something was leaking from inside of them." I turned to Andi. "Have you seen it?" I hoped her answer was yes.

"No, not that I can remember. I mean, I've noticed things lately but not that young."

"I miss it," Pops said. "Since my wife passed, I have been losing the ability a little every day and now it's pretty much gone. It took time to hone the ability once Katie and I became sentinels but it was never black and white. Well, I should say it is rarely black and white. This man, though, was the darkest I had ever seen."

"Like a violent tempest?" I interrupted, thinking about the storm that raged around my father constantly. Even on days when he was somewhat emotionally balanced, the dark mass that surrounded him churned like an angry sea.

"Yes," Pops said, surprised at my description. "He became lost in it, completely enveloped. And that's why Kate wanted to help the little girl. We also knew that this man had to have something to do with why the Christmas clock was slowing down."

"Did you see him again?" I pressed, needing to know more about this man.

"We did. But not with the little girl. A few days went by and the man walked into the library. He asked a few questions about the library's history and wandered around a bit. He told us he was a historian, a professor from California. Kate asked him why he would be interested in our little library. He said it was Kringle Falls that held his interest. Katie tried many times to steer the conversation in a direction that would have given us more information. He wasn't interested in entertaining any of her questions. His gruff attitude had reached a level of condescension, looking down his nose at us as he threw out quick, concise answers. He lingered for a while in several of the rooms and then finally decided to leave. The black mist surrounding him had become violent, its edges sharp as knives. His demeanor was calm but he was raging."

I could feel the tears welling up in my eyes. I knew the description all too well. Sitting here on this couch I was hovering near the edge of an abyss. So many things I had locked away, not because they were merely bad memories, but because my actual survival depended upon it. And now, listening to the description of this man, it was flooding back in, threatening to wash me over the edge.

Andi slid her hand into mine, noticing I was struggling. Her brow furrowed as she looked at me. I hated what this woman was doing to me. She was everything I didn't have. My life was in perfect order, everything had its place and I'd worked tirelessly to get here. Walking away would be so easy, or would it?

"What happened to him?" I asked, my voice just a whisper.

"Just before he left, Katie stopped him at the door and gave him a book to give to his daughter. He looked at the book and then back at my wife. Disdain dripped from his face, so much so that I stepped out from behind the desk to join her. He grabbed the book from her hand, turned, and left."

"Wow, what was his problem?" Andi asked.

"He was used to getting what he wants," I added and Pops nodded his head in agreement. Andi looked at me, her face was puzzled.

"I thought that would be the last we saw of him." Pops got up to refill his mug and grab another piece of gingerbread from the pile of detached limbs and torsos that cluttered the table. He threw a foot to Gris and then retook his seat.

"So, what happened next?" I asked. I felt like I was pushing the story forward, desperate to know the end and worried I already did.

"As he was leaving, he paused for a moment in the entryway. He set the book down on the table and looked around. He was very calculated. That dark mist that surrounded him filled the entire library, and it made it very hard to see what he was doing. The front doors opened, and the black cloud rushed out. He had left the book behind. Seeing the disappointment in Kate's eyes, I grabbed the book and followed him."

"I'm not sure I could have done that, Pops," Sean said, wiping his forehead in disbelief. "That man sounds like a whole lot of no good."

"Well, I either had to face him or your grandmother." Pops winked at me. "I could never stand disappointment on my wife's face, so I ran after him. His 1967 Mercedes Benz 600 had pulled onto the street in front of the library."

"Red interior." I didn't realize I had said it out loud.

"Yes, red interior," Pops added. "How did you…"

"It's a famous car. Dictators around the world use them," I said quickly.

"That's why I thought he was missing the little flags." Pops laughed at his own joke. "Anyway, I stepped off the curb to cross before him, when he revved the engine, not once but several times. For a split second, I was pretty sure he was going to hit me. I walked to the side of the car and waited for him to roll down the window. He looked like the devil himself. By this time, I was pretty rattled and angry. My fight or flight had kicked in, and I was about ten percent flight and ninety percent fight. I was inches from hitting the window with the side of my fist when the door opened. He stepped out of his car, trying to intimidate me. I shoved the book into his chest and gave him a piece of my mind."

"Dad! What were you thinking?" Helen said, shocked.

"I had had enough of this guy coming into our town and waltzing around like he owned the place. He threw the book in the car and attempted to stare me down. I didn't give him the satisfaction. I walked away. I did, however, go around the back of the car. I may be many things, but I'm not a fool." Andi snickered at Pops, as we watched him prop his hand on his knee and his face change to a no-nonsense John Wayne expression. If this family could do one thing well, they could deflect any situation with humor.

"So, you said you averted a global crisis?" Andi said. "What happened?"

"I watched him drive down the road that led out of town. I thought for sure we would never see him again. I couldn't shake the terrible feeling I had that afternoon. I didn't want to worry Katie, so I didn't say anything about it. What I didn't realize at the time was that she was feeling the same way.

"We went home, had dinner, and put up a few more strings of lights. The heaviness I felt was getting worse. I knew I needed to go to the library. I made up a story about wanting to check the fireplace, but of course, Katie would have no part of that. She was going with me. As we left the house, the snow really started to come down. It didn't stop us, though. We both knew where we needed to be.

"The library was dark and quiet. We pulled up in front of it and sat for a few minutes. My wife would always say to me, 'You feelin' it?' And of course, I was feeling it. We decided to pull around the block and hide out across the street, just out of view. It felt like a stakeout. Of course, Katie had hot chocolate and cookies. I don't think that woman ever went anywhere without her hot chocolate."

"That's true, the Kringlas were the best," Sean said. "And always a candy cane to stir the hot chocolate."

"So there we sat, waiting for who knows what. The snow was pretty heavy and had covered our tracks in front of the library. We had just finished off the last of the hot chocolate when a familiar black Mercedes drove past the library, and pulled into the parking lot behind the library."

"And it was just the two of you? Dad, that's so dangerous!" Helen exclaimed, rolling her chair into the circle.

"I *was* feeling a little anxious, but I wouldn't let Katie know about it. We waited for quite a while, and the car never left. I decided to head over to the library and check things out. I begged her to stay in the car and thank goodness she agreed."

"Why didn't you call for help?" Helen asked.

"There wasn't time. Things were beginning to feel urgent. I told Katie to lock the doors and wait for me to come back."

Helen crossed her arms, exasperated at her mother's choice. "She didn't listen, did she?"

"Nope. Not at all. She waited for me to get inside the library and then followed. Of course, I didn't realize it until after I had cleared the bottom floor and looked out of the office window to see Kate peering into the back of the black Mercedes. It was snowing so hard. I could barely see her from the window. I knew I had to get to her. I didn't bother to lock the door. I just ran to her. Looking back, it was an amateur move. When I reached the car, she was staring inside.

"'She's alone,' she said, pointing to the car. I looked inside to see the little girl sitting in the back seat, clutching the book. The car wasn't running, and it was miserably cold. Katie began to take her coat off as she opened the door.

"'Kate, put your coat back on.' I handed her mine. We decided to get the little girl to our car and warm her up. I had a few words I wanted to say to this guy. As Katie was wrapping up the child, I turned to see a flashlight flicker in the library.

"I said, 'Kate! Get her to the car. I'll meet you there.' I ran to the walk-out basement door and quickly jingled the keys to find the right one. I shoved the snow out of the way and pushed through the door. The basement was cold and dark. I stumbled across boxes and old pieces of furniture to make my way to the stairs. A gust of wind blew the outside door open. Snow and wind filled the basement. The door at the top of the stairs rattled and then opened. I thought it was the wind, but I was wrong. The owner of the flashlight was standing at the top of the stairs looking down at me. It was our dark friend who had left his daughter to freeze. He looked as if he was going to run. I bounded up the stairs, taking two at a time when I felt a heavy object hit me in the face. I stumbled, losing a few steps but I didn't fall. He slammed the door shut. I could hear heavy footsteps running across the floor."

"Pops! You could have been killed!" Andi said in disbelief. He pointed to the scar on his forehead. Sean leaned closer to get a better look.

"That's where that came from?" Sean asked. "You told us that happened when you were building your house."

"Well, I couldn't exactly tell you that I got clocked by someone trying to take over the world, could I?" Pops snickered.

"Guess not," Sean said, tilting his head and shrugging his shoulders.

"I felt something warm running down my face and started to feel a little light-headed. Still, I managed to get the door open. The man was frantically searching the vestibule. He knew something was there. I went into the study and grabbed an iron from the fireplace."

Andi and I had used those same irons when we faced our intruder.

"Must be our family's weapon of choice," Andi said, looking like she was swinging a bat.

"No, I'm pretty sure your family's weapon of choice is an AK-47," I said, pointing to all the damage that littered the kitchen floor.

"Good point," Andi said, shaking her head.

"So what happened, Dad?" Helen asked impatiently.

"I remember grabbing the iron and running toward the door. I know I opened it and raised the makeshift weapon, but that's the last thing I remember until I woke up to Katie screaming my name. She was wiping the blood off my face and asking me what had happened. 'Where is he?' I asked, pulling myself up.

"Kate told me the man tried to grab the little girl, and that she begged him to leave her. She held on to the little girl until he struck my Kate.

"Now, when I heard this, it gave me all the energy I needed to get up. I threw the door open and stumbled down the stairs. The black Mercedes was spinning in the driveway, trying to get traction. I ran toward the car. I genuinely believe my guardian angel was present, because if I had made it to the car, I would have killed that man for putting his hands on Katie and treating that little girl like that.

"Just as I was about to open the passenger door, the car's tires found the pavement and pushed it forward. It fishtailed a bit but started to gain speed. The last thing I saw was the little girl's face in the back window, her hand on the glass, still clutching the book. They disappeared in the snow."

"You never saw them again?" Andi asked.

"No, they left town. We checked the entrance hall in the library. He didn't find anything. We decided it was best to spend the night there. Katie made a big fire, and we settled on the couch together. My head was throbbing, but sleep came quickly. That is until my wife woke me up every half hour. She said I had a concussion and wanted to make sure I was okay."

"So, he never came back?" Sean asked. We were all wondering if that was the end of the story.

"Not that we know of. The Christmas clock started working the next day. We spent a little more time at the library than we normally did. I remember we called it 'Holiday Hours' that year. Katie would tell Christmas stories by the fireplace after normal business hours. Word got around and half the town showed up. One person would bring cookies and another hot cocoa. We had enough candy and fudge to last us well into the new year. All those people didn't know it, but they were helping us keep the Kringles safe."

"I remember that," Helen said, letting the memories come flooding back. "I loved that Christmas. We spent so much time at the library. It was magic. You saved the world *and* made some great memories for our family and the town." She paused for a minute, taking a deep breath and smiling. "We had no idea what the two of you were doing every day. Thank you for such a great childhood and everything else you did that I may never know about."

Pops laughed, and I think he may have blushed a little. He stood for a second, stretched his legs, and walked over to his daughter. She looked like a little girl again, standing in front of her father. He bent down and kissed the top of her head. What I would have given to have one interaction like that with my father.

I needed to talk to Andi. There were things I needed to tell her. There was something I needed to show her. I felt her arm in mine.

"We need to go back to the inn. I have something to show you," I whispered in her ear.

CHAPTER THIRTY-FOUR

We left my parents mournfully cleaning up a gingerbread crime scene. Sean was sitting by the fire with Gris in his lap, eating the casualties. Pops had decided it was best for him to go home. He wrapped up some pancakes and headed out. It was the perfect time for us to escape as well.

We sat in the truck quietly, both of us taking a minute. The absurdity of the entire situation finally got to us. The laughter bubbled up inside me, and before I knew it, it was uncontrollable. Luckily, Teddy joined me, and before long, we were both laughing hysterically. That was the first time I heard Teddy laugh without hesitation, very loudly, I might add. It made me laugh even harder.

"That was, without a doubt, the best breakfast I've ever had," Teddy said with the warmest smile.

"Wait a minute, you almost got shot and that was one of the best breakfasts you've ever had?" I laughed, watching her wipe the tears from her eyes.

"Yes, I have never felt more at home. Honestly, I have never felt more warmth or more accepted." She smiled and reached for my hand. My world had changed so much in just a few days. It was frightening, overwhelming, and the best thing that had ever happened to me. Teddy was sitting next to me, holding my hand, her hair pulled back, wearing one of my rowing sweatshirts and a pair of my jeans. She looked more beautiful now than any other time I had seen her. I took it in for a moment, not realizing how close I was to losing it all.

The inn was busy with out-of-town guests coming for the gingerbread contest. It was legendary throughout the Northeast. Nate had done his job of festooning the entire inn with cardboard gingerbread men. Red sparkling ribbons and bows wound their way through anything stationary. Lights twinkled and reflected in the shiny decorations as candles glowed in the lanterns. It was mesmerizing.

We made our way through the lobby, dodging guests who were milling around. I caught Nate's eye as we trotted up the stairs, Teddy leading the way, holding my hand. He smiled, raised an eyebrow, and then continued with his work. I laughed, wondering what he must be thinking. We arrived at the door being guarded by the two nutcrackers. A feeling of guilt washed over me as Teddy reached for the latch.

"I have to tell you something," I said sheepishly, hooking my hand in her elbow and turning her around. "I might have broken into your room while you were gone."

"I'm sorry, you did what?" she asked, very surprised.

"I wasn't looking for anything. Well actually I was, but…"

"What exactly were you looking for?" she asked, obviously frustrated with the situation.

"No, I was looking for you. I was worried. I saw you arguing with the woman, and both of you seemed so angry, and then I couldn't find you. Who was she?" I waited a moment for Teddy to say anything.

"I know, I need to explain, and I will."

"I had no idea what was going on. Sean reminded me that whatever we were going through wasn't as important as what was happening, the bigger picture. I came here to tell you that. You weren't here. I talked Nate into letting me in your room. Don't be angry. I was worried."

Her face softened a little. "I'm not. What you saw had to have looked…odd to say the least." Teddy opened the door and motioned for me to go ahead of her. I walked into a cluttered room and waited for her reaction. "What the hell happened here?"

"Honestly, I'm glad to hear you say that. I didn't think you lived like this."

"You saw me fold my dirty jeans, right?" She went straight to her computer and ran her finger across the top, unlocking it.

"Was anyone able to get in?"

"I can't tell. I wrote a little program to turn the camera on and begin recording when anyone, unsuccessfully, tries to enter multiple passwords." She had put her glasses on and was sitting at the desk, legs crossed, studying the laptop's screen. Did she say she had created a program? I had to sit down to steady myself. Intelligence was quite the turn-on for me. "Are you okay?" she asked, nudging the corner of her glasses.

"Yes…" I stammered for a moment, gathering my wits about me. "I'm sorry. It's the glasses, the program writing."

"So you're into geeks?" she asked, laughing.

"Just sexy ones," I said, walking to the desk and eyeing the screen.

"Whoever was here knew what they were doing." We watched the replay as the camera was covered from behind the screen.

"Any sound?" I asked, hoping for even the smallest clue.

"No, just someone rifling through the room."

"What were they looking for?"

"My guess would be any information I have about the Kringles."

"Like this?" I said, pulling the charred piece of paper out of my pocket. St. Nicholas, draped in blue robes, was visible on what was left of it.

"Father Frost. Where did you get that?"

"It was in your fireplace."

"That is the specific Kringle I am here to get. I was told to purchase the entire set but absolutely, under no circumstance, should I leave without having this particular one in my possession."

"And you didn't put it in the fireplace?" I asked, confused.

"No, it was inside the book." She pointed to the coffee table and the copy of *The Snow Maiden*. "This is what I have to tell you," she said, moving toward the couch. "You're not going to believe me when I tell you this."

We sat down on the sofa together, facing one another. "Remember, you can trust me. You can tell me anything."

"This isn't about trust. It's about you believing me. This is pretty crazy," she said, rubbing her forehead as she reached for the book. "This book was given to me by my father when I was five. Even then, he didn't really want to have much to do with me. He told me we were looking for a place for me to go to school."

"At five? That's insane. You were five!" My heart sank for Teddy. I reached for her.

"You know, I've spent my entire life trying to get his approval. The elusive Olexsandr Tereshchenko approval, to no avail."

"You don't need it, do you? I mean, look at you. Look at what you've accomplished."

"He is the only family I have. I think anyone would want their parents' approval."

While I could sympathize with her, I honestly had no idea how she felt. My parents were my biggest fan club, and they meant the world to me. I wanted to be her family. I wanted to show her how incredible she was and not have her constantly feel the pain inflicted by this man.

"I'm sorry." It was the only thing I could say. She pulled her hand from mine and placed it on the cover of the book.

"We came to the United States and spent several weeks looking at schools. We visited a small town between visits. I remember I liked all the Christmas decorations. It was such a happy place. It made me feel like I was home. The people were so friendly. I still think about it sometimes when I feel alone. During that trip, my father gave me this book." She handed the book to me.

"It's beautiful. I admired it earlier. This is my favorite story."

"It came from your grandmother." She paused for a moment, resting her hand on my arm, and looked at me intently. "She gave it to my father."

The hair on the back of my neck stood up as a rush of adrenaline surged through my body. "I'm sorry, what?" I asked, knowing exactly what she meant.

"I know, Andi, I remember her. She was one of the brightest points of my childhood. She was everything I didn't have in my life. She spent a great deal of time talking to me when we were at a restaurant. It must have been Nick's. My father was too busy to be concerned. I just remember her as being magical." Her last words left her mouth slowly, almost in a whisper. I let it sit in the air for a moment, remembering how special my grandmother truly was.

"She really was magical. I am so glad you have that memory and that you knew her. She brought us together. And knowing her, she probably had the whole thing planned."

"Do you believe that? That this was part of some kind of plan?"

"I don't know what to believe anymore, Teddy. It's not out of the realm of possibility, is it?"

"I took the book from her lap and carefully opened it, revealing the old envelope. I handed it to her.

"I need to open this don't I?" she asked hesitantly.

"Do you know who it's from?" I said, thinking it was from my grandmother.

"My father. It was in the book when he gave it to me."

"What does it mean?" I pointed to the writing under her name.

"Snegurochka? It's Russian for snow maiden. That's what my father called me after he gave me the book. I always thought it was endearing. Something warm and loving to hold on to from him. And now...now I know, he didn't even give me the book. He didn't take the time to pick it out. It wasn't his thoughtfulness. He took it from someone else, gave it to me, and took the credit for it."

"Are you sure it's from your father, the envelope? I can't believe you never opened it."

"I always thought it was. I haven't opened it because in my mind, there were a million things that could have been said, all of them accepting me as his daughter. If I didn't open it, those possibilities still existed. Maybe I just didn't want another disappointment."

"I think it's time."

She looked at the envelope and turned it over, sliding her nail under the flap and breaking the seal. She sat for a moment and then pulled the paper out. Years had changed its color. The scripted words were written in Russian. To my surprise, Teddy began to read it in English.

The storm raged the morning you were born
Within the garden of good and evil
Light against dark
For the soul of a girl
Who might one day lead or destroy
The battle would rage through her life
The darkness
Wrapping its tentacles around her heart
The light
Breaking them free
She would grow to be powerful
Living with purpose
And then there was a choice
The dark
The light
The end
A new beginning
Hero or
Villain

We were both quiet, looking at the paper and then at one another.

"You keep surprising me, you're amazing."

She looked at me for a moment, not realizing her speaking Russian was anything but ordinary.

"Is that about you?" I asked.

"No…why would it be about me?"

"It's addressed to you. It has your name on it. It must be about you. What if I'm not the only one with a destiny to fulfill?"

The weight of my sentence dropped on Teddy. Her eyes drifted downward as her posture changed.

"But why me?" she asked, puzzled.

"Why not you?" I countered as she stood and walked to the fireplace.

"We don't even know where this came from. Who wrote it? This could have been just another attempt by my father to control me."

I saw the look of disdain on her face. I hated that someone had hurt her this much. "Okay, so how do we figure this out?"

"You're the librarian. Isn't this kind of your specialty?"

"Yes…yes it is," I said, realizing I did, in fact, have the ability and tools to research this myself. The past few days had taken me away from a previous life. "Add it to our list of things to do," I said, overwhelmed at what was mounting before us.

Teddy began to clean up around the room, looking to see if anything else was missing.

"I do have a question for you."

"Go ahead."

"Who were you arguing with when I dropped you off?"

"That was my boss. She was furious with me." She continued picking her things up and neatly folding them.

"You gave it right back to her."

"We've been friends for quite some time. We started together. We even dated for a while. I have a very difficult time seeing her as my boss. She is very upset that I have not finalized this sale."

"Oh really? Why is that?" I said, still stuck back on the part where Teddy said they dated.

"Apparently, there is quite a lot of money involved in this transaction with a stringent timeline. I knew this, of course, when I came to town but with everything that has happened…" She sat down on her bed, overcome by everything that had taken place.

"So what did you do?"

"I told her I would take care of everything. I told her she could trust me. I drove her to New Hope to catch the train, promising I would get the job done. I knew I needed her to leave. *We* needed her to leave."

"Does she normally micromanage you like that?"

"No, she's never done this before. I work independently. Something else is going on here."

"Do you know who the buyer is?"

"No idea, but that's normal. There are many times the buyer is not disclosed."

"I think it's time we head to the library. I feel like there are a lot of moving pieces. We need to sort some of this out."

"We still don't know who did this," she said, pointing to her belongings strewn about.

"Nor do we know who broke into the library the night we were there."

Teddy was right. Someone was looking for information and had been pretty brazen trying to get it. As I was beginning to realize that we were not alone in our pursuit, we heard someone at the door. We looked at one another, hesitation freezing us in place. Slowly, Teddy walked toward the bed, slid her hand underneath the mattress, and pulled out a handgun. This wasn't the first time she had held one either. My life, which to this point had been gun-free, was now completely loaded. I began to wonder if the library held its own arsenal. I looked at her with the most discerning what-the-hell look I could muster, but she wasn't in the slightest bit phased by it. She nodded for me to go over behind the Christmas tree, which I quickly did, tiptoeing like the lead ballerina in *The Nutcracker*. The irony was not lost on me as I hid behind one of the many prominent wooden soldiers in the suite. I found myself within reach of a fireplace poker. This would forever be my weapon of choice. My level of training wouldn't allow for any type of firearm, but give me a fireplace iron, and I might just be deadly.

Teddy moved toward the lights on the wall, sliding the switches down and darkening the suite. The Christmas tree sparkled and dimly lit the room. Teddy quickly moved into the alcove that led to the balcony. We waited in silence listening to the rustling at the door.

Light pierced the dark entryway to the room as the door popped open. A figure slid inside, stopping to quietly close the door. The person walked toward the table, dropping something heavy. As they moved to pick it up, I saw my opportunity.

Deciding the iron may be a little out of my league, I went with the all-out blitz and ran for the bent-over figure as fast as possible. I lowered my shoulder just like Sean taught me to do and charged with all my might. I struck the figure hard, knocking them off balance. I, however, did not realize the amount of momentum I had generated and continued careening across the room and right into a nutcracker that could have easily been a linebacker for the Patriots, slamming him against the wall as I heard the wood splinter.

Teddy, amid the commotion, turned the lights on. She stood ready, her gun drawn, and pointed toward the person lying on the floor. I had this odd that's-my-girl feeling, as I saw her walk slowly toward the figure. She quickly reversed her position and shoved the gun in the back of her pants.

"Damn, Andi! What did you do that for?" Nate asked as he lay on the floor. A tray with caviar and a bottle of champagne were strewn across the carpet. Two long-stemmed glasses were in Nate's hands, both escaping the collision unscathed.

I removed the nutcracker's head from my lap and stood, peeking over the furniture at Nate, obviously in pain, holding the two glasses straight up in the air.

"Nate, I'm so sorry. Are you okay?" I stumbled to him, picking up small plates that had rolled in my direction.

"I am never getting the deposit back on this room," Teddy said, looking around and seeing the obliterated nutcracker lying in pieces. "Do you play football?" she asked me, picking up an arm that had landed at her feet.

"I am so sorry, Nate. We thought someone was trying to break into the room."

He carefully set the glasses down on the coffee table and slowly moved away from them. "My parents asked me to bring this to you. It was delivered today. I thought I saw the two of you leave, but I must have been mistaken with the inn being so busy. Wow, Andi, that was quite a hit," he said, grabbing some ice from the bucket, wrapping it in a cloth napkin, and putting it on his face which was already turning bright red from the rug burn.

"You haven't seen anyone snooping around here, have you, Nate?" Teddy asked, continuing to pick up the pieces of nutcracker lying around on the floor.

"Not that I've noticed, no one unusual." Nate brushed his coat and tried to regain a little of his dignity. He lifted the tray, balancing the contents still resting on it. The champagne bottle started to roll. We all watched it like bystanders witnessing a car accident. We knew we were helpless to stop it. The weight of the bottle tipped the tray. The bottle fell and landed directly on the first champagne glass, shattering it into a million pieces. It sat upright on the table, building pressure until the cork popped and a fountain of bubbly liquid spewed from its opening. The cap hit the ceiling and returned to the table with a similar velocity, hitting the second glass and shattering it as well.

Nate sat quietly on his knees, champagne dripping from his nose. He stood, collected what he could on the tray, and said he would return to clean up the mess. I could have sworn I heard him cry as he walked out of the room.

"I hate to see what you do to your enemies." Teddy laughed as she began collecting the larger pieces of glass.

"What about you? What is that in your pants?"

"I don't know. What *is* that in my pants?" Teddy had one eyebrow raised and a half-smile on her face.

"I'm a bad influence on you."

"You really are. That joke would not have entered my head a few days ago."

We picked up what we could and left for the library.

CHAPTER THIRTY-FIVE

We left the bustling inn and luckily didn't see Nate again. We cleaned up what we could and left him an overly apologetic note hoping he would forgive us. Kringle Falls was alive with the spirit of Christmas. The inn was filled to capacity and the streets were busier than they would be any other time of the year. Snow fell through sparkling, lantern-filled, pine-infused landscapes. With the crushing weight of world peace on our shoulders, we really didn't have time to stop and enjoy it.

We quickly made our way to the library. The dark and foreboding clouds were building once again. We were new to the sentinel game, so we missed the signs being shown to us, if there were signs.

The wind began to pick up, something was certainly in the air. It was electrically charged. I searched for my keys as Teddy moved to the side to block the wind. Her arm slid around my waist as she pulled me toward her. I liked her protective side. I felt incredibly safe with her. Putting the key in the door, I stopped and wrapped my arm around her back, my fingers running over the gun still tucked in her jeans.

"I think we need to talk about your past," I said, leaning in to kiss her.

"Maybe we should talk about your past." The voice came from behind us, muffled by the wind. I thought my ears were playing tricks on me for a second until I turned around and saw Jules standing there. "This is awkward isn't it?" she asked, walking toward us.

"Only for you," I said, not letting go of Teddy. I could see something around Jules for the first time, a haze. This must have been what Pops was talking about. She was shrouded by this gray mist, turning and moving around her. I saw Teddy turn to look at Jules. The slightest difference in her eyes told me she saw the same thing. I felt her hand tighten around my waist. Teddy placed herself in front of me, her hand resting on the grip of the gun.

"We were good together, Andi," she said, walking toward us with a gym bag slung over her shoulder. "You moved on kind of quick, don't you think?" She looked Teddy up and down, making the situation awkward.

"Jules, we both know that we gave it our best shot. We're better as friends. I don't want to lose that." I had no desire to follow through on that last statement, but I felt like we were up against a wall. "Let's not make this any worse than it already is. We need to wish each other well and move on."

She laughed, almost manically, as she reached behind her back and pulled out a handgun. She lifted it toward Teddy.

"Still awkward?" she asked, looking at me.

"What the hell?" I asked as her shaky hands held the gun in our direction. "Where did you get that? You can't even handle a Nerf gun!" I said with honesty. "Have you lost your damn mind?" I felt Teddy's grip loosen from around my waist. She was slowly edging her way toward Jules. My hand slipped into her waistband as I held on tightly, wanting her to stay close to me. I didn't want Teddy to make any sudden moves and give Jules a reason to fire that gun. If she did fire it, with any luck, the kickback would knock her out cold. I doubt she had any kind of aim so our problem would be solved.

"Stay where you are...What's your name, Tina?" Jules asked, knowing damn well her name was Teddy. "Let's get that door open and go inside so we can talk a little."

"Seriously, this is ridiculous. Jules, put the gun down and go home. You have no plan, and frankly, you're embarrassing yourself." I turned to unlock the door and go inside. I felt something fly past my head as the window in the door shattered with a pop!

"Jules, you could have hit us!" I yelled, shocked that she had the guts first to load the gun and then take a shot.

"Next time, I will," she said as her hand steadied, and she moved the gun barrel in my direction. "Now, I asked you to open the door. Let's go inside and talk. And you, Xena, Warrior Princess, don't get any ideas."

Teddy rolled her eyes at the prospect of being at the hands of someone so inept at staging a crime. I unlocked the door and led everyone into the library.

"In there, let's go to the study."

"You were never this decisive when we were together," I said, taunting her. My anger was boiling inside because of the audacity she was displaying.

"You, Xena, over there in the chair." She motioned with the gun toward one of the oversize chairs by the fireplace. "Andi, have a seat in the other chair."

"What's your plan here, Jules? Have you really thought this out? You're not winning the argument for getting me back."

"Andi, you are so incredibly full of yourself. You always were. Do you actually think I want you back?"

"You've been at my house more than I have!" I said, very frustrated with the situation.

"Don't flatter yourself." She walked over to one of the study tables, pulled out one of the armchairs, and sat down. She threw the bag onto the table and crossed her legs, resting the gun on her thigh for a brief moment before using the same hand to brush the hair out of her face. She desperately needed a gun safety class. "This was never about you, Andi. You broke my heart too many times. This was about money. About me leaving this town and maybe, just a little, about revenge."

"You're not even making sense," I said, very frustrated.

Teddy was noticeably quiet as I watched her scan the room. The haze around Jules was beginning to mimic the clouds gathering outside. The gray mist was pushed and pulled by small faceless phantoms circling her. A few were bold and lashed out while others were scared and retreated behind her. The cowardly ones far outweighed the bold figures. A storm was brewing. Jules was not the person I once knew. Something else was driving her right now.

A phone rang. Jules leaned forward and pulled it out of her back pocket. She glanced at the screen and quickly answered.

"I'm here. Yes, I have them both." There was a lengthy pause in the conversation as her eyes moved from Teddy to me. "Fine, I'll take care of it." She hung the phone up and began rifling in her bag. Teddy and I looked at one another, both wondering with whom she was talking.

She pulled a long plastic bag out. I couldn't tell what they were until she opened it and pulled out a few zip ties. She headed in Teddy's direction.

"What the hell are you doing?" I asked, standing and moving toward Jules.

"Sit down, Andi!" She swung the gun around and pointed it at Teddy. "I have no problem shooting her." The force with which she said it frightened me, and we had already witnessed a rampant shot. I sat back down, reluctant to make any kind of move.

She quickly tied Teddy to the chair and then came for me.

"You planned this. Who are you working with? Why are you doing this?" Now that we were in this precarious situation, my anger changed to fear. I could see Teddy's wheels spinning. I hoped she had an idea.

"You'll find out soon enough. Just sit back and enjoy the ride." She pulled the zip ties tightly around my wrists and ankles. Too tightly. They dug into my skin. I tried lifting my arms a little off the chair, hoping to give myself wiggle room but lost that advantage when she pulled the ties as tightly as she could.

Jules returned to her seat and rested the gun on the table. She pulled her phone out and began swiping through different images. "Here's a good one. The two of you eating breakfast at Nick's." She flashed the screen in my direction. It was a picture of Teddy and me several days ago at Nick's. "No, I think I like this one better." It was the two of us sitting on the couch in this very study, taken from the hallway. "Look how cute the two of you are…Was this your first kiss? Would you like a copy?"

"You were the one who broke into the library?"

"I watched your cozy little sleepover."

I was not familiar with this side of her personality. I had seen her angry and hurt, both caused by me, but I had not seen this before. She walked over to me, grabbing my face and pulling it next to hers.

"Let's get one last picture of us together." She took the picture and stepped back. "Now look at this. This might be the best picture we've ever taken. You want a copy? I can text it to you."

"How long have you been following us?" I asked, irritated with her attitude.

"Long enough. Don't get me wrong. I wasn't jealous or anything."

"Could have fooled me. Looks kind of pathetic, really." Teddy said, taunting Jules. "The jealous girlfriend was just an act then? If so, you're one hell of an actress."

"You can have her," Jules said to Teddy, not taking the bait. "Do you have any idea how many times she hurt me? Her career was more important, her family was more important, and whatever was in New York was more important. Do you know how many times I asked her to be my wife?"

"Twice," I said, chiming into the ridiculous conversation.

"You can't even get that right. It was three times," Jules said, obviously disgusted with me.

"I think I would have stopped after one," Teddy said, smirking. She was pretty bold considering her current position. "I mean, when someone says no the first time, that's usually your cue to exit. Why on Earth would you do it two more times? You must be into pain. What's that saying? If you're going to be stupid, you better be tough?"

Jules walked toward Teddy, who sat still and tall, not budging. She leaned down so that she was close to Teddy's face. "She led me on each time. Told me she loved me and that she needed just a little while longer." She paused for a moment and inched closer. "She'll do the same to you."

Teddy's movement was swift. She reared her head back and forcefully slammed her forehead against Jules's face. The sound was stomach-churning. Jules fell back, missed the couch and fell onto the floor. I looked at Teddy who was sitting stronger than ever in the chair. Her eyes fixed on Jules, lying on the ground, not moving.

"Where did you learn to do that? Seriously, we need to have some discussion about your past," I said to Teddy as she pulled her belt from her pants. She pushed it through one of the zip ties, pulling sharply with the opposite hand, and broke one of the ties around her wrist. She wasted no time with the other arm and moved toward her legs when Jules stirred. She sat up, blood dripping from her nose down her chin.

"You…" Jules said in a low growl as she stood, holding the couch as she steadied herself, obviously still seeing stars from the hit. She let go quickly and launched herself with all she had toward Teddy, landing on top of her. Teddy was still attached to the chair. Both women and the chair slid across the floor, coming to a stop against the bookcases. Jules pushed herself up so that she was straddling Teddy. The gray cloud that once encircled her as a light haze was now black and pulsing around her entire body. Jagged, sharp pieces of dark red bobbed in and out of the syrupy cloud.

Jules landed multiple punches before Teddy could pull out her trapped arms. The adrenaline rush must have been explosive as Teddy broke the legs on the chair from the sheer force of pushing down against them. In a split second, she grabbed one of the broken chair legs and forcefully landed it on the side of Jules's head. While Jules was doubled over in pain, Teddy barely showed any wear. She stood back, waiting on Jules to make her move.

"You really think you're something don't you?" Jules asked, staggering toward Teddy.

"I don't want to hurt you anymore. This needs to stop," Teddy said, lowering the leg to the chair.

"Aw, isn't that sweet of you? You don't want to hurt me. I don't know how you and your ego can fit in this room." Jules was moving for the gun. Teddy's name escaped me as I tried to warn her. Teddy lowered her head and ran at Jules with her shoulder down, making contact and launching them both across the table. Jules began hitting and kicking like a wild animal as they rolled off the table and onto the floor. I waited for a loud thud, but a gunshot replaced it.

There was silence. I hoped for any sound, terrified.

"Teddy?" I whispered, waiting to hear her voice, my heart pounding loudly in my chest. The silence was deafening.

Out of the corner of my eye, a prominent figure stepped out of the shadows and into the doorway. They were holding a gun, and a small stream of smoke escaped the barrel.

"I should have done this myself." The figure's dark and sinister voice slowly spread through the room like a deadly gas. Jules rose above the table, blood on her face, shaking as she stood. "You are weak and pathetic," the man said.

"Father." I heard Teddy's voice, solid and firm, as she stood, barely disheveled, staring at the figure that had just stepped into the light.

"Theodora. I really thought you were better than this. It was my understanding that you were the best in your field. Not a surprise, however, you have always been a disappointment."

Adrenaline surged through my body as I listened to the words. Everything was surreal. Jules was leaning against the table, holding the gun. Teddy, who had been standing strong, was beginning to deflate. I could see her shoulders lowering. It wasn't hard to picture her as a young girl, being beaten down by constant abuse. I strained against the zip ties, wanting desperately to stand with her and let her know she was so much more and that she wasn't alone.

Teddy's father walked around the table and stood beside me. The man smelled of cigar smoke and thick cologne. He grabbed my chin and forced me to look at him.

"Is this what distracted you, Theodora? I'm not surprised, average at best." I jerked my chin from his large and powerful hand. "And feisty! Is that why you like her?"

Teddy's shoulders straightened just a bit. She looked as if she were summoning an inner strength.

"As usual, you are out of touch and completely unaware of what is happening." Teddy's words were sharp and filled with condescension. She walked over to a defeated Jules, battered and bleeding. She swiftly snatched the gun from her hand and shoved her back into a seat. "Sit down," she said to Jules, putting the gun in the back of her pants. "I'm surprised you didn't kill yourself with this thing. Where did you even get it? Let me guess, did he give it to you? He's good at handing out weapons." Teddy tossed her father a look of disgust.

Olexsandr's face showed only the slightest bit of change, the smallest curl of his lip and the raise of an eyebrow. "Is there something I don't understand, Theodora? It was my understanding that once again, you have failed. That's what you do right? Any dealings we've ever had, you have failed. It's your specialty, correct? I am simply here to complete the transaction and take what I need."

"Typical. There is a lot you don't understand. I came here to do a job. This is part of the job. These are ancient pieces, guarded by a lineage of people who will give up their lives to protect them. And you thought I could just come in here and offer up a little cash and walk out with them. I really thought you were more intelligent than that, Father."

Teddy smirked at the larger-than-life man who still stood beside me. The darkness that surrounded him was pulsing, controlled by the anger that was building inside his dark and vile soul.

I watched Teddy's face for a sign. I needed her to tell me this was part of the plan. Up to this point, Teddy had been surrounded by a lit halo around her entire body. It was comforting. But at this moment, it was gone, replaced by a dark-gray mist. She wouldn't make eye contact with me. I pulled against the bindings but felt no way to escape.

"I'm surprised you would talk to me in such a way, Theodora. It's not very respectful, is it? You know how we deal with disrespect."

"No. You don't get to do that anymore." She paused for a moment, regrouping. Those words were difficult for her to say. Even so, she still stood strong. "I came here to do a job, and I am doing it, quite well I might add. You should have more respect for *me*. This is part of the process. I would have had the artifacts in the next day or two and been out of town before anyone realized it, and you would not have had to pay a penny."

"Please, enlighten me. Tell me how you would accomplish such a feat."

"Do you honestly think I would find anything endearing in this town? It is a means to an end." Her words cut through me, causing visceral pain. After carelessly and effortlessly negating our time together, she finally looked at me. Her eyes were cold and hard. She looked just like her father.

"This is all part of your plan?" he asked, looking suspiciously at Teddy.

"Part of my plan? This *is* my plan. Why on Earth you felt the need to involve her, I will never know." She tossed her head toward Jules, who was still slumped in the chair.

"She was the backup plan. I needed someone inside. She is an assistant to a dear friend of mine who teaches in the Russian Studies department at Princeton."

I looked at Jules, obviously at her lowest point. She looked beaten and ashamed. "I'm sorry, Andi. I needed the money. Everything had run out. I would have to come home with a huge amount of debt and no degree. I can't live here, Andi. I want a life outside of this town. He told me he would pay for everything if I helped him." She began to sob, realizing her choice.

My whole life was careening out of control. My head was spinning, my face flushed, and everything felt heavy. Teddy walked toward me and placed her hand on my face. The warmth felt like home, and then the stinging reality of the situation took over. Her hand slid along my jaw. She placed her thumb on my chin and forcibly pulled my face to meet hers.

"Can you tell my father that I am very good at what I do? I had you convinced, didn't I?" She bent down to kiss me. I wanted her to kiss me, remembering the days that had led us to this. Tears streamed into my eyes and fell down my face. Her thumb left my chin to remove a tear that slid down my cheek. "You really fell hard, didn't you? Maybe I should take up acting? I think I might be pretty good at it." She waited a moment as her last words hung in the air. Taking a deep breath, I found my words.

"All this was a game to you? It meant nothing?"

"Oh, it meant a great deal. My father finally gets to see me in my element. You see, he has thought, my entire life, that I was worthless. Now I have something he desperately needs." She turned to look at her father. "I'm not so worthless anymore, am I?"

"Theodora, you're being childish. Give me what I came here for. I will pay you and be on my way. You can do whatever you wish with these two." He pulled something out of his jacket pocket and handed it to Teddy. It was a silencer. "I find this helps in these situations."

My chest felt heavy as the weight of generations fell upon me. A few days on the job, I had already allowed someone into my life that would destroy everything. I should have checked the book again. Was her name completely gone? I wished I could see the book now. I was sure my name was alone on that page and probably disappearing by the second.

"We're partners now, Father. I will not hand these over to you and let you leave. These artifacts are priceless and I plan to keep them in my possession."

"Theodora, this isn't a discussion. While I appreciate your newfound attitude, it is wearing on me, and I don't have time for this. If you are truly willing to be my partner, you must prove yourself. Dispose of these two, and we'll talk." She took the round cylinder from his hand and slowly screwed it onto her gun. Teddy turned and pointed the gun at Jules. She quickly pulled the trigger. Jules was thrown, her chair flipped back. She lay quietly on the floor.

A groan lifted from the depths of my stomach. I was in disbelief, and then the horror of the situation settled on me as I watched Teddy turn the gun toward me.

"She means something to you, doesn't she?" he asked Teddy as she was slow to pull the trigger. "Why else would you be waiting? I've always told you that any love or affection is a weakness. I would do it myself, but I think you need to learn a lesson. Why have I always had to teach these lessons? Since you were a child, you've always had a soft spot."

I understood why Teddy was the way she was. Who could overcome anything as evil and toxic as this man? Teddy's eyes were still cold as she looked at me and then her father. The gray mist around her had faded to black. Her hand trembled as her finger began to squeeze the trigger. I closed my eyes as a tear ran down my face.

The sound of breaking glass was thunderous. It came from all directions. A cloud of smoke filled the room as everything became chaotic. Sean emerged from the smoke, camouflage bandana around his head, brandishing a sword. My parents burst through the front door, my mom rolling into the study, my dad sliding, both toting AR15s with bullets slung across their chests. The loud noise caught us off guard. Both of us, but not Teddy. She stood, gun drawn, and pointed away from me. It was pointed at her father.

"You are a coward, Snegurochka. I knew you never possessed what was needed to do this job." Red crept up her face. Her hand was noticeably shaking now. I heard a low sob escape her slightly heaving chest as she pulled the trigger. The man she called her father fell backward, covered by the smoke that filled the room. Teddy fell to her knees, shoulders slowly moving up and down.

The room was quiet. Sean was the closest to Teddy and reached to help her up. She took his assistance, walking toward me. She dropped to her knees and placed her head on my lap, her arms tightly around my waist and she cried.

I felt the warm tears stream down my face. Sean moved quickly to cut the ties that bound me to the chair. My arms slipped beneath hers as I pulled her toward me. Her hands touched my face. Her eyes. They were no longer cold but somehow showed her years of pain.

"I love you. I love you more than anything. I choose you," she said emphatically, placing her forehead against my own. "You understand that, right?"

I reached for her face and I held on tightly, remembering the pain I had just left. Remembering my heart crushing under the weight of disappointment. Everything about her was the Teddy I knew, and she was holding me so tightly.

"I don't understand," I managed to mumble through the tears.

"None of that was real. I needed to make sure we were safe. I needed to save you."

"But Jules, you shot her," I said as my voice cracked.

"She missed…" Jules stood up from the other side of the table "…on purpose. I knew I was in over my head when he showed up. All of that about the school and needing money, it's all true. I knew, however, I had made a mistake. Teddy told me to take her lead when she tossed me on the table." She paused for a moment. "So that's what I did."

My parents popped up above the smoke settling on the floor, AR15s locked and loaded.

"We came as soon as Teddy texted us," my mom blurted out, thick black lines below her eyes and her face peppered with splotches of green and black. My dad looked ridiculous. I never, however, knew of a time I was happier to see them.

Teddy still held on to me. "I thought we might need them, arsenal and all." She paused for a moment. "I'm always on your side," she said, "I will always be on your side."

A long and steady breath escaped my body. My world was beginning to right itself. I pulled her toward me and kissed her still-trembling lips. It was a renewal of a commitment we made to each other just a few days ago. "I love you," I said as we pulled away.

"I love you too." The words were strong as she slid her arms beneath mine and lifted me to stand in front of her.

"Guys, we have a problem," Sean said as he walked toward the door. A car door slammed in the distance. "He's gone."

Sean was looking down at the floor. The terror of his survival fueled Teddy's spring to the door. We blasted through the vestibule to see the old Mercedes barreling down the road. The clouds hung low as the setting sun poured between two layers of darkness. The car pulled a long dark shadow behind it like a cape. We watched it disappear into the darkness as the clouds enveloped the sun.

CHAPTER THIRTY-SIX

My family cleared the library, at least that's what they called it. Teddy followed, which gave me a bit more comfort. The Kringles were safe in their resting place, fortified in the cellar, but they would need to be moved. And Teddy was the Teddy I had fallen in love with. To say her performance wasn't jarring would be an understatement. I didn't realize what she had become to me.

She spent the next several days reassuring me that her performance was just that, a performance. She explained to me how she would become this other person to deal with her father. It was hard to understand how much of that different persona was real and how much was truly an act. I watched the mist around her change to dark gray and then black when she was in the heat of battle with that horrible man. That person she had become was part of her, no matter how much she tried to deny it and that frightened me. Which part was truly her? Which side would win, the dark or the light? We still had so much to learn about each other.

My family packed away their battle gear and picked up spatulas for the last stretch before the Kringle Falls Gingerbread Competition. They never missed a beat. I found my mom in the kitchen still wearing camo with dark lines under her eyes, sifting flour and making icing.

Sean had cleared the streets of Mom's gingerbread village. Dad had rebuilt the various motors and installed LEDs throughout the town. Gris was lying on his back under the construction site, back paw in his mouth, overstuffed with gingerbread. Mom had baked several walls ahead of time and kept them in case of an emergency. This was an emergency. The blueprints were tacked to the wall, and everyone was on deck. It wasn't as elegant as it had been before the war zone that exploded a few days ago, but it had charm. The best part about it was my family completed the entire thing together. Teddy and I finished the last piece, the library. We carefully placed stained glass windows we made from Jolly Ranchers. I sat it down in the middle of the town and switched on the light that sat beneath it. Brilliant colors lit the area surrounding the library as the light spilled from the windows. Teddy wrapped her arms around my waist and nestled into my neck.

"It's beautiful," she said as she kissed me on the cheek.

Snow began to fall gently outside the window. Doris Day crooned her Christmas tunes softly in the background. This would be one of the best Christmases I ever had. Teddy and I danced near the tree as Gris wandered around barking at the neighbor's cat that was on the porch. The snow picked up, swirling with the wind that was driving against the windows, almost growling as the storm grew. I was glad to be in her arms, slowly swaying to the gentle music.

The years ahead would be filled with joy and sorrow. We would come up against our worst demons, and evil would rear its ugly head again. But tonight was perfect.

CHAPTER THIRTY-SEVEN

A dark figure stood in the snow, watching two women slowly dance by the light of the Christmas tree. The dog paced in front of the window, watching the man who stood in the darkness, cigar smoke swirling around him and wafting into the air.

His anger grew. The black mass gathering around him swirled and pulsated. The ground began to freeze, tiny cracks forming from the man's feet. A low guttural growl escaped him without any movement from his lips.

This was far from over.

Bella Books, Inc.
Women. Books. Even Better Together.
P.O. Box 10543
Tallahassee, FL 32302
Phone: (800) 729-4992
www.BellaBooks.com

More Titles from Bella Books

Mabel and Everything After – Hannah Safren
978-1-64247-390-2 | 274 pgs | paperback: $17.95 | eBook: $9.99
A law student and a wannabe brewery owner find that the path to a
fairy tale happily-ever-after is often the long and scenic route.

To Be With You – TJ O'Shea
978-1-64247-419-0 | 348 pgs | paperback: $19.95 | eBook: $9.99
Sometimes the choice is between loving safely or loving bravely.

I Dare You to Love Me – Lori G. Matthews
978-1-64247-389-6 | 292 pgs | paperback: $18.95 | eBook: $9.99
An enemy-to-lovers romance about daring to follow your heart, even
when it's the hardest thing to do.

The Lady Adventurers Club - Karen Frost
978-1-64247-414-5 | 300 pgs | paperback: $18.95 | eBook: $9.99
Four women. One undiscovered Egyptian tomb. One (maybe) angry
Egyptian goddess. What could possibly go wrong?

Golden Hour - Kat Jackson
978-1-64247-397-1 | 250 pgs | paperback: $17.95 | eBook: $9.99
Life would be so much easier if Lina were afraid of something
basic—like spiders—instead of something significant. Something like
real, true, healthy love.

Schuss – E. J. Noyes
978-1-64247-430-5 | 276 pgs | paperback: $17.95 | eBook: $9.99
They're best friends who both want something more, but what if
admitting it ruins the best friendship either of them have had?

Printed in the USA
CPSIA information can be obtained
at www.ICGtesting.com
JSHW020930031223
53121JS00001B/2